WHO IS ANGELINA?

WHO IS ANGELINA?

A NOVEL BY **AL YOUNG**

UNIVERSITY OF CALIFORNIA PRESS
Berkeley · Los Angeles · London

University of California Press
Berkeley and Los Angeles, California
University of California Press, Ltd.
London, England

First Paperback Printing 1996

Library of Congress Cataloging-in-Publication Data
Young, Al, 1939–
Who is Angelina?: a novel / by Al Young.
p.   cm. — (California fiction)
ISBN 0-520-20712-2 (alk. paper)
I. Title.   II. Series.
PS3575.0683W48   1996
813'.54—dc20   96-21669
CIP

Designer: Sandra Kandrac
Printed in the United States of America
1 2 3 4 5 6 7 8 9

"Boogie Sunday," © 1973 by Al Young, originally
appeared, in slightly different form, in *Yardbird Reader*,
Volume Two, Yardbird Publishing, Inc.

In Memory of Roland Navarro (1939–1961)
Painter, Poet, Soldier & Friend

There are years that ask questions and years that answer.
—Zora Neale Hurston
Their Eyes Were Watching God

The farther a woman goes out on the end of an arm the more power she has. That power is for good and power for evil. It is also power over weather, over plant growth, and power to cause transformations. Girls in the Middle West often decide to stay at the center of the cross, where they will be safe. That strange passive quality in so many American women comes from that decision. A woman's problem is that if she does leave the center, and go farther out, which Mother will she find there? Whichever she finds she will become, for she is that one already. Many women in a patriarchal society then elect to remain near the center; but if they do that, their spiritual growth stops, and they die, spiritually. If a Scorpio, for example, forbids her radiation to go out, the rays will turn back on her, and turn her to stone.
—Robert Bly
Sleepers Joining Hands

The essential American situation is a flat tire.
—Renatus Hartogs, M.D.
Four-Letter Word Games:
The Psychology of Obscenity

BOOK ONE

BOOGIE SUNDAY

She woke up crying. The devil moon had turned into a devil sun and the light was hurting her eyes.

Once when she was younger than young, her daddy'd told her that life was both too long and all too short and that she'd be surprised one day to find out what it was really all about. He'd said this seriously, snickering, with a Pall Mall glued to his lower lip, parked, as usual when he visited her, in the dorm parking lot at Ann Arbor. He never came in. They would cruise, snack at a drive-in and then sit like captives inside that Buick and talk the time away to curfew. Sunday was his visiting night and Sunday for her had always been the loneliest night of the week.

"Many a night, Angie," he told her, "youre gonna drink your drink and smoke and reach for the phone to call somebody but there wont be anyone to call—unless you ring *yourself* up." He'd laugh, coughing smoke. "And that's no kinda fun, now is it?"

She thought it peculiar at the time for him to come on that way. All she drank in those days was a lot of soda and a little beer, and she never really smoked except at parties or with smoking friends to make some type of silly impression.

But time, time, time'd made all the difference in the world and, God, she'd grown sick of time and the world. Even sunsets over the Bay were no fun anymore. She'd loved them when she first moved to San Francisco and thought they were poetic as hell, but slowly all the poetry in her seemed to be drying up. Sunsets, like most of the people, all over the world, grew saddeningly predictable and, worse yet, boring. Once she'd read in a book on how to paint that the best way to paint a sunset was to turn your back on it and paint the objects and scenes that reflected it.

She'd dreamed she was walking alone by the Bay, happy to the blue skies nappy with cloud. But just as she was taking off her sandals to dip her naked feet in, the water vanished, evaporated the way it does at low tide, and she ended up squishing around, walk hungry, in chilled mud. A male angel who somehow loved her (perhaps it was the ghost of a child she'd lost) flew down and nestled his feathery wings around her so comfortingly that she became aware in the dream that she was dreaming and never wanted to wake up. Feathers, the mud, herself —everything smelled sweet and she wanted it to stay that way forever. A trip was a trip but a voyage was something else again.

She woke up crying with that Sunday pang caught in her throat like a choking tear, Rahsaan Roland Kirk's inflated tear, and intuitively she touched a finger to her eyes. It's OK to cry in your sleep, she thought, so long as there's nobody around to make remarks about it. It wasnt like yesterday, waking up next to sweaty old Curtis.

"What's the matter, sugar?"

"How do you mean?"

"I mean, like, you woke up groaning and carrying on like you were coming up outta some dream about hell or someplace."

"Nothing's the matter."

"Then how come you made all those weird noises coming up outta sleep? I mean, you kinda had me worried there."

"What sort of weird noises did I make?"

"O, they were awful!"

4

"Awful? How?"

"I cant describe them really. I was laying here watching you, thinking about how funny it is to go to bed with somebody and they be one way and then turn around and wake up with them and theyre completely, well, different, you know."

She'd had enough of that. It was almost sweet to wake up all alone, in private, in her own bed with sunlight gushing through the upper portions of the window where the bamboo curtain didnt reach. Patterns danced on the walls, reflections of quivering tree leaves and passing traffic. She wasnt sweating like yesterday. She wasnt panicked.

Coolly turning her head to one side, she spotted her bra and bikini panties hung neatly over the back of a wooden chair. Where was her long dress? What'd she done with her shoes?

She felt tired but rested. What time was it? Had she been with anyone? Had she thrown up? Was this the Tuesday she had an interview at the department of employment? Hadnt Margo said something about driving down to Monterey? Or was it up to Mendocino? Rationally, it couldve been Saturday she was waking up to or Monday, but in her throat she knew it was Sunday and her whole body grieved for the hours.

Her mouth tasted sour and powdery.

What party had she been to?

What substances had she taken into her system?

What man had she let drag her home to die with and at what hour had he eased up, dressed, and tipped cleanly away?

This is no way to do it, she told herself. Ive got to go away somewhere and think it all over again.

For breakfast she turned on the FM, fixed herself boiled eggs and toast with jam, and drank a tall can of beer.

From Scoot's kitchen window, she could look down on her own bedroom window. Her lights were out and the bamboo shades were drawn, but just the same, she wondered whether he and Tanya had ever stood around in the dark of their place and peered for laughs down into hers. When she lived in New York on West 93rd Street, she'd look across the way and check out a middle-aged black couple, not unlike Scoot and Tanya, who fought all the time around the clock, pulling knives on one another, wrestling and screaming. Once or twice she'd gotten frightened enough to think of calling the police as she watched them set about doing one another in. She'd even flashed on the same thought when she'd first moved in next to Scoot and Tanya Harper on Grant Street, Berkeley, and heard them go into their traditional weekend knock-down-drag-em-out—

"Nigger, I know you weak-minded but you aint no good, aint never been no good and aint gon never be no good!"—but by that time Angelina was enjoying the absurdity of it all too much to want to interfere. Besides, the Harpers always made up and drank jubilantly after Tanya fixed a conciliatory meal.

"Baby, you wanna know somethin?" Angelina could hear Scoot grinning. "It aint nobody in the world can throw a meal in me good as you can. This gumbo, these greens, these biscuits, these black-eyed peas—*mmmMMM!* And this here sweet-potato pie! . . ."

Now here she was next door, up in their house, partying with them, the same people she'd always suspected of sniggling about her behind her back. "There go old Angelina Green with her little stuck-up black hincty self. Broad hang out with spooks, japs, chinamens, mexicans, honkies, jews and aint no tellin what all!"

Standing in the kitchen helping Tanya slice ham, she had to strain to forget the times she'd overheard this matronly brown-skin lady tell her husband: "Sugar, if you think these here dumplins is somethin—and this chicken and okry and cornbread and squash and buttermilk—just wait till all this good gin go to seepin on down and we get to boogie-woogin shonuff back up in there on the bed. I been savin it up for you all week, Scoot, and, now, you talk about *ready*!"

Tanya had a daughter by a previous marriage. She lived with them and her name was Etta Jean. As far as Angelina could figure, Etta Jean was in her late twenties and had also been

6

married before but had never had children. Watching her drive up evenings, wearily dragging herself out of her car in her sad uniform, she'd easily pegged Etta Jean for a domestic. She felt sorry for her. She felt sorry for Tanya and for Scoot too. Mother and daughter, when they werent working—Tanya cooked for a fraternity house—each took turns looking after Mama Lou who was Tanya's mother, an invalid theyd brought up from Louisiana to live out her last days with them. Angelina never saw Mama Lou but had often heard them speak of her and her eccentricities. For one thing, Mama Lou got awfully finicky, even downright mean, if she didnt get her double shot of whiskey with sugar stirred in it three times a day. Etta Jean had told her this and it still cracked Angelina up.

"Thank you, darlin," Tanya said, easing the ham slices onto a big serving plate with a fork and turning toward the dining room where all the food was laid out. Etta Jean was standing close by, talking with a fat man in mod clothes. Tanya broke in. "Etta Jean, baby, you see how nice Angelina been, helpin me slice this meat into thin respectable-lookin slices? Child, you better learn how to carve meat."

"I already know how to slice meat, Mama." Etta Jean was a little high and didnt like Tanya interrupting her conversation.

"You can tell me anything, but what if you get hold to a good man and he want you to carve him some meat?"

"What you say?" Etta Jean snickered, baring her teeth. "That aint no big thing, I'll *hunk* it off!"

The whole kitchen laughed.

The fat man Etta Jean'd been talking with laughed hardest of all. He'd been eyeing Angelina all along, giving her stupid blurry-eyed glances and winks. All she really wanted to do was mix herself another rum and Coke and get back to her sofa seat in the living room by the window with the breeze and let her mind roll on. There were too many people in the kitchen generating hotness. All during the ham-slicing, this portly drunk, got up in a fancy dashiki and an ascot, had been getting on her nerves. He made her think of old movies of Fatty

Arbuckle that she'd seen on TV as a kid, a black unfunny Fatty Arbuckle gone absurdly native. Maybe Etta Jean dug him but, to Angelina, he looked like a damn fool. Occasional drunk herself though she might be, Angelina didnt like drunks.

Before she could get away, Etta Jean asked her over to introduce her uncool friend whose name was Tolby Crawford. She stood there, like a captive simpleton, while he ranted on about nothing—his Elektra 225, how much he spent on clothes, rent, good-timing, his government job. The joker was fifty if he was a day and had the nerve to brag about what a good dancer he was.

Suddenly, spotting Scoot at the refrigerator door, the fool broke out into a number that seemed to even embarrass Etta Jean. "It's just like," he began, clearing his throat, "it's just like Franklin Delano Roosevelt say." Angelina knew he was signifying but she couldnt tell what about or why. She just didnt like being used this way. "If it just so happens you cant stand the heat, then get your nasty, stinky, sweaty, doofus-lookin Afro-American ass from out the kitchen! Aint that right, sweetnin?" Laughing at what he'd just said, the clown stuck his corny hand out for Angelina to shake or to slap. She wasnt sure which. She knew she wouldnt be staying at the party much longer.

Scoot, who'd also just about had enough, rushed over and wedged himself in between them and, looking grizzlier than necessary, proceeded to get Tolby Crawford told.

"Look here, chump! Look here, Tolby! In the first place, you doin your act in fronta two young ladies I happens to be quite fond of—my daughter Etta Jean for one, and the other young lady's name *aint* Sweetnin. She my next door neighbor and we good friends. I believe in treatin my friends right, OK? Her name is Angelina, Angelina Green—Miss Green to you! In the second place, you got the thing ass-backward bout 'If you cant stand the heat, get outta the kitchen!' It wasnt Roosevelt put that out, it was Harry S Truman and thats *all* he said. He didnt put in all that sneaky shit you slipped in with your signifyin self. Which brings me to the third place, and the third place is you been sloppin round back here layin into all my good Cutty Sark and Johnny Walker Red Label until you cant even walk straight no more—and just cause I ask you to go easy cause it's other folks that like to drink scotch too now here you come with your ass all up round your shoulders signifyin bout me bein stingy and doofus and every other old evil thing you can think of. Well, I dont play that! I'm a hardworkin man down at the Chevy plant and when I gives a party, I *gives* a party, do you hear me?"

"Now, wait a minute," Tolby shouted.

"Unh-unh, aint no waitin no minute. It's my house you gettin drunk in and I'm doin the talkin. I dont know who in the hell you spose to be. You told me you was a frienda Jug and Patsy's else I'da never let your old whiskey-pootin butt in here in the first place. You treat my friends and relatives with some type of respect or else take your wino manners back down on Seventh Street in Oakland or Sixth Street in San Francisco or wherever the hell you hang out! I aint nobody's sucker chump. You dont come up in my house insultin my people. Facta business, you owe everybody here a apology."

Angelina, who'd finally mixed her drink while Scoot was sounding off, tried again to break for the living room but this time it was Scoot who held up a hand to stop her.

The kitchen was silent and tense. The whole party, all the guests, at the sound of Scoot's voice, had stopped what they were doing and gathered in or around the kitchen doorway to watch and listen.

"Listen," Tolby Crawford blurted, a little pathetically, slurring his words. "I could go home right now and get my .44 magnum, stand your ass up next to a tree, pull the trigger and blast you *and* the tree away with one bullet and then turn around and organize me a defense committee to see to it I dont do no time."

Scoot laughed in the dude's face. Etta Jean laughed nervously, both eyes on her stepfather. Somebody had to grab Tanya and force a fork out of her hand.

Growing sick to her stomach, Angelina remembered that she'd been drinking rum and Coke for a good two hours as though it were only Coke. She'd even arrived with a hangover from last night. She couldnt stand this fatuous man who'd drawn so much cheap attention to himself. Her head was pounding.

"You wanna know something?" she told Tolby Crawford without so much as stopping to think.

"What's that, baby, you fine, foxy little sophisticated thing you?"

"Youre repulsive."

"Repulsive?"

"Stupid, sick, jive, ill-mannered, gross, and very corny."

Scoot moved in closer now as if preparing himself for the worst. "Come on, Angelina, I'll talk to the fool if you dont mind, aint no sense in you gettin mixed up in this."

"No, I mean it, Scoot. I mean every word. This is one aggravating corny Negro."

Crawford was trying to keep cool but it wasnt working. "Check yourself, pretty, I aint hit a woman yet but—"

The crowd shrieked, screamed and gasped and then fell silent as Scoot pulled the .32 from his inside jacket pocket. Some wisecracker way in back shouted, "Git down, Scoot, with your bad, bad self!"

Scoot leveled the barrel of the pistol at the dashiki'd belly of Tolby Crawford who, by now, was beside himself.

"I want everybody out the kitchen," Scoot shouted, "except for my wife, my daughter and Miss Angelina Green! Go on out and turn up the record player and keep on drinkin your drinks and eatin the food and enjoyin yourself. We got a little private business back here to take care of. Everybody out!"

Angelina, who'd never seen anything like this before in her life, was aware of a sizeable spurt of adrenaline spreading through her body, connecting with every nerve. Suddenly she felt soberer than she had in weeks. She wished she'd stayed home and read or watched television and turned in early. She wanted to be in San Francisco or New York at a quiet gallery opening, or in Paris chatting with talented Africans or expatriate Afro-Americans, or at sea in Barcelona cashing a Traveler's Check at American Express to go out on the town with new-found friends. She wished—and all of this shot through her head in a flash—that she and Larry were together again, avoiding all outside hangups as they stumbled through and improvised a fun romance headed, as it turned out, nowhere.

"I want you to apologize to each of these young ladies personally," Scoot ordered.

Tanya, arms folded, was grinning.

Tolby Crawford, wide-eyed, back to the sink, hands held high in the movie-like air, was still clutching his drink. It was so quiet in the room that Angelina could hear the ice tinkling in his glass as he trembled. "Uhh . . ."

"*Uhh* nothin! I want you to apologize to the ladies and then apologize to *me* and then get your repulsive ass on outta my house quick. And if I ever hear tella you sayin *any*thing to *any*body about *any* of this, I'mo get a contract out on your sorry ass so fast you aint gon never know what hit you. I might joke but I dont play. I know a whole lotta outta-work hired killers from the old school thatll up and off they own mama for a hundred dollars and a bottle—*bad* niggers, chump! And dont think I wont pay it and dont think they wont do a clean professional job!"

Apologies delivered, much to Angelina's discomfort, the offender was promptly sent packing. Scoot, .32 concealed in his coat pocket, even walked the fool outside to his car and stood watch while he started it up and roared away.

The party continued as though nothing had happened. Angelina wondered what she was doing here. It wasnt her crowd. The vibes were all wrong. Out of politeness, she danced to a couple of 45s with a necktied garbage man mostly to show Scoot and Tanya that she wasnt upset, but inwardly she'd had it.

"What you say your name was, honey?" Mr. Garbage Man asked.

He was a dark, wiry man with short hair in his early thirties who was taking night courses at Berkeley Adult School to broaden himself. He really wanted to break into real estate. He was a good dancer.

"Angelina."

"Well, Angelina, you sure are down, baby. I could dig a smart little college girl like you."

"How you know I'm smart?"

"I can just tell by the way you buck them pretty little eyes. They so sweet and . . . well, I kinda like the way they slant. You got some Indian blood in you back there someplace, don't you?"

"Probably," she said, glad that the record would be over soon.

"Yeah, me too—Blackfoot, what else?—on my daddy's side. Where you from?"

"Michigan."

"Michigan? What part?"

"A little town called Milan, it's about forty miles outta Detroit—farm country."

"You from Michigan, hunh? Well, I'm scared to tell you where I'm from. Yeah, no lie. But I can tell just by lookin at you, you kinda on the smart side."

"Can you tell that I'm sleepy too?"

"Where you live? I'll drive you home?"

"I can . . . I can manage," she lied. "I got my own car." She excused herself, saying something about the bathroom. Once out of his sight, she made her way through the hard-partying crowd of working people to find the Harpers and dutifully thank them for a fun evening.

Tanya Harper gave her a tipsy embrace and said, "Slow down, Angie. Slow down, child. I been watchin you and you

12

dont seem to be doin so good these days. Tell you, it aint nothing you goin through that I aint already been through and aint nothin worth runnin your poor self into bad health. Slow down, hear?"

"Sorry about that outburst," Scoot told her.

"No big thing," she said, smiling, smiling, smiling. She smiled all the way out the front door.

It was her fifth straight night of partying and, for the first time all week, she hadnt ended up with some vague man to hold her close through the terrible night.

Boogie didnt get it.

Drink didnt get it.

Being around a crowd didnt get it.

She still felt that pang.

It was still Sunday in the world and there was nothing she could do about it.

PEPSI GYPSY

The gypsy woman, with her comical earrings, took another sip of Pepsi and blinked at Angelina. "Youre an attractive young woman, you know." Her gown was dark paisley and her head scarf purple.

"Thank you, Madame Lola."

Angelina leaned forward, extending her right hand, clearing her throat out of nervousness.

Madame Lola took the small hand in her two large ones. Angelina felt the spiritualist's dry fingers brush across her own moist palm several times. She mightve felt embarrassed if Margo Tanaka hadnt already just gone through it all only minutes before. For a moment, with her eyes closed, she imagined that she was really putting herself in the hands of an exotic manicurist. She felt very confused and self-conscious being in a fortune-telling parlor. It was, after all, Margo's idea and not hers to drive down the freeway to Menlo Park for a consultation with a real freeway gypsy, as Margo called them. But here they were in a little stucco house nestled among Kentucky Fried Chickens and Taco Bells, antique dealers, liquor stores and car lots on El Camino Real. "I know my rotten luck's gotta change and yours too," Margo had told her, "and besides it oughtta be fun. The whole three years I was living down there on the Peninsula with my first old man while he finished up his doctorate, I always wanted to visit one of those psychics but that Marxist sonofabitch'd never let me."

MADAME LOLA, the neon sign out front read, SPIRITUAL READER & ADVISOR—CARDS PALMS PAST PRESENT FUTURE. Hungry at the time, Margo'd picked this particular gypsy, figuring that she and Angelina could go next door afterwards and gorge themselves on tacos and burritos.

Over the whirr of TV airplanes, gunfire and bombing, Angelina could hear children's voices and squeals coming from another room. She wondered what the Madame's husband, if there was one, did for a living.

"Well?" the gypsy said tentatively, eyes staring tiredly from her chubby tan face. "Is it the past, the present or the future you want to know about?"

Like any good American, Angelina wanted to get her money's worth. "How about a little taste of all three? Is that possible?"

The gypsy shrugged. "Sure, why not? In your case it's worth it. Most people have uninteresting lives any way you look at it. Yours fascinates me."

"How so?"

"Well, to begin with, youve led a pretty lucky life so far. Someone you loved, a man, just walked out of your life and you cant take it. There's been tragedy but youve always had good friends who've stood by you, especially one parent in particular —a father perhaps?"

A chill passed over Angelina but she couldnt help laughing out loud. "My father, yes," she said, "he's about the only family Ive got left. Is there anything else you can tell me?"

Madame Lola, the delicate lines around her eyes crinkling as she smiled knowingly, took a big swig of her Pepsi, let go of Angelina's hand and looked directly into her eyes. "Yes, but of course, my dear. You may feel old, very old but youre still young. Dont be so impatient. You want to know everything all at once. Youre looking for something, more than just answers. Youre looking for something important and before long youre going to realize that this past year's been one of the most important in your life. The new year will be even better."

"What am I looking for, Madame Lola?"

"I see you devoting yourself to a special path, call it what you will—the path of righteousness, the spiritual path. In your heart you like adventure. You want to know the truth about yourself, the real truth, because by finding that you feel that then youll know all there is to know about everything under the sun. Youre a lost little woman, Miss Green, but even so there's still times when you wonder if it's all worth it. Lately, for example, youve been on a sort of, well, crazy binge. It's as if youre at the end of something—a certain phase of your life that you dont want to see ending. You miss old friends, old times, all the gaiety you used to enjoy and take for granted. You miss being free and going from one moment to the next with no thought of yesterday or tomorrow."

Another draft passed over Angelina and she broke out in goose pimples. Now the woman was getting too close to home. She was telling her things about herself that she'd never even told Margo for fear that she wouldnt understand. Through soft traces of tears that were filling her eyes, she could see Margo slumped in a beat-up wicker chair, one room away, playing around with *Newsweek*.

"You even have reservations about being here this afternoon," the gypsy continued. "It's OK, I understand. You dont know this but lately youve been worrying unconsciously about something that's beyond your control. Someone else you love very much is ill and you dont quite know what to do about it."

Tears were streaming down Angelina's cheeks. Madame Lola handed her the napkin that the glass of Pepsi had been resting on. It was damp but Angelina patted her eyes and cheeks with it anyway.

16

"You stand at a street corner, my dear. You can go either this way or that."

Angelina remembered the I Ching reading that Margo had interpreted for her two nights before:

> Nine in the fifth means:
> In dealing with weeds,
> Firm resolution is necessary.
> Walking in the middle
> Remains free of blame . . .

"Madame Lola, I—"

"I know . . . youre afraid, but there's really no reason to be. All around you there's good people, good spirits. No harm is going to come to you except what you create to punish yourself. Youre complicated. What's your first name, Miss Green?"

"Angelina."

"Youre complicated, Angelina. Youre good at explaining everything but you. One look at a stranger and you know who he is, most of the time at least. The hardest thing for you to explain is yourself to yourself. Youre always asking yourself, 'Who am I? Who is Angelina?' You wont be satisfied until you can come up to some picture that you have in your mind and it isnt simple. Youre always trying to go one step beyond."

"Beyond?"

"Yes, beyond—beyond everybody around you, beyond yourself even."

"Is there anything wrong with my being this way?"

"No, no, no, of course not! When I was a young girl I saw in my own heart many of the things that youre beginning to see now. It's nothing to be afraid of. We all got to go down secret paths sooner or later. Like the rest of us, you suffer because of your wants. Dont forget that, but that's another matter. I have one other thing to tell you."

Angelina leaned forward to listen, her eyes completely dry by now.

"I see a man—very tall, very dark . . ."

Now it was Angelina's turn to smile, actually chuckle in a private way. "And very handsome no doubt, right, Madame Lola?"

"Handsome? Well, that's up to you, I'll leave it up to you to decide. Be patient with him, more patient than youve ever been with anyone. This way youll be helping one another. I wish that I could tell you more but now, well, it's up to you."

Sensing that the worst was over, Angelina sat up straight, adjusted her skirt and shyly touched the gypsy's hand. "Tell me, Madame Lola," she heard herself asking, "do you ever bother looking into your own future?"

"Not as much as I used to when I first discovered I was blessed with this divine gift. It's no fun really. I mean, knowing the future is no fun."

"But it seems to me that knowing what's going to happen automatically puts you in a good position to control things. Like, if I saw some disaster coming up in my life, wouldnt this beforehand knowledge somehow help me in taking steps to avoid that disaster?"

Madame Lola poured the last of the Pepsi into her ice-filled glass and sipped at it, looking lost for a moment. Angelina could almost hear it fizzle on the way to her stomach. "I would have to say no," the gypsy said finally, "at least not necessarily. You see, we all have a certain amount of control over our lives. We have free will. We're born with that—the freedom to choose between this and that. At the same time, we're each born with certain weaknesses that we have to struggle and put up with all of our lives, do you see?"

Angelina's eyes lit up. "How do you account for these built-in weaknesses?"

The gypsy laughed. "Now youre getting in a whole different area. Youre leading me into philosophy and religion and all that kind of stuff. I really dont want to go into it. Besides, you already know the answer, Angelina."

By this time, Angelina was trying hard to control her thoughts. She'd been in the company of psychics before and didnt want to be embarrassed. For fun, she pictured herself on a vast, sun-drenched beach by the bluest of seas, walking, conversing with Madame Lola. The thought of infinite space surrounding them made her glow.

Madame Lola glowed back at her. "My dear," she said in hypnotically soft tones, "youve always been basically a happy person. I can't explain why but youre going to go through some really tough times pretty soon now. Youll just have to trust yourself and what you believe in. There'll be family troubles. Youre going to take a trip that will mean a lot to you. Be patient."

"Will I travel alone?"

"No, not by any means, but a lot of the time youll feel as if youre genuinely alone. Nothing will be easy. You have much to learn from all this. When you feel yourself becoming ill, rest, cure yourself in cheerful surroundings. Above all, trust yourself. Be patient."

Angelina didn't know what to say, so she sat, saying nothing.

"You have powers you dont even know about yet."

"Is that as specific as you can get, Madame Lola?"

"I'm afraid so. Dont be so restless. Let yourself go a little. I mean, relax, really relax and stop trying to do yourself in."

Of course, none of it seemed to make much sense, but Angelina trusted the gypsy. Two years ago she mightve written down her every word but now she was tired, tired of living inside her own head, tired of herself most of all.

When Margo was called back into the room, she asked the Madame: "You wont accept Bank Americard, will you?"

The gypsy frowned. "Well, no, but I'll take a personal check . . . if youve got I.D."

The two women laughed and went into their purses for money.

"Thank you and bless you both."

A big-eyed child poked his head through the opening in the bead curtain that divided the rooms. "Mommy, are we ever gonna eat again? I'm starving."

His mother rose from her cushioned seat and waved him away as she saw Angelina and Margo to the door. "Please come again," she told them, "any time you feel the need." She was beaming. "Ive really enjoyed visiting with you both. Please . . . take a few of my cards and pass them out among your friends."

They sat in Margo's little Toyota. It was beginning to rain again. "Well, do we eat now or wait till we get back to Berkeley?" Angelina asked.

"Whatever you wanna do, Angie. Me, I'mo come into a considerable sum of money soon and spend all my time in plush, overpriced restaurants."

"O yeah? Well, I'm gonna meet me a very tall, very dark man who's handsome, depending, and go on a trip with all kindsa hassles. I'm too excited to eat."

"Ha, well, what say we grab a snack before we drive home . . . just to celebrate."

"Celebrate what?"

"Bein so lucky."

"Doesnt sound to me like I'm in for all that much luck."

"You know," Margo said, laughing, "did you notice how uptight Madame Lola was gettin when she thought I was serious about that Bank Americard stuff? If she such a good soothsayer and all, it seem like to me she woulda known I was just jokin."

"Maybe she put away too many of those Pepsis. Just because she can tell you a lotta things about yourself doesnt mean she knows everything. Besides, most people I know dont fool around too much when it comes to money."

"I guess you right."

"Maybe," Angelina said, hands gently patting her fluffy, simple hairdo, "I dont know. I dont know anything anymore. Let's eat in a real restaurant with menus and waiters, OK? I'm *so* sick of bullshit!"

ANGELINA
DESCENDING

When she got home everything was missing. Well, almost everything. Her Kenyan woodcomb, which she'd thought she'd lost, was on the kitchen table where she'd left it. There was soap, cosmetics, most of her books, the furniture that'd come with the place, a few clothes and a couple of useless pieces of luggage. But the rest of her belongings—typewriter, art books, clock radio, turntable, amplifier, speakers, LPs, new boots, her best clothes, her mother's jewel box and ring, the $112 worth of change she'd been saving in a coffee can, the little Sony TV set Larry had given her—all of it was gone at last. It was a comedown and a half!

She turned to Margo who'd come in for a drink and to use the john. Twilight hung in the sad room like blue smoke. "Well, Margo, I knew it had to happen sooner or later."

Margo squeezed her hand consolingly. "Who you think did it?"

"Had to be somebody in the neighborhood, that's all I can figure, someone who's been watching the place."

"You suppose it coulda been that fat drunk dude you was

tellin me about, the one from the party that your neighbor pulled the gun on?"

"I dont think so. I think it was probably one of those simple-ass junkies that just moved in upstairs in the house out front. I dont know why in the hell Montego rented to them in the first place."

"We all make mistakes, honey," Margo said, walking to the refrigerator door and opening it. "Hah! You lucky! At least they left you somethin to eat. Last month when I got hit, the bastards even cleaned out the fridge, ripped off all my meat and cheese, frozen stuff, everything. They even copped all my liquor and expensive wines, the assholes!"

Yes, but Angelina couldnt help remembering how Margo, with all that enviable alimony pouring in by the month, had been able to laugh it off. Besides, she'd had theft insurance. Angelina, stuck with unemployment checks, was secretly thankful that theyd at least left her with a couple of wicker chairs, tables, cushions and a floor mattress to sit and sleep on.

She sat cross-legged on the living-room mattress that served as sofa, trying to be calm, trying to be poised, unattached. A few afternoons before, coming home on the F bus from job-hunting in San Francisco, she'd watched a seagull coasting over the polluted waters as the bus crossed over the Bay Bridge. She loved letting her mind float out across the water, letting it cleanse itself that way over the hum of bus engine and passenger chatter. This afternoon, trapped in Margo's car, she'd had a premonition, a feeling that something was going on wrong back at her little brown shingle cottage. *Be cool, Angelina,* the voice at the back of her mind had said, doubtless inspired by the gypsy's talk, *no matter what happens just be cool, be calm, be what you strived for so long to be.* . . . Over the past year she'd learned to trust these hunches, flashes, intuitions, whatever you wanted to call them. Not only did her secret mind whisper; it was disturbingly right about 100 percent of the time. When it spoke—and it hadnt much lately until the Madame Lola visit—she listened, straining to learn from it all she could.

22

"Where do you keep your booze, Angie?" Margo wanted to know. "That's the real test of how bad you been ripped." Margo was a problem drinker and it was getting to be that time of day.

All the liquor and wine was in its cupboard untouched. Margo found glasses and poured them both some port. Lighting up a cigarette, she eased herself down next to Angelina on the mattress. "Berkeley sure is changin, hunh? Hell, I can remember back when I used to leave my doors open day and night. I'd go for a walk at two in the mornin if I felt like it and didnt need to carry no dog or chain with me. Cops wouldnt bother me and neither would the creeps. There wasnt no creeps then and if there was, I didnt have sense enough to know they was. Ah, beautiful days, amazin days. I cant even believe I lived through em."

"It was kinda like that when I arrived on the scene," Angelina put in wistfully, the port softening her. "I remember I'd be out walking down a street—Dwight Way, Ellsworth, Benvenue, didnt matter—and hear music, Marvin Gaye or somebody coming out of a window, and if I was in the mood for partying, I'd just go up and knock at the door and the people'd say, 'Come on in and join us, we're short on chicks,' or something like that and we'd have a good time just sitting around talking or dancing all night."

"Wasnt it somethin, honey? This was really at one time the only place to be—if you had to live in this messed-up country. I'd take off and go to London, Paris, Mexico, New York, but I always ended up back here where I knew I could find easy-goin basic everyday people just tryna make it that I could get down with and have a good time. We mighta all been crazy but we really had what they call today a sense of community, some kinda understandin."

"Youth," Angelina whispered.

"How's that, honey?"

"We were young."

"Maybe, I dont know. Youre what now—twenty-five,

twenty-six? I'm thirty. Big deal. You pass a certain point—in experience, if you know what I mean—and age has nothin to do with it anymore. You havent been tied down to two, count em, two men like I have, and youve never had children. I'm the one oughtta feel old. You act older than me, Angie! What the hell's the matter with you?"

"Margo, what am I gonna do?"

Margo gulped the last of her port and poured another generous slug. "You mean, whatre you gonna do about this rip-off? Same thing I did, chalk it up to fate and take it from there."

"But . . . You've got an income. I'm flat on my ass. Ive got nobody to turn to. I—"

Margo's eyes moved past Angelina to the darkening window. Montego's orange cat, an enormous tom, was perched in the middle of it asleep on a porch railing, shining in the light from his house out front. "I'll lend you some money, Angie. I'm your friend, you know that."

"I'm not asking for money. Everything's been going wrong in my life lately. I'm getting to be a drag, a drag to myself, a drag to everybody around me."

"Ever think of takin a trip?"

"A trip?"

"Anywhere, anywhere but away from here."

Angelina laughed.

"What's so—did I say somethin funny or somethin?"

"No," Angelina said, getting control of herself, "I was just thinking about a time Larry and I were talking about opening up a business, jokingly of course. We decided on a travel bureau, and the only names we could come up with for the place were When Do We Leave? and Anyplace But Here."

"He's really what's been botherin you, isnt he?"

Angelina was fingering the woodcomb, teasing the tip ends of her hair with it. "I miss him sometimes."

"I understand. You miss him but youre glad it's over, right?"

Music was what Angelina felt most like hearing now, but

there were no longer any records to play, no radio to snap on. Despite the warming port and Margo's company, she still couldnt get over the fact that she'd been robbed. She still wasnt sure whether to cry or celebrate.

"Angie. Angie, why dont you go to Mexico? I got friends there could put you up. You know Spanish. You got a degree in it from Cal and you been to Spain. I could lay a few hundred bucks on you and—"

"Aw, c'mon, Margo, that's asking too—"

"No, really, I mean it. I get a grand and a half a month from the settlement with Seishi—he's back in Tokyo workin for his old man, the sonofabitch!—and Booker just landed a heavy TV contract actin in a series outta L.A. and sent me a check for seven hundred fifty dollars, guilt money. It aint like I'mo be hurtin or anything like that. I think it'd do you good to get away from here for a while, at least long enough to get yourself back together, clear that sad little head of yours. I hate to see you this way, baby. I mean, I'm plenty screwed up enough myself but, heh, like you say, maybe I can afford to be."

"But what about my unemployment checks? I filed for a job at that new alternative school!"

"Youll have to figure that out yourself. I know you need all the help you can get right now but—couldnt you just tell them people in so many words that youre out to lunch for the time bein and sorta pick up the pieces after you get back?"

"I'd have to buy new clothes, new everything."

"Come on, Angie, what do you need for cryin out loud? I got clothes. We're around the same size. Quit makin excuses. We all get ripped off sooner or later one way or other. You dont mean to tell me Larry didnt rip you off emotionally when he split on you?"

"Please, Margo, please leave Larry outta this. That was complicated, hard to understand. I'm not sure I even understand it yet."

Margo put a hand on her shoulder and said, "Listen, I gotta go pick up my kids. You can stay at my place tonight if itll make you feel better. If you wanna take me up on my offer, fine, just say so and I'll write you out a check. If not, that's OK too. I'll still dig you for just bein you. That's my angle and that's all I care about."

"I dont think I could stand being alone here tonight after what's just happened."

"I hear you," Margo said, dousing her cigarette in a saucer next to the wine glass. "Pack your overnight shit and let's done went!"

As Angelina went about gathering her nightgown, tooth-brush, cosmetics and things to read, she felt glad having a friend like Margo, a crazy not unattractive redhead from South Carolina who, in many unofficial ways, was blacker in express-ing herself than Angelina was or would ever become.

Margo had soul, and soul, like blood, went way beyond pop ideas of sisterhood or brotherhood.

BASIC
AMERICAN
LIGHT

It was almost like old times. She was actually doing something again. Because of the gypsy and Margo, here she was all packed and organized, carrying out what, a few dreams ago, had only been a casual suggestion. Talk about excited! She was like the twenty-year-old Angelina who'd decided to leave New York one rainy summer afternoon and arrived in San Francisco a day later with less than a hundred dollars in her purse to parlay into half a decade of intense and so-so living. She remembered the way her mind worked in those days: *The only way to get something done is to do it!*

Placing her borrowed bags in the trunk of the Toyota, she flashed for one endless moment on the time she'd sailed for Europe, again with something like two hundred dollars in Traveler's Checks that lasted for the better part of a year as she schemed and partied her way through Tangiers, Madrid, Barcelona, Paris, Nice, Rome, Florence, and London. So now it was gonna be Mexico City, OK, all right, she'd do what she could.

At twenty-six, she felt terribly old. She'd felt old at twenty-two in Europe—unmarried, no steady man, a year of teaching high school Spanish behind her and any number of meaningless desk, counter and lab jobs. What was life supposed to be all about anyway?

She'd always been a loner, the friendly outsider, but more and more she thought dutifully about selling out and getting married—if only she could find the right man and work out a suitable arrangement. He wouldnt necessarily have to be rich—a modestly successful artist would do—but he'd have to understand that she needed time alone and, at the same time, someone to love and relate to on a permanent part-time basis. Larry came closest and Larry was gone.

Angelina sat at her side of the table, petrified with emotion. They were drinking Bloody Marys in the airport lounge and Margo was winning. Decked out in jeans and turtleneck sweater, Margo looked like an old-time 1950s bohemian at the onset of the Beatnik era. There shouldve been a chessboard in front of her, a pack of Kools, some Thelonious Monk thunking away in the background and a discussion of what Albert Camus said to Jean-Paul Sartre going on at the next table. With her shoulder-length hair, which framed her sly face perfectly, Margo looked classic.

They shared a lounge seat that overlooked the airfield. Planes taxied, roared off and set themselves down. Angelina was in twentieth-century heaven. She loved airports. She loved the idea of everything, everyone, being in transit, and nothing dramatized it more for her than hanging out in some plastic, streamlined structure, waiting to get on a plane or to get off of one. It lent direct and instant meaning to everything else that was or wasnt happening in her stupid, sealed-off life. Hopefully, the future would help her justify and make sense of this chaos called now.

"What's the first thing you gon do in Mexico City?" Margo asked.

"Find a room and go to sleep, sleep for as long as I can, then go find Chapultepec Park, walk through it till I'm exhausted."

"Why Chapultepec Park?"

"Because I read about it in all the books. It's supposed to be beautiful, really beautiful and safer than Central Park."

"Anywhere's safer than Central Park. After that whatll you do?"

"Find a man?"

"You askin me or tellin me?"

"That's for me to know, as my cousins used to say, and for you to find out. Who knows what I'll do? Wish I was back here probably."

"There you go with that old defeatism again. Send me a card, naw, a letter so the postman cant read it. I want you to be—*ta daahh!*—intimate."

"Listen, Margo. Thanks. Thanks for everything."

"Big deal! Send me a letter and some pictures and if you really get to havin a good time, call me up long distance collect and I'll come down and join you. I aint like you. I aint got scruples *one!*" They were walking the long spacious distance to the departure gate. "I'm just jokin, honey. You know me. I'm basic. I got scruples all right but I'm a good American too. I wear my scruples light. I love you, Angie. Take care yourself."

FLOATING

Snuggled into a window seat at the back of a jet plane zooming toward Mexico City, Angelina felt more than virginal again. She felt almost innocent and absolutely vulnerable, a little like a nun who was shedding her habit, resigning from the Order and setting foot back in the world on her own tentative terms.

Suspended this way, between heaven and earth, she felt happy to be free and uncommitted for the time being, at least until the plane set down.

The simple sight of the impossible world laid out so neatly below—measured off into ridiculous squares, humps, slices and circles with roads and highways snaking through—was enough to bring back the child in her who'd known by the third grade that doors and fences meant nothing in the end.

Thank God for woods and forests, jungles, mountains, streams, lakes and rivers that splashed into oceans!

Plane trips always did this for her—put her back in happy touch with herself.

She thought about absolutely everything. All that water! All that sky! All those clouds beneath her now! If her little life back down there on the ground had seemed like a slow dream, now she really did feel like a bubble in some private, mysterious sea.

She spoke Spanish with a little boy, couldnt have been more than seven, who told her all about his daddy's huge undrawable house and airplane and fast cars—mmmmm, the pleasures of weekday air travel to impossible places!—and she talked with a somber American who'd been shuttling between San Francisco and Mexico City for the past thirty years, a shy Lebanese importer-exporter, a man whose balding head was polished gold.

Food was delicious again.

Head clearing, body resting, heart softening, she felt surrounded by millions of years, every nameless moment of which was once now.

WHAT MEXICO?

The first thing she did was to have the taxi driver rush her through the afternoon rain to a good second-class hotel, El Azteca on Calle Bolívar, described in the cheapie travel guide she'd been studying as "clean, well-lighted with plumbing that works and a charming elevator, one of the oldest in the capital." She had to use her firmest Spanish to keep the driver, who looked like a mestizo Raymond Burr, from diverting her to another hotel, one from which he no doubt received a kickback on every tourist he delivered to its lobby. She'd been through this kind of thing before in Europe. Once in Madrid, fresh off the train with the business card of a particular pension in her hand, a cabbie had actually lied to her, insisting that no such place existed and that she'd do well to check into his friend's pension which turned out to be one of the biggest bummers in the Western world. Two days later, walking, she'd discovered the nonexistent pension and decided she'd never trust another train station or airport cabbie for as long as she lived.

Because all singles were booked up, the Azteca's desk clerk, a wheezy little Syrian in a seersucker suit who affected dark glasses, offered her a double on the fourth floor at single rate on condition that she'd move into a single as soon as one became available. It was raining, she was tired, so she took it.

El Azteca was close to the *Zona Rosa*, the so-called Pink Zone where fashionable tourists and monied Mexicans mingled. Many of Margo's friends lived there. Angelina decided to shower, relax, nap a couple of hours, dress and make a few phone calls before hitting the streets for a late supper. Maybe she'd even end up saving money if someone offered her a free place to stay, but for now she planned to do her own independent number and enjoy a little privacy. Accepting the hospitality of others, she'd learned too long ago, had its drawbacks.

Bathing her face with Noxzema after a tepid shower, she wiped a clean circle in the steamy mirror and looked at herself. It'd been a long time. Since April (it was October now), she'd been too busy being self-involved to keep track of herself. All that drinking and bad food had left its mark. She thought she looked terrible—puffy cheeks, flabby neck, wrinkly eyes. Her whole body seemed to have changed. Her eyes felt dull, her tongue thick and useless, her spiraling hair unalive. "Youre getting old and fat and ordinary, Angelina. Pretty soon nobodyll wanna look at you anymore!"

Dried off, a nude, she climbed into one of the beds and read a long article in Spanish in a magazine, *Siempre*, about the Mexico City subway, pausing between paragraphs to daydream about the time she and Larry set out for Baja California in his Volks and got as far as Carmel where they checked into a dumb motel and spent the evening watching the Miss America extravaganza on clear cable TV. They drank a lot of beer, smoked a little grass and, between visits to the john, made love like hardcore professionals.

Missing Larry now was like missing a part of herself that set no limits on the pleasure of being with a man who dug you as much as you dug being his. It had taken her a year and a half to find out what she'd always known anyway—that no one belonged to anyone. She was still having trouble getting over the rediscovery.

Bone tired, she rang the desk clerk and asked him to ring her back at six. He explained that he went off duty at five but that he'd leave a message for his relief man to buzz her.

"Muchas gracias, señor."

"De nada, guapita," he told her, *"de nada."*

She didnt like his uncalled-for familiarity—"Youre welcome, cutie, youre welcome"—but she was too exhausted for the moment to call him on it.

She lay back, stretching and squirming, and pulled the cool, starchy sheet and skimpy blanket up over her, groaning to lose herself in two hours of delicious sleep.

Somebody's snoring kept waking her up. It took her forever to figure out it was her own. Except for the flashing of a sign in pink neon that seeped through venetian blind slits, it was dark in the room. For an instant she wondered where she was. How had she gotten here? Whose joke was this?

Lying very still, she heard voices oozing through the wall from the next room. They were in Spanish and slurred. A man and woman, in passionate discussion were using a lot of slang she couldnt understand. There was heavy breathing and long silences between words. The woman said something incomprehensible that made the man laugh. Laughter being infectious, the woman laughed back as Angelina made out what she imagined to be the sound of them crashing down together across their rented bed. Finally the man said, *"Chhhsst!"*—Spanish for "Shhhh"—and from then on out it was bed springs, coughing, giggling, moans and grunts.

She knew she was in Mexico and she knew that the desk clerk had simply forgotten or neglected to ring her like he'd said he would. The whole layout of the room came back to her. She reached for the light which, sure enough, was there at bedside. Clicking it on, she saw what Mexico she was in for the time being and winced at the sight of her borrowed belongings spread all over the room.

She was hungrier than she'd been in months. Her watch,

which lay on the nightstand, read 2:00 A.M. If she were a man, she'd simply get into some clothes and go out into the night to forage for food, scoring chicken perhaps or rice, tacos, enchiladas, burritos, refried beans, chili dogs, chili, sloppy joes, pizza, pancakes, cornflakes, a chocolate malt, pork and beans—anything! Chicken Delight wouldve been all right. She caught herself thinking so extensively about La Fiesta, the Mexican restaurant on Berkeley's Telegraph Avenue, that she scrambled out of bed to her feet and immediately began searching her bags for the candy bars she knew she packed there somewhere.

The thin portion of herself that was some kind of make-do intellectual registered: *Aha, America, land of instant gratification! All-nite eateries, computerized cheeseburgers and fries to go . . .* FOOD GAS TELEPHONE RESTROOM NEXT EXIT

She found two enormous Hershey with Almond bars and wolfed them down shamelessly seated on the bed's edge. How long to morning? Why hadnt she thought to pack anything to drink?

Cigarettes she did have, up the kazoo, and she smoked them to stave off hunger the way a panicked diabetic munches sweets.

She was wide awake now. It was going to be one of those nights. She knew that between now and the time all the light came back into the sky she'd be thinking through everything that'd ever happened to her, but from some strange angle based on her changing self being in this pitiful room at this particular bend in time.

Back home she'd simply snap on a good FM station, keep the volume low, get her head nicely messed up and groove with her thoughts till morning.

Tonight she chain-smoked, something she never did in real life in the States. She drank dangerous Mexican water from the tap and read her thick pulp travel guide from beginning to end, pausing to wonder what the hell she was doing here.

A LETTER FROM THE NORTH, A LADY FROM THE SOUTH

dear angelina,

a herd of deer, a pride of lions, a pack of wolves, a lepe of leopards, a sedge of herons, a rafter of turkeys, a nye of pheasants, a flock of pigeons, a school of fish, a gaggle of geese, a nest of ants, a hive of bees, a tribe of indians—what do they all have in common?

even though we only spent a night together, i still find myself thinking of you all the time. i know you were pretty wasted at the time because i was too & you were further out than me, walking around your house naked with the tv on in one room, the record player grinding out marvin gaye in another room, and the radio blowing scott joplin ragtime in the only room left, the bedroom, that cozy little bedroom with the blue light & the posters of ray charles & muhammad ali where we made do so beautifully that my head was permanently taken apart.

you're some lover, ms. angelina green, & i don't only mean this in a gross physical context—i'm saying that the subtlety of your appeal—the secret ways in which we communicated—was enough to make me rush home & write at least a dozen poems in my head. as the days passed, i managed to get a few of them on paper to send to you but my better judgment said no, that i should wait.

i am not a poet, angelina, as much as i would like to be and have tried to be. i am only a poor, lonely dreamer; a thirty-year-old bachelor who by day attends classes at san francisco state with the express purpose of securing a masters degree in business administration. my b.a. which i took at a small black college back home in missouri was in sociology. i've always wanted to be a creative individual & almost majored in english or art history but the pragmatic side of my makeup told me to go into something practical. i still admire creative people, more especially those who perceive that creativity need not be relegated to mere practice of the arts. you strike me as being a person who is creative in everything you do.

you may wonder about my writing this letter. i can assure you, however, that i am not a nut or a chump. i was very much taken with you that night even though we were only two lonely people who met at a party. i knew fred, the one who was giving the party, from my old track-running days in high school back in st. louis, therefore he invited me. i'm sure glad he did. have you ever seen a picture called *The Loneliness of the Long-Distance Runner*? well, to me that was a very moving picture (see, i do keep trying to be a poet in spite of myself). i was a long-distance runner & even though i'm not one any longer, i'm still very lonely.

i hope you're having a charming time of it down there in old meheeco. i used to go with a puerto rican girl who maintained an intense dislike for mexicans. i never understood it & used to tell her so. after all, puerto ricans & mexicans speak a mutual language & have both been exploited by the same oppressor— the blue-eyed devil, the "gringo" if you will—so why the conflict? what's wrong with human beings anyway?

i tracked you & your whereabouts down through fred who knows an honorary soul sister named margo tanaka—a friend of yours, i believe—& hope that during your broadening travels you will perhaps find time to respond to my little discursive hello.

reply to my riddle if you can or so wish. i hope you're getting over your sadness & crying spells & that this awkward missive will not have annoyed you in any way, shape or manner. don't eat too much hot, spicey food & watch out for those latin types. i wouldn't want any of them to steal your sweet little heart.

yours shyly & respectfully,
curtis

p.s.: like I say, I think about you all the time & your pretty little mouth is something more to me than a functional organ designed to receive food, drink, smoke, or to issue forth words.

It was her fourth day in Mexico, her second visit to American Express on Calle Niza to ask about mail. The friendly lady had handed her this envelope sent air mail, special delivery.

At first Curtis's letter annoyed her but more for Margo having told him where she was than for anything he'd said. In fact, she rather admired his straightforwardness. She'd felt that way about more than one man on brief encounter but lacked the nerve to try and put it into any form as elusive as language. The general tone of it made her think of all those old records she'd grown up dreaming by and dancing to as a kid where, in the middle of a song, the band would relax into a soft background riff for a chorus while the lead bass singer'd come in with some spoken nitwit soliloquy:

> My darlin, I craves you.
> If only there was more time
> in the day for me to kiss on you
> is my one sincere desire, for you see . . .
> from the bottom of my deep deep heart
> I salute your cold cold eyes and
> your bold bold thighs as we pretend
> that a youthful young love

like yours and like mine
did not flare up . . . between us . . .
And I know . . . cause you told me so . . .
that in our very souls we connected
(O yes we did)
in that teen-age paradise called eternity.

Jammed between four other passengers in a *pesero,* one of the jitney-style taxis that shuttle the length of La Reforma, the city's fashionable main thoroughfare, she read the letter over and over again, wincing and chuckling.

A Latin-looking lady, a portly beauty-parlor blonde in elegant middle-aged dress, nudged her and said, "That must be what you call good reading matter, yes?"

Angelina ignored her.

"I like to see people when they are responding so apparently to a letter well written, dont you see? It makes me also feel like my day is made of course." The lady was beaming.

Angelina wasnt sure how she'd handle this. She herself was nosey to the core but wasnt fond of this quality in others. Should she play dumb and ignore the woman one more round, do her *no comprendo* number and play the non-English speaking foreigner, or cop out and be Latin too? As was often the case in the States, everybody's racism and her own skin was going in her favor. She could come on anyway she wanted because, no matter what she did, no one would really take her seriously, the way they would a regular universal individual, a white person.

"*¿Mánde?*" she said, meaning "Beg your pardon?" as she folded the letter away.

"*Ándele pués,*" the lady zipped on, "*usted habla el español. ¿De dónde es?—¿de Panama, de Costa Rica, de Puerto Rico, de Cuba?*"

Angelina had a good mind to tell Her Nosiness that she was from Uruguay, descended from a powerful but little-known Afro-Indian family (her grandmother being of pure Charruan blood) that had once been the talk of all Montevideo. Instead she decided to put the lady on with the truth which somehow was always more confusing than sarcasm.

"Soy de los Estados Unidos," she said. Everybody in the taxi, driver included, turned to have a look at her. *"Soy de Michigan y de California."*

"¿De qué parte de California es, jovencita?"

"Del norte."

"Ah, de San Francisco, ¡no me digas!"

"Vivo en un pueblecito muy cerca de allí."

"Ay, eres de Berkeley—eso sí que es, ¿verdad? Debe ser la ciudadita mas bella que visité durante mi breve residencia en su gran país. La conozco bien pues mi hijo mayor es estudiante universitario allí. Dígame, pués, ¿dónde aprendiste el español?"

"Lo estudié desde mi niñez . . . en la escuela secundaria, la escuela superior y además fue mi estudio principal en la universidad."

"Ay de mí," the lady said, "there's for certain no need of us continuing to do the chitchat in Spanish, yes? You speak it beautifully for a Michigander and a Californian but since you are now from the famous Berkeley then let us why not express ourselves in English. I love the language, the American English, you know. My oldest son is a student of electrical engineering at U.C. Berkeley. I received my doctorate in Education from U.C.L.A."

"What do you teach if I may ask?"

"Certainly you may ask, *jovencita.* I am now professor of Art History at the University of the Republic at Montevideo."

"Are you headed for the Museum of Anthropology too?"

"In fact I am, yes. Have you ever before seen it?"

"Spent all of yesterday here. I love it. Ive never really seen anything like it."

"I am here for a convention of Latin American university professors. This is my one free afternoon to do with myself what I please and I am spending it all touring this remarkable museum which I have already visited four times before. Tell me, what is your occupation?"

Angelina hated that question. "O, I teach—Spanish."

The lady was delighted. "I thought so as much. Spanish, as

you must know, is such a universal language. It should be taught everywhere, throughout all the world, yes? We tour the museum together, OK? I show you things. I know it by my heart, OK?"

Angelina felt uneasy but what else was there for her to say except OK? She was growing to like being by herself. Besides, she could always fake a headache if necessary, if Her Nosiness got on her nerves too much, and split to return some other anonymous day.

OCEANS

They did the first floor of salons and displays together—Introductions to Anthropology, Mesoamerican and American Origins; Pre-Classic, Teotihuacan, Toltec, Aztec Mexico, Oaxaca, the Gulf, Western and Northern Mexico. The lady from Uruguay turned out to be knowledgeable indeed. Angelina even found herself enjoying Sra. Ruiz's lively commentary and opinions on various artifacts and crafts and the peoples who'd produced them.

As they entered the Oaxacan salon, Sra. Ruiz said, "You must know that the *indios* of this region, the Zapotecs and the Mixtecs, never could they live at peace with one another. Each group wanted the throat of the other group, *comprende?* The Zapotecs built the great stone-made cities of Monte Albán and Mitla—you hear of them, yes?—and the Mixtecs came and destroyed their fantastic temples or, how you say, churches. Well, it is in this way that I see it. . . . The Zapotecs always thought the Mixtecs was a mistake, you see, and vice-versa, you understand?" The lady laughed.

Angelina laughed, not so much at the pun as at Sra. Ruiz's

impressive capacity for enjoying herself and getting a kick out of very small things.

"Forgive and pardon me for making what you call a witticism but I like to play with the words."

"Yes, youre something else," Angelina told her, hungry again by now. Theyd been traipsing the halls for hours it seemed. Sra. Ruiz wanted to know what it meant, this "something else," and Angelina explained it to her in American and Spanish the best she knew how, adding politely, "I dont know about you, señora, but I sure could use a bite."

The señora surprised and delighted Angelina by answering, "Yes, but of course, my dear, I too could stand to be bitten myself, above all by a delicious hot dog. After we take lunch then we tour the Mayan salon, OK? In my opinion, it also is very something-else."

In the expansive cafeteria, they rested their cameras and munched on sandwiches and salads; drank coffee, smoked and played with their sunglasses while Sra. Ruiz told Angelina all about herself: her upbringing in Punta del Este, the resort town out from Montevideo where her father ran a first-class hotel near the beach; her "wild" grad school days at U.C.L.A.; her marriage to a wealthy Argentine meat-packing heir and his death by cancer seven years ago, leaving her with their two sons—Mario, the EE student at Berkeley, and a younger boy, Antonio, who was stashed away in some Swiss prep school. Like everybody else, the señora was lonely and not particularly happy with her work.

Angelina promised her she'd look Mario up when she got back to Berkeley and told the strange, peculiarly glamorous older woman about her own travels and stupid moves; the little farm she'd lived on in Milan, Michigan, before her mother died and her father moved to Detroit to take a civil-service job. He never married again but took as a common-law companion a sweet, resourceful woman who respected Angelina and accepted her as a daughter. Dad was now a moderately successful administrator with the postal service. They kept in touch by mail and phone calls. Sra. Ruiz didnt understand why they lived so far apart. Angelina explained that in America it's the individual who matters most and that she and her family, such as it was, lived at separate ends of what's called reality. She too was lonely and fed up with the kind of life she'd been leading.

In the middle of all this, two men who'd been sitting at a nearby table walked over and introduced themselves. One was white, the other black.

The white one, in suit and tie, said, "I believe that Ive met you before, at least one of you. Were you at the recital I attended last night on Calle Tokyo?"

Both women shook their heads no.

"Then perhaps it was at the reception given for my good American photographer friend Anthony Borowitz at the Mexican–North American Cultural Institute last Monday."

"I wasnt even in town then," said Angelina.

"I dont like photographs," said Sra. Ruiz.

"Well, how bout this," the black man said, "instead of all this formal oompty doomp, what say we join you lovely young ladies for some coffee?"

Both women waved for them to be seated.

The black man, who seemed to Angelina to be all of seven and a half feet tall, was very big, football size, and had a broad, cheerful Toltec-looking face—or had she been looking at too many statues and potteries? He introduced the white man. "This here is Theodore Robinson from Winnipeg, Ontario, Canada. He taught . . . what was it you told me you teach, man?"

Theodore Robinson cleared his throat. "I'm an associate professor of geography at the University of Manitoba."

Angelina watched the señora's face brighten.

"Yall can call him Ted," the black man smirked. "It's all right if they call you Ted, aint it?"

Obviously bugged, Ted adjusted his tie.

"Me, my name is Sylvester Poindexter Buchanan, but

everybody call me Watusi. I'd be pleased if yall'd call me that too. I'm from everywhere."

"Everywhere?" Angelina couldnt help asking.

"That's right, young lady, everywhere. You name it, I been there. You point it out on a map and I can circle it and add footnotes. My man here a geographer but I'm kinda whacha might call an explorer."

"How interesting," the señora broke in, "an explorer."

"That's right, madame, aint nothin to it. Little babies could do it if you jacked em up to it! I like to wander around through countries and cities and towns and mountains and valleys and various settins, especially those situated on the surface of that vast ocean the human mind as it's commonly called."

For the first time all week, Angelina felt herself on the verge of loosening up. All the little pressures, trivia really, that had been stacking up at the back of her head—her incurable loneliness, the burglarizing of her cottage, the need to find a job, paying Margo back, Curtis's letter—it all began to dissolve softly like pain from a body that's just been shot up with Demerol. There's nothing the matter with me, she thought, that a little imagination wouldnt cure.

"So," said Ted, hands folded gentleman-like atop the little formica table, "we finally get a chance to chat up close. We've been admiring you young ladies for the better part of half an hour now. It's certainly a pleasure to be sitting here at table with you. Is there anything you want—coffee, more food, dessert perhaps?"

Sra. Ruiz, who was suddenly all smiles and blushing girlishly, shook her head no.

"No, thank you," said Angelina, placing the edge of her hand at her throat, "we're full up to here. Whatre you guys doing down here?"

"Aw, you know," Watusi volunteered, all but winking at Ted (or so it seemed to Angelina), "we come down to the cafeteria same as yall to fuel up on some scarf."

Ted shot the black man a funny glance and Sra. Ruiz, for a moment, looked lost.

Angelina, amused but still in control of her side of the table, said, "All I meant was whatre you guys doing down here in Mexico?"

"I'm here writing a book on Aztec ecology," said Ted.

"And I'm just here," Watusi sang, hands tugging at the chest of his elaborate serape, like some nighttime peasant dignitary straight out of the movie *Viva Zapata*. He took off his straw hat and Angelina cracked up out loud. His bushy natural, parted down the middle, was packed down tight where the hat had rested but fully puffed out on each side of his head. To her he looked like an old-time Fiji who'd been banged on the head with a plank.

"You are the both of you so amusing," Sra. Ruiz said finally. "I do not know what it is I am to make of you."

"What say we all four of us take in the Mayan room together," Watusi suggested. "They some down very together brothers and sisters. Any of yall ever been down to Yucatan? They generous, fun-lovin people that after all these years managed to hang on to they own language."

"A highly intelligent race of people," Ted put in. "Why, the ancient Mayan priesthood was well aware of the revolutionary significance of language. They kept strict control over the written word which—"

"Who dont know that?" Watusi broke in. "The mysterious Mayan codices and Chicken Itza and all that stuff, right?"

As they strolled the Mayan salon together, Sra. Ruiz outdid herself explaining this fetish and totem and that style of handicraft and dwelling place. She knew more about it than anyone in the group and obviously took perverse pleasure in conducting her own private tour within a tour.

"How is it you know so much about Mayan culture?" Ted wanted to know.

"She's a professor," said Angelina.

"At the University at Montevideo where I lecture," chimed the señora, "we are involving ourselves with all manner of what you call pre-Columbian cultures, do you see?"

"Yeah, I see," Watusi put in, tapping his forehead, "you lettin us know how heavy you are bout your own territory. Rap on, sister, I hear you! I hear you! Back home you'd be drivin all the MCP's up the wall and blowin em away with your fabulous brain and your fine, foxy olive-complected self! And I'd be right there in the background rootin for you."

When the señora blushed, Angelina knew it was because she hadnt the vaguest idea what this loud, rambunctious man was raving about.

Ted, who'd been messed with once too often, tightened the knot on his tie again and gave the so-called Negro smart-ass a look that sent shivers down Angelina's back. "Have a little respect," he ordered, visibly upset. "She isnt a señorita, she's a señora. If you want to get down to, well, the true nitty-gritty, she's a full professor, chairman of her department for crying out loud!"

Watusi—who at this point was standing between the two women—took them by their free arms and added, "Am I forgiven?"

"What does it mean this . . . MCP?" asked Sra. Ruiz, shining.

"Male Chauvinist Pig!" Angelina and Watusi answered simultaneously.

"What's this particular sculpture all about?" Ted threw out, cuddling closer than ever to the señora. "Is it from Uaxactún or Tikal? I've seen it described in a number of studies if memory serves me correctly."

Angelina and Watusi, each recognizing that the other was about to die laughing, hung back, moving spontaneously toward another display far enough away to allow them momentary privacy.

"Do you consider him your friend?" Angelina asked as soon as she figured they were beyond earshot.

"That dude? We met up in the Oaxacan room bout an hour ago just before we come down to the cafeteria and run into yall. He come up and ask me if I had a cigarette, said I reminded him of somebody name Rahman X or somethin like that, some blood workin outta Montreal that's sposed to be some kinda light-weight militant or somethin, be on TV all the time. Aint too many niggers up there, you know, so I guess this joker been havin a pretty easy hustle of it scarin the white folks and Frenchmens, pullin de wool over ole massa's eyes like they say."

"Shhh, keep your voice down, he might hear you!"

"Dont care if he do. I knew he was jive from in front. He knew I didnt look like no Rahman X, he just wanted a smoke. I cant stand a damn liberal! It's a lotta niggers do but I aint one of em. I met a nigger once in Copenhagen, Denmark, married to the daughter of a furniture tycoon, and do you know this poor nappy-headed ex-patriate, got his two brownskin, blonde-headed daughters in the back seat of his Volvo—I was hitchhikin and he picked me up—had the nerve to lean over and confide that even tho he been living up there in the Land of the Midnight Sun—remember that Lionel Hampton tune on vibes? —he was really a Panther?"

Angelina hadnt expected all this. She'd only wanted to find out how two men who'd introduced themselves together, presumably as friends, could be so hostile toward one another.

She sighed. "But you really gave us the impression you were pretty good buddies, acquaintances at least."

"Look here, sister," he said, changing everything. "Can I call you Angelina?"

"Only if you let me call you Sylvester."

"Watusi, Watusi—that's the name I go by. Where you from?"

"California."

"Big country. You from L.A.?"

"San Francisco."

"Now we zeroin in. San Francisco or Oakland?—or for all I know you just might be from someplace like Richmond or East Palo Alto, or have the people raised enough hell by now to get East Palo Alto changed to Nairobi?"

"How about Berkeley?"

"Unhh-hunhh! Now I hear you, Angelina! You like me."

"I do?"

"I mean, you *are*. If you from outta someplace like Berkeley then you kinda like me—in the sense we share certain unarguable affinities and similarities, dig it. I'm from all them outta the way places too—them offbeat settins where niggers do all right for themselves living by they wits between the cracks."

"I dont know if I agree."

"Aint no need to agree or disagree, baby. I'm from the States too, you know, and if it's one thing I know about it's this shadowy AA."

She was attracted to him, no doubt about that, but he made her nervous. "OK, Watusi, here we go again—AA, what's that?"

"This Afro-American. . . . You . . . me . . . even that stone monument we standin in front of."

"I'm afraid I dont get it. How's that sculpture supposed to be Afro-American?"

He towered above her by a good foot and a half. He looked as if he should be on exhibit. He must have weighed 250 pounds to her 110. She thought of her father and her father's father, both big flat-nosed, barrel-chested men with willpower to spare and senses of humor as sharp and shiny as machetes. "It's a whole lotta shit I got to school you about," he said. "We got oceans yet to cross. How long you in town for, Angel?"

"I'm just trying to clear my head—a couple weeks maybe."

"That's long enough, plenty long enough. What's your girlfriend's plans?"

"O, you mean Sra. Ruiz? We just met."

"Yall just met too? This planet gettin tiny enough to fit in my backpocket. Where you stayin?"

"A little hotel, the Azteca over on Bolívar."

The dude from Winnipeg and the lady from Montevideo caught up with them and suggested that they all have dinner together at, say, Bellinghausen's, a German joint in the Pink Zone specializing in seafood.

Angelina made up her mind to come back and do the Museum all by herself some neutral afternoon when she could take it all in without the slightest interruption, no matter how pleasant.

BLUES

Dear Curtis Benton,

The night has at least a thousand eyes but it has a lot of ears too. Through five hundred eyes I'm looking at Mexico City out my window and the lights are blinding me. My ears hear sounds I could never describe. The sum total of my audial-visual impressions is sufficient for me to conclude that this is one dirty, noisy town. At night before I go to bed, I take a kleenex and wipe my windowsill clean. When I wake up the next morning and do it again, the tissue's all black and grimy. What can I conclude except that they've finally hit the bigtime here: lots of smog, lots of exhaust fumes and too many cutesy-poo car horns for a country girl like me. The haze hurts my eyes and the din is definitely deafening.

Your letter surprised me to say the littlest. I myself am not much of a letter writer. I mail off my bills and grind some form of greeting out to my folks when the guilties overtake me but a correspondent I ain't. I guess you could say that, at base, I'm a very shy person. O, I shift into some other gear when I've had a few drinks or tokes but, generally speaking, I like to do very quiet things alone or with someone very special that I trust and like. Now that you've forced me to peek out of my shell, there's something I should tell you.

Less than a year ago, I broke up with a man I loved more than I love myself. We'd been together going on two years. He was a kind, thoughtful, passionate man; rather reclusive like myself. Before meeting me, he had spent most of his adult life working to support his aging mother who was an invalid. She needed so many things—specialized medical attention, orthopedic devices, registered nurses in the home and, possibly, above all else, the love of her son, her only child. It nearly killed him. From the age of twenty until he turned thirty, he was tortuously guilt ridden even though it wasn't his fault that she'd contracted some hideously complicated form of leukemia. When he wasn't working terrible jobs to raise money, he lived in with her. Occasionally he'd sneak out to a movie with some girl he'd met on the job or get drunk with buddies. After she died, I inherited him. He needed a mother, and I needed somebody to mother so we got along fabulously for two springs, two summers, two autumns and one very long winter.

He split. I don't want to lay all this on you but tonight's the night, as they say in the song, for me to do my confession thing and, Curtis old boy, you're my arbitrary confessor. He split and I flipped. By the time you met me, I was still flipping. I still am. I wanted to disappear. I wanted to pull the good-bye to end all good-byes. One night I actually took the AC Transit Bus from Berkeley to San Francisco and walked all the way (don't ask me how) from the main terminal on First and Mission over to the Marina, Lombard Street, straight out to the Golden Gate Bridge. I walked out onto that bridge, drunk on adrenaline, and started visualizing in my mind what would be the best spot to jump from. A full moon was out, one of those life-size illustration moons that you poets like to romanticize and publicize, and I just looked at it real hard, the way I used to look into my Aunt Jujie's face, which was also a planet unto itself, trying to imagine people on other planets and wondering if they had to go through all the sad changes we have to go through down here on this ground called Earth.

It's funny, Curtis, how it all comes back. Even now as I write all this in my unhappy room, I feel that night swooshing in my face, chilling my neck and shoulders and face and breasts and hips, nipping at my panty-hosed legs. Nobody's ever written about, I realize now, what it's like to strut out onto the Golden Gate with the idea of doing what that bridge is most famous for making you do. People say that your whole life passes before you as you're dying. That rainless winter night my silly little life started flickering across some dumb screen in my head like an uncut B movie shot on location under the worst conditions: the loneliness I'd known all my life; the stupid things I'd done and regretted and every precious change I'd lived through; the time my folks took me to the Michigan State Fair, for example, and I got sick in the fun house; the first boy I ever fell in love with who wasn't out of a comic book or a movie or some dumb TV program (Hank Graham in the 9B who'd taught himself to play piano and could imitate any singer out); the day my mother died and I was sent to live with my way-out Aunt Jujie and Uncle Roscoe; my early days at the University of Michigan (Aunt Jujie had predicted correctly that I'd get a partial scholarship there) and my saddening discovery of where mainstream America was coming from. I won't bore you by going on and on about all the scenes that flashed in front of me as I strutted, shuffled and creeped toward that bridge, determined to make some kind of messy peace with myself.

Well, I got out there finally in the middle of that structure, that landmark, and, preparing to make some awkward leap, I noticed how uncomfortable I really was. It was too cold and windy to be out so late at night. Besides, I had to pee. For a moment, I pictured myself mounting the bridge railing and, pulling the balancing act of the century, hoisting my skirt, pulling down my pants and panty-hose, and squatting carefully to relieve myself. The thought of it made me giggle. Some old feather-headed drunk—God only knows what he was doing out there that time of night—wobbled by and held up a $20 bill that flapped and snapped in the wind at his fingertips, mumbling, "Baby, all this is yours if you just come home with me tonight and gimme a good back rub, have pity on a stoned old man!"

I actually saw myself going home, wherever that might be, with the pitiful old buzzard. Once you've decided to do yourself in, any act, no matter how absurd, becomes a positive yea-saying event. I held my territory, said no to the drunk, and rejoiced in the new strength and power I sensed welling up inside me just because I'd decided to take that ultimate chance. With nothing to lose and absolutely nothing to gain, I felt myself coming alive again.

Suddenly I heard my old Aunt Jujie's voice sputtering into my shivering head. "You can fool around and fool around and die if you want to, but don't think for a minute that the world's gonna stop just on account of you done somehow slipped out of it. You come here a stranger and that's pretty much the way you'll be going out! This world, Angie, sweetheart, ain't nothing but a big old fake. God didn't put you down here, you know, to make no home but He did put you down here for a purpose."

I heard that voice and at the same time saw myself written up in the papers and talked about on television—MYSTERIOUS BLACK WOMAN LEAPS TO DEATH. There would be statistics about how many haggard souls had made the plunge to date and all the overpaid psychiatrists, black and white, would rush out to make a killing analyzing and packaging my misfortune. How corny it all seemed. I'd rather die what passes for a natural death—MILITANT ASSASSINATES WIFE or BELOVED AUNT ANGIE KICKS BUCKET AT NINETY—than goof and wind up sorry.

This is how it all came down, Curtis, just a few quick-moving months ago. I decided to stick around the Karma Circuit (as I'm told the Hindus call it) and let everything that follows be gravy. The left side of my head said You're a Fool but the right side of my head said Live Each Day as if It were Your Last.

This is what I've been going through, and I wanted you to know so that you might understand where my head was at around the time our paths crossed so fleetingly. My life to date's been a series of misses and near-misses. I never get a bargain, it seems, I always have to pay the full going price and then some. For years now I've lived in self-imposed exile from my family and all the people I grew up with. You could say, I imagine, that I'm something of a recluse and misfit who wants desperately to be a part of something bigger than this stifling little cocoon of flesh and nerve endings that we so glibly call Self. I feel as if I've been in the world all this time without accomplishing anything of importance.

Just before I left Berkeley, my place was robbed. Margo Tanaka, bless her crazy old heart, was kind enough to lend me enough money to come down here for a couple of weeks to try and get my poor head back together. You probably already know all this. Your letter, which I thought was nakedly and beautifully put, sent me through a few changes that I'm still trying to figure out. Mainly, it made me think about how eager we are (or, rather, I am) to try and touch someone by establishing bodily contact only. Frankly, I had forgotten the details of the night we passed together. I only remember that you were quiet and thoughtful and very gentle.

I'll stop now before I go completely mushy on you. I'm glad you followed your impulse and took the time to write me. I haven't the slightest idea what your riddle means but your letter meant a lot. What do all those creature units have in common?

Let's get together for a drink or something when I get back to Berkeley. Making friends with someone new certainly wouldn't hurt since I feel as though I'm starting life all over again.

Best wishes,
Angelina

She finished the letter in one sitting at a reading table in the Benjamin Franklin Library, the U.S. Information Service facility on Calle Niza between Insurgentes and Londres, where she'd gone to find San Francisco, Detroit and New York directories to look up the addresses of acquaintances she wanted to send postcards to. She folded the letter without reading it, slipped it into a thin Mexican envelope, pasted on a colorful air mail stamp, and dropped it into her big purse with the untouched postcards.

There'll be plenty of time, she thought, to think over what I've said before I mail it.

Stepping out into morning sunlight, she felt as if she'd just gotten some kind of minor complaint off her chest. Writing all that stuff to Curtis had been pure catharsis. Her cluttered head felt lighter now, the way her whole system felt after she'd had a good cry or interacted with a good blues.

Except for a good-bye luncheon engagement with Sra. Ruiz and some afternoon shopping for herself and for Margo, the day ahead was open for her to indulge in the kind of unscheduled and imaginative loafing she never seemed to have time for in the States anymore. Here she was free in Mexico City at eleven o'clock in the morning!

For fun she bought a strawberry ice from a street-corner vendor to enjoy while she strolled around with no possible destination. Most of all she loved being on top of time as it flowed on and passed by and simply slipped away.

A GEMINI
INVITATION

Wiping the last of the green sauce from his mustache with the back of his hand, his eyes narrowed and he spoke very urgently but simply. "I gotta go outta town for a few days and, well, I was wonderin if you'd like to go along with me."

She knew that he expected her to be startled, and she was, but was too full of food and drink to put up much of a show. It had all happened quickly, too quickly, but she was getting used to the pace. "Just like that!" she said. "Youre leaving town and want me to accompany you—just like that?"

"Well, did you have other plans?"

"I'm supposed to look some people up, friends of a girl I know in Berkeley. In fact I shouldve looked them up as soon as I hit town. They have a house in Lomas and could put me up. That damn hotel's been getting me down."

"Lomas, eh? Pretty fabulous part of town. They Mexicans or what?"

"Americans, I think, but they could be English or Swedish even. The name's Hansen—Francisco and Laura Hansen."

Watusi's eyes lit up. "He's American and she's, uh, Mexican, I think, but German descent—you know, her folks suddenly turned up down here around 1944 or somethin like that. It's a whole lot of em immigrated here right around that time, no questions asked, if you can get to that. Did pretty good for theyselves too. All they kids got names like Pablo Wurstistfertig, Pedro Auerbach and Maria Luz Hitler, and they be cruisin round in Porsches and Mercedes-Benzes with they blue-eyed yellow-headed selves talkin Mexican like a mariachi!"

"You mean you know the Hansens?" Angelina asked, this time forgetting that she was too stuffed to act surprised.

"*Know* em! I aint even hardly been able to get away from em since I been down here. They be at every party I show up at and they tight with just about everybody in town, specially on the foreign set."

"What do they do?"

"Dont do nothin!" Watusi laughed, producing a toothpick. Angelina thought he looked nice in his blue shirt and lemon tie, a hell of a lot better than he had in that damn serape at the museum. "They aint *got* to do nothin. Between em they got enough pesos to spend the rest of they life in a taxicab with the meter runnin—even in New York!"

Angelina hadnt intended to laugh for fear of making Watusi think that she approved of his dramatic advances but she couldnt help herself. At the same time she felt bad about not having contacted the Hansens. Margo hadnt said much about their backgrounds but had stressed the fact that they knew how to live.

"Well?"

"Well what?"

"You gon stay round here in the big city and goodtime with Frank and Laura—and I mean they will naturally get down and goodtime you to death—or you gon make this run with me?"

From the moment she'd laid eyes on him that silly afternoon in the museum cafeteria and all through today's spastic changes, she'd been trying to figure out, among other things, his age. The other day she'd put him in his early thirties. When she'd arrived at the Azteca this afternoon and found him waiting in the lobby, playing chess yet with the flippant desk clerk, she'd pegged him for middle-aged, forty-five, say, if he was a day. During the walk through Chapultepec Park, a beautiful excursion that she felt had brought her back to life, she thought of him as being closer to her own age. Now that theyd lingered over drinks and dinner and coffee at El 77, a bullfight fan rendezvous on Calle Londres—"I know this OK joint over on London Street," he'd said, "where all the bullshit bullfight freaks hang out but the eats is for real and they keep the lights right"—he looked positively ageless.

Was this what she was looking for—some fast cozy action? Her head felt blank and cushiony. During the meal her thoughts had drifted to Billy Strayhorn's tune "Lush Life," the part where the singer whispers about "relaxing on the axis of the wheel of life to get the feel of life."

The answer was "Yes" but she wasnt pronouncing it yet.

"Where you going?"

"I'll level with you, baby, if I might be so presumptuous as to lay that term of endearment on you."

Right away she figured she was in for some masterful shucking and jiving.

Watusi waved the waiter over and, without consulting her, put in an order for some Kahlua liqueurs. She'd have preferred brandy but her mellowness kept her silent. Would the day ever end?

"I'm runnin a little business deal down here. Me, like I told you, I'm one of them dudes that hopscotches the globe like they use to say on the news. I aint in it for headlines. I'm in it for all I can get. I'm workin with a dude, a most resourceful young man from California, San Francisco as a matter of fact, who's in the import-export business. We sorta formed whacha might call an informal partnership. I deliver certain goods to him—ethnic artifacts that I come across in my travels around—and he make it worth my while, OK? I dont go round advertizin it but I'm a pretty good judge of authentic jewels such as jade and the real down-on-the-ground pre-Columbian arts and crafts. I gathers it up, turn it over to him and he carry it up the States for retail. We split the proceeds and that's how Rock and Roll was born."

"You still havent answered my question."

Watusi sat back and held up his half of the two newly served liqueurs. "The name of the place is Guadalajara or, if you wanna get personal, a town called Chapala situated in the grand old state of Jalisco."

As soon as he said Jalisco, pronouncing it in the genuine Mexican way, a paunchy party of four at the next table, two dull couples, took immediate interest in them. Angelina felt the way she did in similar Stateside restaurant settings when common white people made it a point to theatrically acknowledge the presence of her and her black date. She didnt hate white people; she simply was careful in her personal associations with them. As for Mexicans, there were times when she wished she couldnt understand the language as well as she did, particularly here in the capital where people hurt themselves grinning in your face and then muttered murder under their breath as you walked away.

"As a good Gemini to a steadfast Libra, shall we, hee hee, clink to our forthcomin journey?"

She touched her glass to his automatically and then asked, "How do you know I'm a Libra?"

"It's a pure sign, Angelina, one of the purest. I can spot you people a kilometer away. Yall all hung up with justice and balances and pretty things and lookin good and the world got to be just so-so for yall or aint nothing doin."

"Do you have any feeling for me?" she heard herself asking.

"It's been six years," he said, "since I made a fool of myself like I done over you today."

TRACKS

It'd been a long time since Angelina had taken a real train anywhere. O, she'd ridden on BART, the Bay Area subway, when it finally opened up, and now and again she'd grab the SP commuter train over in San Francisco and roll down to visit someone on the Peninsula, but her last rail trip of any length had been from Madrid to Marseilles that European summer when she'd grown so weary of dragging and having her body transported from place to place. She loved trains and told Watusi so.

"Good," he said, apparently set on pleasing her in any way he could now that she'd decided to take a chance and accompany him to Guadalajara. "I dig em too. Aint nothing like a nice long train ride to relax the body and mind too and dont have to worry bout fallin out the sky or dozin off behind the wheel. I use to really get into it when I was a kid and my folks'd send me back down south every summer from Chicago to Mississippi to stay with my daddy's people. The Chickenbone Special they called it—all them box lunches. Me and my brother we'd sit up there in our seats for a while and then walk around the car and get to know everybody. I remember one summer it was a joker

61

on the train kept everybody up all night, crackin jokes and walkin from seat to seat, sittin in on card games and all that kinda stuff—this was back in the days when they put the colored off in separate sections, you probly too young to remember any of this shit—and everybody kinda liked this old tall basketball-player-lookin Negro. He even got in tight with the colored porters and cooks and kept talkin bout how he wanted to get in on some of them crap games he knew they had goin on somewhere on that train. Nigger kept flashin his sucker roll, you know, a big wad of bills, probly wasnt nothin but a gang of ones with maybe a couple twenties and tens on top and at the bottom. Well, I stayed up all night and seen the joker break into his thing after all the chumps'd finally done gone to sleep. What he was really into was sellin watches and rings and shit and I set there in my seat, curled up next to my brother—wasnt worried bout a thing cause I knew the Travelers Aid people was gon look after us at them stops—and watched that cat sell two-three hundred dollars' worth of jewelry in a hour's time. Said to myself, 'Well, yeah, so that's how you do it, hunh?' "

Angelina thanked him for dinner and the cab ride home and said, "Tomorrow at noon, OK? I'll be packed and ready."

She'd planned to sit in her room and think things over carefully and soberly. He'd given her his number in case she changed her mind in the middle of the night. Instead she went straight up and carefully packed. Too tired and fuzzy to think anything through, least of all the consequences of what she might be letting herself in for, she showered leisurely and fell into deep sleep—no dreams.

When the National Railroads of Mexico train (with the letters *F.F.N.N. de M.* stenciled on everything connected with it) pulled out of Gran Estación Central de Buenavista at midday, Watusi and Angelina were safely on it, seated right up in a first-class compartment with the window shade half-drawn to keep out sunlight they didnt need.

Her seat faced his. At the bookrack before boarding, she'd

picked up a photo-joke magazine, *Foto-Risa*, which she thought might help her catch up on current Mexican slang. She also bought, out of curiosity, a terrible pulp novel called *Los Hippies*, and an expensive copy of *Newsweek* in English to get some idea of what people thought had been going on in the States while she'd been smugly absent.

Watusi stretched out—hands behind his head, feet propped up on the unoccupied portion of her own seat—and yawned like a man who'd just come home to rest after a hard day in the onion fields or the insurance office. In his simple slacks and sport shirt, pen in pocket, he looked like the last man in the world she'd ever be attracted to on a voluntary basis. It was that warm, plentiful face and the body that went with it that made her feel so relaxed around him. What was it, this sense of well-being that he touched off in her? Words just didnt say it for her. His sense of humor? Yes, maybe. For certain, she hadnt met a man who'd made her laugh the way he could since freshman days at U. of M. when she dated Winfield Shattuck from Atlanta. But that was about all Winnie, as he was called, could do. He was funny as hell, especially in bed where she least wanted jokes, but never got over the fact that he was from an old-line colored aristocracy family back in Georgia in whose eyes she was only slightly better than poor white trash. After going out with Winnie and a couple of other bourgie Black brothers, she'd come to the unhappy conclusion that she was a misfit, at least in college Ann Arbor. She befriended and dated one or two white guys from classes but that hadnt worked out either. As long as they related to colorless activities and topics of conversation, OK, but as soon as she wanted to break loose and really be herself the walls went up again, firm and solid, and sex in those days was secondary to everything else as far as she was concerned. She never, for instance, forgot the time a white date had insisted she listen to a certain Woody Allen comedy album. Pipe in hand, with lots of good wine and a couple of joints on the side for good measure, he'd sat there meticulously checking *her* checking it out. Angelina had heard the album before and thought it pretty hilarious. She didnt want this young man to know she'd heard it before so she was particularly careful to laugh and respond appreciatively in all the correct places. Besides, as with everybody else in the country, there was a part of her that'd been raised on this type of comedy. At the time, they were both psych majors and had just read Freud's *Jokes and Their Relation to the Unconscious* which concluded, as she understood it, that humor, like every other aspect of human personality according to Freud, was essentially unhealthy. When she played this serious young white date some tracks from a Moms Mabley LP the following Friday night, he absolutely hadnt known what to make of it. He made a poor show of pretending to laugh (in all the wrong places) and later asked in all seriousness, "What did she mean when she said, 'Thank you, Lord, for puttin me back here round people that *know* what I'm talkin *about*!'?"

"Are you happy?" Watusi asked out of nowhere.

"Let me turn this page"—(she was reading *Foto-Risa*)—"and I'll tell you."

"Well?"

"Yes," she said, lightly brushing his ankles with her fingers, "very much so."

"I registered us as Señor and Señora Sylvester Poindexter Buchanan, you know."

"You what?"

"Aint no big thing, pretty eyes. We aint signed up for no Pullman service or nothin. I just thought for the sake of convenience it might probly be better if we travel as man and wife insteada havin to go through changes with these simple-ass machos and petty officials. They aint never heard tella Womens Liberation—even though it's more women lawyers and surgeons and professors down here than it is in the New Knighted States—and I dont wanna have to go up side nobody's jaw behind no trivia. Beside, since we both off-color they gon take it for granted we legally together anyway dont care what you tell em. In short, the customs and mores of these fascinatin people are very much at variance with our own, wouldnt you say?"

Stretching out her own long legs, Angelina grinned like a rag doll as she thought about towns theyd pass through, people she'd see, the sights, the smells, the music; the imagined thrill of being vibrated across the land as though she were riding a giant version of one of those old-time foot revivers she used to stick a penny into for a buzzy foot massage when she was a kid and that was what you did.

Watusi'd dozed off almost as soon as the train had got rolling. At first Angelina felt deserted because she'd been thinking how much fun it was going to be to take in the landscape as it flashed by, just the two of them, swapping and matching comments and glances. After a while, however, she rather appreciated his quiet little fadeaway. It freed her to be alone with her own thoughts again, and it was nice to have some changing scenery to think out across. It was even nicer to be going someplace. She had no idea what Jalisco, the state, would be like; hadnt even taken time to read up on it much, and that's what was nicest of all.

Like the rest of the passengers, Mexicans mostly, she kept her eyes glued to the window and took visible delight in anything novel that popped up—farming families at work in green fields, for example, who'd wave at the train with hands and hats as it roared through their little native planet. Even the urbanized Mexicans got a kick out of zipping past some kid in a sombrero mounted on a burro or leading one loaded down with beautifully tied bundles of sticks and firewood. Idyllic wasnt the word for it, it was downright comforting just to know that there were still places on the earth where people still poked along, the way her grandparents had, sweating out a way of life that had to be better than hustling in a city, dying in a factory or making do on grants or welfare.

Was she being romantic and simplistic? What about feudalism? What about capitalism? What about the way the Indian was treated compared to the mestizo to say nothing of thriving fair-featured Mexicans of Spanish descent and foreigners out to protect their investments in the national economy?

For one long, unbearable moment, all the old orthodox Berkeley-style rhetoric came rushing into her head, but she was having none of it. She felt too good, too secure in the privacy and warmth of this moment to be brought down by social concepts.

The world's always been impossible, she thought. The gloomy side's always been here from the beginning but to dwell on just that aspect of being alive to the exclusion of little joys which, like everything else, were painfully momentary . . . well, was that really telling it like it is? What was it all for anyway?

Angelina, slouched in her seat, let it all run through her brain but it was really the gorgeous unphotographable light shining down on the whole world, dirt and loveliness, that astounded her at this moment, reinforcing what little faith she had in the importance of keeping afloat.

"It's a whole lotta Mexicos, *verdad*?" Watusi said, waking up suddenly from a very long nap.

Theyd reached Celaya, a fertile little outpost in the state of Guanajuato. As at all the other stops, vendors of all ages invaded the compartment to hawk their wares and foodstuffs.

"*Cajetas! Cajetas! Cajetas de chivas!*" was what they all seemed to be shouting. A tattered little girl who couldnt have been older than eight thrust a tray in front of her. It was filled with various-sized containers that appeared to be made of delicate wood, balsa perhaps. Angelina took one look around her and saw the Mexican passengers going into their pockets for money, many of them grinning with excitement. One elderly gent had already cracked open the thin balsa top of his goodie with a wood spoon and was smacking his lips contentedly as he licked up its brown, syrupy contents. She knew that *chivas* had something to do with goats, but *cajetas de chivas* meant nothing to her. All that high-flown Spanish she'd lost sleep over for grades in college, and now she didnt even know what all the fuss was about!

Watusi wiped his face with a handkerchief and yawned. "This the Mexico where they make this stuff they call *cajetas de Celaya*. Some call em *cajetas de chivas*. All it is, is a kinda carmel-like sweet made outta goat milk, but everybody really be into it. I mean, they be's *diggin* into it. Check out that old dude cross the aisle!"

"Have you ever had any?"

"Yes, yes, yes, and it's so good I even stock up on the stuff. Try it on pancakes sometime. Here—"

He handed her a twenty-peso note. She passed it on to the little girl who carefully counted out four large glass jars of the village specialty.

Curious, she opened one of the jars and dipped out a fingerful. It was so sweet and delicious she wanted to shout.

Celaya was also a rest stop. Angelina had the munchies and so did Watusi. "We better not wander off too far," he advised. "These trains down here got a way of sneakin away without givin you warnin the first. Sometime the dude might toot his whistle a coupla times but you sure as hell cant count on it. Let's eat in the train station so we can keep an eye out."

"Youre really an old hand at this, Watusi. How many times have you traveled this route?"

"Not all that much really. Maybe half a dozen times. I'm a fast learner, baby. One time I had to pay a cab fifty pesos—four dollars American—to drive me to the next town to catch up with a train that'd done slipped off while I was foolin round gettin a shoeshine."

"That happened to me and some friends in Spain once. Our luggage and everything was already checked through from Barcelona to Madrid. The taxi driver caught up with the damn train but wanted more money for the trip than we could afford."

"Ripped yall off real righteous, I hear you. What'd you do?"

"One of the girls, Connie, her old man was some kinda

67

big-time black gangster outta Chicago, laid a fifth of American whiskey on him she had in her big straw purse and a cheap transistor radio. We got together about three hundred pesetas between us—"

"That's around five bills, right?"

"Yeah, about—and that seemed to do the trick. The three of us got out and rushed for the train. I looked back and saw the taxi driver actually sniffing the whiskey before he took a big slug of it right from the bottle."

"Yeah, well, them jokers . . . I been burnt in Spain myself, burnt bad. It aint one of my favorite places, not even to visit, except maybe for Málaga. You ever been there? They got some fine little Afro-Gypsy-Hispanic sisters round there! The Moors, whoever the hell they was, sure took care of a whole lotta business in them seven hundred years they laid round the Iberian Peninsula. They got a lotta nerve talkin bout *limpia sangre,* 'clean blood.' They got to be the most mongrelized race of people in the world, you wanna look at it on that level. Everybody—the Phoenicians, the Romans, the Carthaginians—everybody'd done run up into Spain and done they thing before the so-called Moors got there. And what was the Moors anyway?"

"They were Arabs out of North Africa, right?"

"*Noooo,* no! They was first and foremost Africans, honey. Come up into Spain, as it's now known, without woman the first, and spread they technological know-how around—very advanced, you dig—mathematics, architecture, administration—and even now you got hundreds of words, probly thousands, that you can track straight back to Arabic. This town we headed toward, Guadalajara, for instance, mean somethin like stony river in old-time Moor talk."

"You arent a Muslim, are you?"

"The Nation's all right with me," he said, picking up a plasticized menu, "but where matters of religion're concern I take the ultimate fifth. I'm strictly me. Hear people talkin bout 'I'm a Freudian, I'm a Marxist, I'm a Christian' and all that, not necessarily in that order, historically speaking, y'understand, and all I got to say is I'm me, a stone Watusian if there ever was one."

A band of what-you-see-is-what-you-get mariachis darted toward their table.

"We play all kind of music," its spokesman bragged.

Angelina had put her X on mariachis, having noticed that the city natives called them coyotes to their face and quipped about what would happen if they had to hold down real jobs.

"What you want to hear? We at your command—a ranchero, a bolero, chazz, a bluez, anything you like. May we suggest for you 'The Tracks of My Tears' made famous worldwide by your fantastic Smokey Robinson and the Miraculz—or whatever you may desire?"

"If I wanna hear Smokey and them," Watusi shouted on his way to the men's room, "I'll hire em. Tell these parasites to play 'La Bamba,' a beautiful Mexican tune from Veracruz, Afro-Mexican, check it!"

They played it smoothly and mechanically. Angelina handed the lead guitarist-singer, leader of three, the ten pesos Watusi had dropped on the table. Having honored the request, this middle-aged man, who reminded her of a vagrant ex-uncle-in-law, under his big professional hat, grabbed up the money and had the nerve to linger, to ask her for the pleasure of having dinner together, just the two of them, alone.

When she insisted in Spanish that her husband would violently object, he came back with: "Hokay, hokay. Just take it easy, buddy. I was only having the fun, you know?"

"Whew! They sure be's blowin a whole lotta soul down here in these roadside johns in the provinces," Watusi breathed, seating himself again. "*Too* much soul! What you havin? I want this thing they call an American Cheese Sandwich with a taste of refried beans on the side and a Coke. What time is it? You enjoyin your trip, pretty?"

SMOOCH

"Well, what you think?"

"I think it's great. You know that dive I was holing up in back in Mexico City, the Azteca. No comparison!" Even as the words rolled off her tired tongue, she couldnt believe she was pronouncing them. She thought she sounded like some quaint MGM gun moll from the 1930s.

"I dig it too and I'll tell you somethin else. It's my sincere intention to sleep a hole in the bed tonight and dont get up till I'm good and you-know-what. It's buses leavin for Chapala all day long way into evenin so aint no hurry bout that. I just want you to be happy seein as how I talked you into jumpin down here with me on a hype anyway."

"On a hype?" It was bad enough that he'd spoken so brazenly back in Celaya of how attractive the girls were in Málaga. She'd been in Málaga. They werent all that hot. In fact, they were mostly bummers as far as she was concerned. Besides, who was he anyway?

"I dont mean what you think I mean by hype, Angie. I'm just tryna apologize gentleman-like for comin on so strong from outta nowhere. You dont know me from Adam, and I dont know you from Eve but we both been in the world long enough to know what apples is."

"My whole life's been a hype," she said.

They were sprawled across their respective beds. Watusi had phoned ahead to reserve them a room at the Francés, a moderately priced hotel on a quiet side street close to the center of town. Not too long ago it had been a charming old monastery. According to Watusi, all their rooms with double beds for couples had been booked up and so he'd settled for the twin beds. They'd only be stopping over for a day or two before moving on to Ajijic, the little fishing village less than an hour's drive away where his business associate was based. Angelina was glad about the twin beds but was cool enough to keep her feelings to herself. The thrill of being in a different place again with someone whom she really didnt know but thought she could get to like was excitement enough for the time being.

"Your whole life," Watusi drawled, at the same time yawning into an enormous fist. "Dont be talkin bout your whole life until it's been lived out. Me, I'm kinda like Satchel Paige. I really loved that old dude when I was a kid. He played baseball the way Cholly Parker blew music—all funny-style and offbeat, or, like the so-call critics say, unorthodox, heh—but all the same old Satch like Bird was a mammy-grabbin genius! Dare anybody! The man was too much for them old stiff academic ball players and didnt nobody even know how old he was. I dont even think *he* knew. Just kept pitchin that ball and catchin that ball and runnin them bases with his old off-the-wall homemade technique till the Caucasian sportin powers finally got together and said, 'We gon have to do somethin for this old nigger or else history gon catch up and embarrass our ass! What say we elect his butt to the Baseball Hall of Fame?' Old Satch got up and accepted they award real gentleman-like. I seen it myself over the CBC up in Montreal, Canada, and like to broke out cryin."

"Never look back," said Angelina, sitting up, super-weary.

"That's right, pretty. Never look back. That's what he said

and the man was consistent with it. Never look back—somethin might be gainin on you. That's my philosophy. I might do a little thinkin ahead based on past performance, but I try to live every day like it might be the last. We could be lollygaggin round this hotel room for the last time checkin one another out. Like I say, you dont know me and I dont know you but, dont care what nobody say, the best time of your life, you mysterious little thing you, is right now and dont you forget it!"

She thought about herself perched up there on the Golden Gate Bridge. What an extravagant gesture! Now, seated upon a well-made bed and with everything in the world she needed close at hand, she saw how silly it'd been. Perhaps Watusi was right and telling the truth despite his half-ass way of putting it. That business of having your life pass before you as you went down for the second or third time still fascinated her. There were specific moments she'd give anything to re-live. Was another one taking shape now?

Apparently they were both going to play it cooler than cool. He hadnt made any overt advances so she hadnt yet found it necessary to dip into her dwindling reserve of defenses. They really were putting up a pretty good show, she thought, of being an old-line married couple—an easy-going colored couple from the States on holiday, as the English put it, in a Mexico that was straight out of the books. There'd be time enough for foolishness, an innocent touch of smooch, as her Uncle Roscoe used to call it, maybe, somewhere down the line.

They both slept till noon and breakfasted in the hotel dining room on Mexican-style eggs, *huevos rancheros*, tasty and spicy, served sunnyside up on a moist tortilla. Watusi had beer with his, dark *Dos Equis*; she had *café con leche*, strong coffee with lots of hot milk.

Now in the park, slouched on a bench in the early afternoon, he sorted through endless scraps and sheets of paper, scribbling on some of them in ballpoint, while she watched the people lolling about and strolling. One little girl, a real cutie who couldnt have been more than four escaped from her mother to wander over and ask Angelina where she was from.

"California," Angelina told her in Spanish.

"From Los Angeles?"

"No, but not very far from there."

"My papá lives in Los Angeles. We're going to visit him."

Angelina reached into the big straw purse she'd bought in Mexico City and gave the little girl an orange.

"What do you say?" asked the sad fat mama, prompting.

"Thank you," the girl said, covering her whole face with that bright orange and turning away shyly to run back into mama's arms.

"Theyre all so cute these Mexican kids."

"What was that?" Watusi looked up from a long list of numbers he was adding.

"I really love the kids down here. They arent like kids in the States. There's something really dignified about them. Theyre so beautiful but at the same time there's something so old and grown-up about a lot of them."

"I was like that."

"Remember that lady on the train, the one who'd lived up in San Jose?"

"I musta been asleep."

"I think you were. She was around thirty, I guess, it's hard to tell with people here sometimes. She was sitting across the aisle from us having a beer and we're talking about all the violence and stuff on TV in the States—I forget how we got on the subject—but all the time her two kids, a boy around four and a girl maybe six, they sat there next to her, the girl with her little legs crossed and the boy real still and he smiled out the train window. Impressed the hell outta me. Back home the kids wouldve been wrestling all over the train and bugging their parents to buy them something from every vendor that came through. Not these kids! The mother was pretty together too though. Told me she used to go with a soul brother in the States. I kept trying to picture what he mightve looked like."

"Kids in the States expect too much," Watusi said. "Kids down here might look cute like you say but wait a few seasons and check out that very little girl you just give the orange to when she turn, say, fourteen or fifteen. Chick be lookin olllld! Unless they folks got plenty bread, they end up scufflin so hard to make a go of it that it make em look rough in the face before they even get into they twenties good. It's changin though, it's a whole lot more money circulatin round the country than it was when I first popped up down here fifteen-sixteen years ago. That's probly how come dont too many of the other Latin American countries go for Mexico. You take Guatemala for instance. You go down there and tell em you from Mexico and they get to actin all funny, snigglin and crackin snot like them little poor Southside niggers use to do back home in Chi when they get up round some black doctor's son that live on the Near Northside. A Guatemalan gon do his best to try and beat a damn Mexican outta everything he got cause he schemin on him the same way the Mexican be's schemin on the gringo."

"Do you have any kids?" Angelina asked point-blank.

"Yep. But what you really askin is do I have an old lady."

The term "old lady" turned her off. She'd grown up hearing it used all around her but, all the same, she never applied the "old man" tag to any of her male friends. It was just another one of those little things about Watusi that annoyed her when she gave it any thought, like his excessive use of the word "nigger" even though it sounded natural, almost affectionate at times when he said it.

"Do you ever see them?"

"The women or the kids?"

"Well—both."

"Sure, I see em when I can, send em money too."

"Where do they all live?"

"That's a little complicated, honey, but, lemme see—my

oldest girl, Anita, she fifteen and. . . ." He put his papers down and looked up grinning into the warm blue sky. "Chick gon turn sixteen next month, damn! I gotta send her somethin special for her birthday! Thanks for remindin me. You talk about a beautiful young lady—and she really is a lady, always was—she a stone fox! My goodness! Sweet little sixteen! Remember that record by B.B. King? Her old lady wasnt much past sixteen when I met her. Nice woman. She teach school in Queens. They live in New York, naturally."

Angelina felt something melting inside her. In her mind she was picturing her own mother as she remembered her—something about cobblestone streets, darkness, old-time dress shops and barbershops with real candystick poles stuck up outside them—O yes, the time she toured the Detroit Historical Museum with Mama and they clicked down antique streets restored to look like the original eighteenth- and nineteenth-century settings—Mama's telling her all about grandparents and great-grandparents and Angelina's drunk with thoughts of time, generations, the woody-ringed histories of big fat trees (theyd been studying some elementary botany at the time in Miss Ludlow's class, the sixth grade). She loved her mother so and knew she was probably still looking down on her now from wherever she'd gone to—the dead can float anywhere and see everything—it was just the way things were. Why had she been so afraid of Mama's looking over her all these years, for so long now? Had she done anything all that wrong? Mama'd once been young herself and . . .

"OK, next on down the line come Giselle, a little bundle of cocoa joy if it ever was one. She must be around ten by now. Her ma's French but was workin as a B girl in Brussels—and blowin the gig, I might add—when I met her. They live in Paris, the Montmartre section you probly heard so much about. They spent a lotta time in London so when I talk to my little sweetheart she put all this old funny-style cockney on me, crack me up! She just like her mother—clever and pretty easygoin. Her mother's remarried, some dude outta Martinique I dont too

75

much go for but they doin all right. I get along pretty good with all of em and any time I'm in France I take Giselle around with me and she act as my interpreter. She can talk that shit like a little championess—is that right?—and steady rackin up points in school. Little broad's a genius. The Repoobleak Francez dont know what they got on they hands. Giselle gon one of these days up and turn em out!"

She forced herself to stop re-living her own origins and ask about his youngest child.

"Now, this is one little joker I'm proud of. His name is Tomás—his mama named him. I wanted to name him Sylvester after me, but she kept sayin it meant somethin ridiculous in Spanish and—"

"Sylvester in Spanish is Silvestre," Angelina said automatically, years of romance-language training surfacing in the instant. "It means," and here she paused, holding back an unexpected giggle, "wild, of the forest or woods, kinda, you know, uh . . ."

"Yeah, I know and that's how come I wanted to pass the name on to the little crumb snatcher. But Susana—that's his old lady—she wasnt goin for it. Any one of these mestizo or Indian women woulda gone for it straight out, but this chick got our blood, black blood in her veins—brought up in Veracruz, you understand—and she just wasnt goin for it! She like the name Tomás and so did her folks and seein as how we got married with her whole family gettin in on the deal I didnt think I had much choice. There I was a black gringo they didnt know nothin about with a little taste of change, more than any of *them* was makin at least, so I didnt think I had much choice."

"How old is he?"

"Tomás? Around five, I guess. Great kid, muscular, sharp, slick to be more exact. I was with him a couple of weeks ago. Susana hates me because I'm never there, but yet all the same she loves me for givin her Tomás."

Angelina was very still. She knew there'd be some dukey in the game somewhere around the bend.

She scooted over on the bench until she was smack up next to him, her hip and thigh pressed next to his, her arm looped around his, their hands intertwined as she squeezed and squeezed, waiting, hoping for some token response. She'd been playing this little game by ear and now all she wanted was pure human touch, some indication, any indication that he had some real feeling for her despite all the personal history she'd just prodded him to volunteer. So he's got kids, so he's had wives, so he's been around. I should hate this bastard but I dont. I like the way he lives on the run. I'd probably do it myself if I were a devilish man. I dont care. We've got no commitment. Mama's dead. I couldve been with her but I'm not. A thousand times I couldve faked inserting the diaphragm or pumping the foam in or dropping the pill with a little swig of beer—but I didnt. I never got pregnant. I never copped out. I never put anybody through that lifetime commitment.

"So legally youre still a married man."

"How's that?"

"Well, you know . . . that girl you married in Veracruz who gave you a son."

"Nope. It didnt work out. I tried, Angie, I really did but it just didnt work out." He placed his giant arm around her and pulled her closer to him. "How's it feel to be settin up here on this bench in Guadalajara, Mexico, scrunched up next to a three-time loser?"

"When do we leave for Ajijic?"

He peeped at his watch, a handsome little pocket model. "In about three-four hours. It's buses leavin for Chapala every hour till tonight. We can take a taxi to Ajijic from there. Anything you wanna do before we take off?"

She let her head drop against his shoulder. "Can we go for a long walk around town, Watusi? A long slow walk with no particular destination? That's all I came down here to do anyway—just to sorta wander around, look at things."

"Aint no big thing, baby. That's what a good halfa my life's been about, doin just that—wanderin and wonderin and tryna duck the shit."

"Youre so silly," she laughed, gazing down at her own brown hand gobbled up by his.

What she really wanted was to go back to the Hotel Francés and be held.

She wanted to be whisked up and sailed far away without ever leaving the ground.

"Do you love your children?" she asked for no apparent reason, too chicken just yet to inquire too closely about his women.

"*Love* em? You better know it—a helluva lot more than I love myself."

This pleased her. This pleased her. Tingling to the soles of her feet, she felt rested enough now to walk across this whole flat, smokey city—and back.

CHICKENS

The first thing to catch Angelina's eye as they pulled into Chapala late that Friday afternoon, besides the quiet villagey beauty of the town, was a lanky man with collar-length hair and an imposing Pancho Villa mustache walking across the main street with a fishnet shopping bag full of groceries.

"Hey," she said, nudging Watusi and pointing, "that's Seishi!"

"Who?"

"Seishi, Seishi Tanaka, my friend Margo's ex-old man. Margo. I told you about her. Well, I'll be damned if that guy there doesn't look exactly like her last husband."

"What is he," Watusi asked as he leaned toward the bus window to get a better look, "Chinese?"

"Japanese. Cant you tell the difference?"

"Ive shipped out for Hong Kong and Ive shipped out for Tokyo, but from where I'm sittin now on this Mexican bus, they all look like Mexicans to me."

"If you'd been living on the west coast as long as I have, you'd know the difference. Seishi's the youngest son of a wealthy Tokyo industrial family—I think his old man . . . I mean his father's into some esoteric branch of the computer field. Margo met him at Cal in Berkeley when she went back to school. They got into some kinda complicated romance and got married."

"What's he into now?"

"I don't know. He dropped outta Cal to get in on the underground filmmaking scene which was going pretty big around the time they met. Margo lost track of him after they got divorced. His family back home must still back him up because a lotta alimony and child support gets pumped Margo's way— like, more money in a year than I'd make in two teaching Spanish full time."

"Don't talk to me about no alimony."

"I thought he'd up and gone back to Japan but if that's him I just now saw—and it really couldnt be anybody but him—he's got to be into a whole different kinda thing. I never could dig him completely. Hard to tell where he was coming from. He could be charming when he felt like it, but the last few times I was around him he was obnoxious as hell, trying to be some kinda homemade hippie just when the hippie thing was playing out."

"Everything plays out, sweet thing. I go back a helluva lot further than you do and I can assure you it's all gon run its course. Bebop done played out. Beatniks done played out. I got this play I wrote back in 1959 I thought I was gon get rich off of bout this dude that built a bomb shelter and got his family all crammed down it and they all end up dyin from a leaky gas pipe and I couldnt sell it now for twenty-five cent. Aint nobody scareda the Bomb no more. Bomb shit done played out. Psychedelic shit done played out. Bullshit revolution done played out. Hippies done played out and, look here, I'll tell you somethin—nigger shit done just about played out too! That's how come I dont spend too much time hustlin round the States no more. All them psychotic Negroes. All them dangerous-ass Americans! You cant win. If the white folks dont get you, the niggers sure will! You start some new kinda beautiful shit you

80

think gon shake up the country and change it around—for the *better,* you understand—and next thing you know some old corny Madison Avenue clown that dropped acid back in the sixties or somethin done figured out how to use it to sell toilet paper or feminine spray deodorant. It's like back when the civil rights thing was comin down heavy and you look up and there the governor was sittin in with you on the Capitol steps. It dont make sense."

"I know, Ive just come from there. I was involved with all of it—in my own funny, half-ass way of course. Now I only wanna know one thing."

"One thing? I can relate to that, as the kids use to say not too long ago, and now before the bus come to a full standstill why dont you mash it on me?"

"I wanna know where we're staying tonight?"

All the Mexican passengers who'd ooo'ed and ahhh'd at the sight of water as the bus wound around Lake Chapala a little ways back were now scrambling to line up for the grand central get-off. One Indian woman was carrying a live chicken under one arm. Angelina, who was behind her in line, couldnt take her eyes off the chicken, a fat red hen. She'd raised one as a pet back in Michigan when she was ten years old.

"You see that, Watusi?"

"See what?"

"The way that chicken looked at you?"

"How he look at me?"

"*She,* it's a chick chicken—looked at you like you was stone crazy!"

"Chicken got plenty sense, got *plenty* sense!"

BOOK TWO

CARTOONS

The taxi driver, as professionally sullen as any of his Manhattan counterparts, drove them around Chapala and waited patiently while they fooled around in the little supermercado, stocking up on groceries and liquor. Angelina resented finding the store, which reminded her of compact Speedy 7–11 Markets in California, filled with resident gringos buying canned and frozen goods along with enormous half-gallon containers of Oso Negro gin and Bacardi. She thought she'd left these people with their odious consuming habits back home where they belonged. But here she was and here was Watusi wheeling their cart right down through the tiny aisles scattered with retired Texans and bored pensioners, grabbing items off shelves like all the other lonely Americans.

Outside, loaded down with two sacks apiece, Watusi spotted a man selling late-season watermelons from a truck. "What's the word for watermelon?" he asked her.

"*Sandía.*"

"That's right." Watusi ambled over to the truck and, with a nod of his head, told the man that he wanted one sandía. "Una muy bonita." The paunchy straw-hatted man smiled that he understood and followed them to the taxi with a classic-looking melon.

Everything paid for—Watusi had worked out a fixed price beforehand for the driver's time and services—the rattly Ford Galaxy motored them out of central Chapala with its tile roofs and comically gnarled bougainvillaea trees onto the dusty two-lane blacktop that wound and stretched into dirt-roaded Ajijic.

Something in Angelina died in that dusk that found them in front of a lonesome-looking Mexican dwelling with a high iron gate.

Had some business to take care of in Jocotepec, the note they found read, *so make yourself (selves?) at home. Good news. Carmen's coming in with us. Jade. See you in a few days. Baxter.*

Suddenly she was hit with things to be aware of. It was, after all, October and she was horsing around south of the border with a man she had to figure out as she went along. The note taped to the icebox annoyed her. *So make yourself (selves?) at home.*

"Does your buddy Baxter always expect you to turn up back here with a female friend?"

"Jealousy, jealousy," Watusi said by the icebox door where he was busy unloading perishables. "Round here we party a lot, Angelina, and my boy Baxter know it aint no tellin who I'm subject to turn up with. Last time I showed up with a buncha Mexican hippies I met over in Guad. Baxter like to flipped! He cant stand no damn hippies irregardless of race, color, creed or national origin."

"You wanna know something? I cant stand em either."

"That's cause you from Berkeley where they make the hippies."

"Youre probably right. They got many of em around here?"

"Use to, but the Mexican government done just about shut the door for good on that jive. They tolerate the native hippies cause all of em come from upper-class families that's got a lotta power and pull, but long-haired freaks from Gringoland got to straighten up when they step cross that border cause these crazy people down here dont be playin! It use to be a gang of em layin out round here in Chapala and Ajijic but they was so uncool—and aint nobody unhipper than an uncool hippie—until the local people got to where they couldnt put up with they shit no longer and teamed up with the law and run they doped-up boodies clean out the state. I mean they naturally swabbed deck!"

"Well, I'm for anybody creating their own life-style just so long as they don't try to force it on me."

"That's a pretty right-on way of lookin at it, but these idiots would get all lit up and spaced out and go right up into town and start fuckin with the populace. One clown even laid some LSD on a twelve-year-old girl, and the little girl, whose old man work over at the courthouse, decided it was time to start takin names and kickin asses. Beside, the dumb hippies be down here tryna *make* money insteada droppin some into the Mexican economy and you know the government wasnt about to let them get away with that shit. Tourism still the number one industry down here and after while all the gringos even started complainin bout the hippies. Here a dude done slaved his ass off dealin insurance or somethin so he can take his family on a nice vacation in sunny Mexico and get down here and here them same deadbeat motherfuhhh—scuse me, Angie—them same deadbeat eyesores they thought they was gettin away from back in the States talkin bout, 'Got any spare change?' Shit, I'd be mad too. Spare change my foot! You wanna pull a gun on me or whip my ass and take my money, OK, but dont be leanin up against no parkin meter lookin like Beowulf with your nasty hand stuck out at me whinin bout spare change. Hell, I use to shine shoes and throw papers all day for—"

Angelina was smiling and shaking her head. "You're getting pretty worked up, you know. I think youve made it clear how you feel."

He leaned down and gave her a little kiss on the forehead.

"You right, baby, you right, you right. Lemme show you round the place. It's a pretty together little villa and Baxter bein compulsive like he is keep it in pretty good shape."

"So Ive noticed."

"Wanna get high?"

They were sitting in the patio in the cool of night, watching the sky fill up with stars. Angelina had pointed out Orion and the Milky Way to Watusi who confessed that, for as long as he'd sailed with the Merchant Marines, the only constellations he could safely sight were the Big Dipper and the Little Dipper. Angelina told him she was a country girl who used to sit on the front steps and study the skies at night in the summertime. Also, she'd taken a course in astronomy in her sophomore year at U. of M. The teacher, Miss DeLoach, was a wiry little old lady with a weakness for athletes and football players in particular. All the jocks got A's from her whether they knew the material or not. Angelina had to work her tail off for her modest B-plus, but the charts and details she'd sweated over so were still very much with her.

"What I really need is to come down," she said.

"Hmmm," he sang, extracting a jumbo joint from out of nowhere, "then how bout we both get high and then get down?"

For weeks now she'd been meaning to try an experiment: to lay off alcohol and drugs in any form just to see how she'd feel. During those last hectic days in Berkeley, preparing for the trip, she'd made up her mind to put herself to the test in Mexico. "Bad place to go cold turkey," Margo had quipped when Angelina told her of her plans, "unless you do it with a little mole sauce."

My poor body, she thought as Watusi handed her the enormous reefer freshly lit, always having to put up with the garbage I keep dumping in it. It's a wonder it doesnt rebel. In the same instant, it flashed through her mind that her body had rebelled many a time. Well, what the hell! A couple of tokes wont make that much difference now. But tomorrow, well, she was down here in the Land of Mañana, and mañana she'd start cooling it. She wanted to get back in touch with her natural, untampered body rhythms and check out the world with a clear new head. "I'm higher right now than most of youll ever be," she'd once heard Hubert declare from his soapbox. Hubert was the spindly, freckle-faced, red-haired Bible-thumper who preached the gospel, socked it to the kids at Sather Gate on Berkeley's campus. Some wise-ass had cracked: "Hubert, what you need is to get high!" and Hubert's reply had stuck with Angelina. "That's right, I'm high, but I dont need any of your acid or grass or speed or smack to get me there. I'm high on God, young man, and let me tell you something—God is gooood!"

One toke and Angelina was mellow. Two tokes and she was all giggles. By the third toke, everything was cartoons! The sky, stars, the chirp of crickets, the clean leafy smell of the garden surrounding the patio, the squared-off U-shaped villa, Gato the little black cat asleep in her lap, the sound of the Mexican announcer gunning out the news from the kitchen radio, Watusi in his fuzzy sweater and herself in ankle-length dress with one of his jackets draped around her shoulders, even the smell of the grass itself—it was all one big ridiculous ha-ha, an animated cartoon she hadnt expected.

"This some pretty good shit, hunh?" Watusi had to say in his devilish way.

"It's awfully strong."

"Yucatán, baby! That's where this smoke was raised. The Indian women use it only for medicinal purposes, but the men—yes, yes, yes—they know some other uses for it."

They stroked one another's legs and laughed.

THE NIGHT THAT
NEVER ENDED

Dreamer though she was, it was still hard for Angelina to picture what planet Sylvester Poindexter Buchanan had zoomed in from. His broad black face, despite its magnetic sunniness, was still a mask to keep her and the world at large from entering his worlds.

Now that she was tingling in that secret way again (she hadnt felt this relaxed in months), it was occurring to her that the best way to find out about the rascal—at least a little something— might be to sit back, relax some more and let what happens happen.

By mid-evening, they were lounging around what passed for a living room, a spacious, shadowy make-do den filled with the kind of wooden, stone and metallic curios she'd seen passing for ethnic artcraft in tourist shops everywhere she'd traveled except in mainstream USA.

The floor made of stone was carpeted with thick straw rugs braided into designs she was afraid to study too closely; afraid she might trip off into them the way she'd just about disappeared into the patio sky before Watusi'd mentioned how cool it was getting, and hadnt they better put up camp for the great indoors?

There was even a real woolen rug, a very expensive-looking one in one corner. Two mattresses, soft lamplight, a hanging Mexican ceramic candelabra and a quaint hip poster left over from the Mexico City Olympics rounded out the homey effect. The poster brought to mind stories she'd heard Margo tell about the hundreds of students who'd been wiped out during the riot that year. Margo, who was living in the capital that year, had known several of them. Angelina's stomach tightened as images of the massacre flickered across her mind.

Watusi put a Bessie Smith LP on, a newly re-issued one with "Black Mountain Blues" on it where the Empress of the Blues sings braggingly about herself and her razor and her gun—"I'm gonna/cut him if he stand still/and shoot him/if he run!"

Some funny shit to be playing, she thought. "I use to have that album."

"O yeah?"

"Yeah, my old man—my father I mean—laid it on me along with four or five others the October I turned nineteen."

"When's your birthday?"

"October first. I just celebrated it not long ago."

"And your old man was into Bessie Smith?"

"He's into music, any kinda music. He use to play trombone in a little semiprofessional band back in Georgia long before he came north and got to farming and postal clerking and carrying on."

"What's he do now?"

"Works in the post office, poor man. He really couldve done better. He's got such a good mind, a really deep perspective. I mean he can really see things the way they are even though he doesnt talk much, you know?"

"Yeah. I know dudes like that. Black geniuses except nobody'd ever know. Heavy dudes that keep real quiet and so people take em for ordinary. He put you through school, didn't he?"

"Sure did. He sure did." She paused, staring into the dark

corner of the room where the stereo was lit up. "I love him too. He's a good man. I really love him."

"I know you do," he half-whispered, reaching out suddenly to pull her toward him. "Do you dance?"

As her head shifted gears and her tender armpits dampened, she heard herself saying, "Sure, but I never danced to Bessie Smith before."

"Bessie Smith, Jimmy Smith, the New York Philharmonic, it's all about the same right now. I wanna know all about you."

"Only if you tell me all about yourself."

"You already know that but I'll fill you in for the hell of it. Is it a deal?"

"Youre the dealer."

It *wasnt* all the same. Everything was getting different fast. The way he moved, the way he spoke, switching out of and back into his sly Niggerese—"The Negro delivery" she'd read in some ante-bellum book, "is always sly and elliptical"—brushing his slick cheek against her dry one, breathing into her ear (oooo she couldnt *stand* that, it felt tooo gooood!)—all of it was making a difference, *shhhh,* she wanted him to stop, *shhhh,* she didnt want him to stop.

Uh-uhhh, night was getting in the way! Look out! She wanted all that poetry sizzling her senses to fizzle. Touch had to mean something this time. She wanted it to mean something. She dared it to mean something. It had to mean something. The tongue plunged quietly into her wet mouth now had to mean more than a kiss. The woolly head her hands caressed, the delicious warmth and juices they playfully shared and exchanged—it all had to be part of something bigger to come this time.

Angelina. Part Angel. Part lean little bawd. Surely in some recent past life she'd taken her pleasure on the fly, or, perhaps as a desirable slave, had staged regular raids on her mistress's or master's larder and laughed up her flaxen sleeve about it.

As Watusi's arms tightened around her, that old familiar feeling, now stronger than ever, of having been here before—in

92

this place, with this person, doing this very thing—began to overtake her. The world might be one big dream of a re-run, after all, but who was it doing the dreaming?

Suddenly it was raining moments, moments that stretched into soft, fleshy years. Some ancient tune was sweetening the silence inside her head, some song that conveyed without words just how her mother mightve felt the instant her father's seed entered her womb and—

How easily she rose up out of herself now to hover above those figures below. Some part of herself slipped clean away and took it all in now from an angle of delicious detachment.

How gentle the man seemed now. How selfless the woman. How easily they undressed one another in perfect random time to the music.

Naked now, their beautiful bodies made the walls quiver with prehistoric shadows, all of it undrawable, unfilmable. The whole room trembled for a moment with the fat drone of a jet passing overhead in the Mexican night, drowning out Bessie and crickets and distant Friday night gunshot sounds.

High voltage, she flashed. I'm a part of this action and at the same time standing apart from it. Just like old times. Their bellies touched as waves of pleasure current rippled through her body like high voltage.

She didn't want it to change. She wanted everything left exactly as it was: the taste of his sweat and private zones gathered on her tongue, the tender crush of his moist meat straddling hers, the churning reversed, the breezy position in which they lay back to belly, puppy ritual, prickle of his head and facial hair as it rolled from spacious outer thigh to sensitive birthmarked inner thigh, her shoulders cushioning his own enormous thighs, his lips at her breasts, his mouth at her throat, the music circling her, encircling her, ringing in tight around her heated body like soft invisible ribbons drawing tighter and tighter and tighter and tighter, the summer of his breath, the rocking the rocking the rocking the *ooooo* and *ahhhh,* his laughter, her *hisssss* and soft squeals, the two of them lost now, impossible to tell female from

93

male, it's all so fuzzy, it's all so clear, O slow endless merging baby, O darling unngh unnnnngh nnngh! How much forever can you stand? Unnngh! Ohhhh! Dont dont dont dont no no no no *please!* Ahhhoooouhnnngh!

She didnt want it to change. She wanted it all to continue and continue without ever changing ever.

Consider the two of them now, sipping cool drinks in total silence, collapsed on their bed of that eve, looking too deeply into one another's faces lover-style, she still not knowing him from Adam, demon sun, devil moon, about to start from scratch again, from scratch, from stroke, the squeezing of a forearm, the assessment of a calf, her own toes (she didnt like toes) no longer just toes, her whole cage of a body no longer just hers now that this stranger's laid strong claim to it.

Room bathed in apple light, the rosy edge of her blueness cooling, theyre about to do it all over again.

She didnt want this moving picture to change. It would be filed securely away in her brain, a thrilling mind-film that'd fill the screen of her consciousness again and again, O not so much the seeable part as the hard-to-get feeling of Yeah that went with it. Bessie Smith had been part of the soundtrack, to be sure, but only accidentally; it couldve been any music or no music at all. The creeps who'd ripped her cottage off had got away with the album, but she'd find it again and use it as a souvenir if necessary.

From the moment theyd stepped off that bus in Chapala to the moment of her second explosion, a century passed for Angelina in a night that never really ended.

"Dont the moon look lonesome?" he paused to whisper at one point.

"Yes, it do," she said, licking his ear, "but you dont have to say it, I can see it myself."

THE CALL

Around the time that crazy night was heading into its fourth straight day, Angelina's thoughts flickered toward home again. What was happening back in Berkeley?

Before leaving, she'd applied for a part-time teaching position with a federally funded alternative high school in Oakland, working with Black and Chicano dropouts. She thought she might stand a good chance of landing it since word had got out that the woman who'd been hired originally had withdrawn in advance for reasons of health. Angelina had wasted no time in applying for the vacated opening.

Since Margo had kindly agreed to go by and pick up her mail every couple of days, Angelina was eager to telephone her and find out if any promising-looking letters had turned up.

"I'll make it a collect call," she told Watusi who was snuggled beside her at the time, fresh shot of tequila at his fingertips, not unlike a Doberman Pinscher nestled up next to a poodle. "I already owe the phone company for two months' service anyway."

"You can charge it to this number, baby. It's all right. You a guest of mine."

"But that costs money. I dont mind if—"

"You a guest of mine. I'm the one enticed you to come here in the first place. I'll pay for it. Make your call!"

She'd been with him long enough to know that he meant it. The few days theyd spent together had been like a tight little fistful of years. She'd also fooled around with time long enough to know that it was strictly a confidential concept, possibly the most intimate of concepts.

Already she was resigning herself to playing the disinterested mate who hadnt the blurriest idea of how her partner made his money. What Watusi was really into, what he actually did for a living, was beyond her. All that mattered was that they spent meaningful time together.

Mornings she'd make coffee, fix breakfast and theyd take a taxi into Chapala where he'd press a few twenty-peso notes into her hand for shopping—to buy fresh produce in the market-place, groceries and liquor in the supermercado and anything else that caught her eye—while he "took care of a little business" at the bank or telegraph office or mailed letters at the post office. He usually got up at daybreak, even after turning in way past midnight, to sit at Baxter's little Olivetti portable to tap out letters and notes addressed to companies and individuals scattered throughout the Republic as well as the rest of Latin America, Europe and the States. She never got to read any of them. By the time she'd appear on the scene, he'd be hunched over licking stamps to paste onto envelopes or adding up columns of figures in that fat little notebook he carried and was always consulting.

"Where'd you learn to type so fast?" she asked him once.

"In high school, baby, in high school. I was runnin track and playin football like everybody else, but I knew the commercial curriculum was where it's at. Learned to type, keep books, all that shit." He laughed. "Can you imagine what the teacher—a lil old biddy broad, Miss Schmidt, musta been a hunerd years old if she was a day—can you imagine what she musta felt like havin a big old rusty athlete-lookin nigger like me settin up in her typin class bangin out the quick-sly-lazy-fox with all the resta them lovely little things?"

Morning duties carried out, theyd get together for coffee or beers and even lip-smacking afternoon luncheons, *comida corrida,* at one of the restaurants. Angelina loved the local fish and would order it just about every time even though, on their walks afterward, she'd take one look at the mud-gray waters of Lake Chapala and feel her stomach twitch.

"See all that algae out there in the water?" Watusi told her one afternoon while they were enjoying cans of dark Tecate Beer brimmed with lime and salt at an outside-inside joint known as El Beer Garden. "Some better-thinkin old gringo lady once brought in some type of water buffalo outta India to eat that jive up but the people found out it's the algae that keep the water halfway clear, so you gotta be real careful if you brave enough to swim out there. I use to kinda try to swim in it but I gave it up. I do my swimmin in Acapulco now."

He'd taken her along to visit acquaintances—Karen Pérez, an American girl in her late twenties who'd been a junkie in New York but had straightened out and married a sort of Mexican traveling salesman, and who now passed the time writing her so-called memoirs; an elderly English couple that collaborated on travel articles for British and American magazines; a middle-aged freelance photographer named Rafael García Valdes who worked in Guadalajara and lived in Chapala. Like Watusi, or so she figured, they all led off-beat unscheduled lives that wouldve seemed fascinating five years ago but which now made Angelina want to yawn and stretch.

Am I growing old? Will I be hopelessly conservative by the time I'm thirty? She was tired of people with their hassles and fronts. She knew herself too well to romanticize about the real world anymore. The moment mattered. Yesterday Watusi got on the phone and blurted out all kinds of fuzzy details that passed for business to Baxter over in Jocotepec. Now that Baxter had taken off unexpectedly for Yucatán to "look after a few things" as Watusi put it, they were more or less safely alone and that's what mattered. She dug it—the setting, the being halfway alone—despite the silly intrigue which could become a pure drag if she let herself think about it, and despite her down to earth soreness.

"I'll make it short," she said, the call to Berkeley having been put into motion, clinging to her *cuba libre,* the rum and Coke drink he'd fixed.

You figure out your whole life, she thought, in weird little unexpected rooms along the road. It was something she'd experienced in Portugal years before and had written down and memorized from her brilliant-insight notebook of the time.

It took forever to get the call through but eventually there Margo was on the other end of the line carrying on excitedly in her familiar Afro-Caucasian twang.

"Yes it's me, Margo, I'm calling from Chapala. What's going on back there?"

"Listen, Angie, I dont know how to break this to you but I'm afraid I'mo have to hit you with a little . . . well . . . a little news that's kinda on the heavy side."

Angelina held her breath. "O no! That's all I need. What is it?"

"A telegram arrived here from Detroit. I found the notice for it on your door when I went by to pick up your mail yesterday, so I shot over to Western Union and picked it up. Hope you dont mind but . . . under the circumstances . . . well, I had to open it."

"Is it from my father?"

"No but it concerns your dad. It's from a Julia Green Holmes. She'd be your aunt, right? Well, here . . . Ive got it right here in front of me. It says: PLEASE GET IN TOUCH WITH ME AT ONCE. YOUR DADDY IN CRITICAL CONDITION AT HERMAN KIEFER HOSPITAL. URGENT. GOD BLESS YOU. AUNT JUJIE. And then there's a phone number where you can reach her."

Angelina heard the frantic tinkling of ice and glanced down to notice that it was coming from her own glass. Watusi sat up and took the drink from her trembling hand. Her head was spinning. She flashed on Tolby Crawford the obnoxious drunk and how he'd trembled, drink in hand, the night Scoot Harper pulled the gun on him. Now she was the one under the gun.

"Somethin the matter, baby?" Watusi asked, sitting up and buttoning his shirt.

"Shhh. What's the phone number, Margo?"

Margo gave her the number slowly while Angelina repeated it aloud, gesturing dizzily to Watusi to write it down. He plucked a ballpoint pen from his shirt pocket and scribbled it on the inside of his wrist.

"I'm really sorry to have to lay this on you, honey," Margo went on, "but—"

"It's OK, Margo, it's no fault of yours and—" Her voice was beginning to quiver. She couldnt think what to say next so she didnt say anything.

"Listen, Angie, I know how you probly feel. Gimme a ring after you talk with your aunt. Call collect. If there's anything I can do . . . I mean, if you need money to fly back or anything like that . . ."

"Youve done enough for me. I'll call her and . . . I'll call you back."

She'd planned to rap casually with Margo about all the things that'd been happening to her lately, about seeing Seishi in the bus station and Watusi and how much better she was feeling and thank you and I'll be coming home soon. But this was a whole different trip, and—O Daddy, I shouldve written you!

She hung up, still trembling, and lay back across the bed, her eyes flooding with tears.

Watusi lay back next to her. He surrounded her with his enormous arms and wiped at her tears with his fingers. "I understand, baby," he kept whispering. She knew he didnt; couldnt possibly even know yet what Margo had conveyed to her, but just the words, his well-meant words, "I understand," touched something.

99

"Daddy's in the hospital," she moaned, "my daddy's in the hospital and it's critical."

"Come on, come on now. Go on and cry. Let it all pour out. It aint nothin you can do now but get to where he is as fast as you can."

What hurt more than anything else was her messy realization that this sudden bad news, still very generalized and abstract for the time being, had triggered off so many complicated emotions in her that it was hard to figure out which were genuine. Was she feeling sorry for herself or for her father? Ten thousand strong feelings lumped up in her throat. She felt devastated, abandoned, guilty, self-pitying and ashamed in the same instant. It was for real and it was all much too much.

GOOD-BY/DON'T GO:
A PRIVATE MOVIE

Like a zombie she sat drifting in and out of the world while Watusi navigated the borrowed Volkswagen, Karen Pérez's car, toward Guadalajara's airport through the rain.

Even now, even in autumn, overwhelmed by gray and brown and watery green, the colors of Mexico were still too much for her to take in on the fly. One part of her regretted not having brought a camera along while another part of her regretted not having mixed with the people more—whoever they were.

She was half-thinking of Enrique the chunky orphan boy from town who begged to carry her packages for coins and who looked a few seasons older than the ten years he claimed. The afternoon she'd asked about his parents, his eyes had moistened and he'd said, "I'm not living with them anymore." It broke her heart in the same way that she'd been shattered sitting by the lake that afternoon at the sight of a hunched old widow with a smile on her face bending to retrieve a scrap of yellow newspaper that'd probably been blowing for weeks in the wind. The lady then sat on the same bench where Angelina was waiting for Watusi to turn up and devoured every inch of that newsprint with her smile intact and broadening.

Life could be simple. Life could be hard. Life could be simply hard. All she wanted to know for now was how long it would really be before she'd be close to her father. She was passively rolling with all of these images when Watusi's voice broke into her private movie.

"Sure hate to see you have to cut out this way."

"You do?"

"Of course I do. What you think? I been through a lotta this stuff too. Lost my old man when I was round twelve years old but—"

She was crying again, fumbling with her purse for tissues.

"Aw, come on now, Angelina, look here. I didnt mean nothin by that. I guess that was a bad example. Look like everything I say's the wrong thing to say today. Listen. Your daddy probly cant wait to set eyes on you. He probly settin up in the hospital right now, hair all combed, got a big tray *fulla* good food on his lap, new sheets, some fine big-legged nurse spoon-feedin him right off the tray. You aint got nothin to worry bout, betcha anything."

Half an hour to go. For Angelina their universe was coming to a close. Maybe it'd been fun. Maybe there'd even been some love exchanged or gotten across. She'd have to think about it. She'd know later.

He offered to buy her something to drink. She settled for Sidral, an apple-flavored soda. He offered her a trip to Acapulco just the two of them if she'd come back and see him after Detroit if everything went down OK naturally. She settled for a promise that he'd write her in Berkeley.

"From all you done told me bout your old man, he sound like a pretty together dude for the generation he's comin from." Watusi reached out with his free hand, squeezed her knee, whispered "Sorry!" and took both her little hands in his. "You know, Baxter was back in Detroit a few months ago. Had to visit his stepfather who lives round there. Hamtramck. He told me it's pretty much a jungle these days—everybody on smack, armed guards every place you go. Sound like it's pretty scarey."

"Ive heard that. I'm not looking forward to going back."

"Well, all I can say is I hope your daddy aint in too bad a shape. Considerin the environment there he been livin in, dont be surprised. Sound to me like it might be a high-risk area."

"Hunh?"

"I really go for you, Angelina. You know that?"

He couldve been talking Polish for all she heard. Her moist hands clung to his big fingers under the table until he snatched his hand back to go inside his shirt pocket. This time he brought out a wad of American money, peeled off $200 in twenties and tens and pressed it into her hand.

"What's this for?"

"For spendin, what else?"

"O but Tusi, youve already paid for my plane fare to Detroit and back to California and I'll pay you back, honest."

"You aint got to pay me back nothin! That's a gift, you know, outright. You been puttin up with all my off-the-wall shit these past few days. To me that's at least worth some plane rides and a little pocket money."

"I wont accept it."

"You *will* accept it. Drop it in your purse and pretend like you dont know where it come from."

"You know I could never forget."

"Dont never say never. It's some things I thought I could shine on that turn up in my dreams every now and then."

"Where . . . Where do you get all this money?"

"I pick it off trees. Besides, I'm kinda whacha might call a provident nigger. I'm thrifty like a Scotchman. I work hard makin it and I work harder keepin it."

"What do you do?" she asked him at last.

"You ever see that show that use to be on television—'What's My Line?' Well, let's just say I deal in services."

The worst kind of blues was stabbing at her again. Tears slipped down her cheeks. She could feel them. She wanted to be invisible. Tables away, a young Mexican soldier and his

103

girlfriend were openly clinging to one another. She wished none of this critical hospital stuff had happened so that she and Watusi could cling too—freely.

At the departure gate she wanted to tell him a thousand beautiful things but another lump gathered in her throat and she said almost nothing.

When he squeezed her against him more tenderly than usual and gave her the kind of good-bye kiss that attracts a lot of attention from onlookers, especially Mexican onlookers, she came very close to forgetting everything important—why she'd come to Mexico in the first place, why she didnt want to leave and why it was necessary that she leave right away.

"I'll be gettin in touch," he said finally as she hurried to join the moving line of passengers anxious to get this little show off the ground.

She touched her lips and waved him a kiss.

He waved her one back, slowly, lingeringly, and threw in a warm, fatherly wink for good measure.

All the way across the breezy airfield her pulse beat out *dont-go-dont-go-dont-go-dont-go!* and she could barely make out the gigantic plane for the wind and water in her eyes.

BOOK THREE

THE WHOLE WORLD

Aunt Jujie and Uncle Roscoe were both there waiting. Angelina stepped down the carpeted landing tube into the arrival area and right into their warm, ancient arms.

What a trip it is this business of going away and coming back. She didnt so much think this as felt it. It's been a good six years since Ive seen them and here they are, Aunt Jujie in particular, looking about the same way they did back when I was a kid and lived in their house.

"O my goodness, my goodness, child!" Aunt Jujie sang, clinging to Angelina for dear life it seemed. "You done got to the place where you look like a perfect cross between Lizbeth and Matthew. Fact, you kinda favor your mama more, the older you get. Poor Lizbeth'd probly turn a flip if she was to hear me say that. She probly just now did. She always thought you looked more like your daddy than you did her. But you really got her cheeks and nose and eyes and forehead, dont she, Roscoe?"

Roscoe agreed with his smiling eyes that Angelina could feel scanning her diligently but in a way that was friendly and pleasing. "Yeah, she do, and she got Lizbeth's build too. Come on over here, gal, and let your old Uncle Roscoe hug you! You remember all them times I use to take you up there to the Linwood Theater to see them monster movies and things or for a ride on the ferris wheel or the rocket at Edgewater Park or the Michigan State Fair when it came to town and you'd get scared as all get out and be all scroonched down next to me and jeckin on my arm and carryin on? Well, I aint forgot, so come on over here with your little grown-up fabulous-lookin self!"

Uncle Roscoe's style hadnt changed a drop. He'd always had his own special brand of amiable bullshit and it still gushed out of him like block-party water from some summertime fire hydrant of her childhood.

"Angie, your complexion look so nice and healthy," Aunt Jujie put in. "Look like you bout to break out and sprout blossoms or somethin. Must be all that sunshine they got out there in California, hunh?"

Angelina wanted to ask them all about Daddy. How was he doing really? When'd they seen him last? What was it that'd put him in the hospital? But she knew that it would all come out before they even got to where the car was parked, so she strained to relax. Surprisingly, it wasnt that hard. For the first time in years she felt connected to something real again, to something from the past that had more than immediate meaning.

"I sure hope you had sense enough to pack some warm clothes," Aunt Jujie told her, arm looped in hers, as they made their way toward the airport escalator. "I know yall use to it bein July in January out there where you been but we a whole lot closer to the North Pole round here than you probly remember. I told Zalea Mae—remember her, use to live down the block from us? Still do—told her, say, I mighta been half-black—the kids they dont like you to say colored or Negro no more nowdays—say, I mighta been half-black and half-Indian when I first come up here to this Detroit outta Georgia but, behind all this snowin and ice and sleet and mess, I'm one-third Eskimo now."

Aunt Jujie laughed and laughed and laughed at what she'd just said.

Angelina laughed too but not so much at Jujie's joke as at all the long forgotten things she was feeling and connecting up now that she was back among home people again. She knew that within a day or two her whole way of speaking would change. Strange. It had almost happened while she was off goofing and taking chances with Watusi with his flat-out agrammatical self, but, for some reason, and deep feeling had nothing to do with it, she'd stuck to her low-keyed standardized mode. Actually it boiled down to more than speech. She'd simply been a different person then in a different time and place with a man whose strangeness mattered more than his skin color.

"Yeah," said Roscoe, backing Aunt Jujie up, "it naturally be's gettin cold round here even round October. Mister Hawkins be's sayin somethin!"

Although she gave every appearance of being right in there with what was happening between the three of them, Angelina's head, the underside of it that she veiled beautifully, began to drift.

Before Daddy had taken up with Barbara, her stepmother, he'd left her for two years in the care of his youngest sister, Julia, Aunt Jujie, who had her own religion which she lived by haphazardly.

Aunt Jujie was a small-boned peculiarly pretty woman who'd never married officially but lived half-heartedly with Roscoe who was several years her senior. He'd always struck Angelina as being Aunt Jujie's opposite.

Jujie was strictly opposed to drinking, smoking, partying in general, cursing and movies. She lectured regularly to anyone who'd listen on the all-around wickedness of the world to say nothing of the devil and the flesh. She didnt keep liquor, cigarettes or ashtrays around the house.

The only records Angelina remembered her as owning were

by gospel artists: Mahalia Jackson, the Highway QCs, the Pilgrim Travelers, Clara Ward, the Dixie Hummingbirds, the Soul Stirrers, the Five Blind Boys. She played them in the morning while she was getting Angelina off to school, and she played them at night just before bedtime. She also played them vigorously in what she called "times of trial," when she was angry or weary or disgusted with life or simply afraid of everything.

"Let us give praise to God from whom all blessings flow," was the kind of pronouncement she'd make over food at mealtime.

"Jesus wept," Roscoe might add a little nervously, and sometimes contemptuously, when it came his turn to give blessing.

"Jesus wept," Angelina would follow.

In those days Roscoe was a day laborer who worked when he could. For more years than Angelina couldve imagined then, Aunt Jujie had held down a steady job as a domestic for a prominent Jewish family in the Northwest section of Detroit, a well-established middle- and upper-middle-class area that blacks were later to take over completely. The Fishlers, Jujie's employers, had been among the last nonblacks to sell out and head for Oak Park or some other suburb when the neighborhoods around there began to change drastically. The Fishlers were lively, generous people, to hear Jujie tell it, and she'd considered herself lucky to be working for such prestigious, open-handed people—"quality white folks" she'd called them—but, all the same, she encouraged Angelina to be trigger-quick to take on intellectually or socially any white person who jumped up in her face.

Roscoe had always been something else.

Roscoe, who was lighter skinned than Jujie, had never come anywhere near to being as holy. He was, rather, on a totally different trip. He smoked strong unfiltered cigarettes, at least a pack a day. He drank Jack Daniels Black Label Whiskey with as little ice or mix as he could get away with, and he loved to party—five, ten, fifteen, twenty, thirty hours at a time.

Sometimes while Jujie was away and he and Angelina had the house to themselves, Roscoe'd play blues and rhythm and blues records loud, and the two of them, the girl and the grown man, would show one another new dance steps that theyd recently picked up. Occasionally he'd even let her have a sip of his beer, warning her that if she *ever* slipped and told Aunt Jujie he'd never have anything whatsoever to do with her again—or so he let on.

What happy times she remembered from those days! Why do people have to grow up and spoil everything? It'd been so nice being a child and feeling that adults knew what they were doing and what the world was all about. Now that she was one of them, the truth was out, and the truth was breaking her heart by the hour. Even now, smiling and nodding and yessing and no-ing to her elders as they all made their way through the gray afternoon light to the car, she caught herself breaking out in goose pimples just recalling all the times Aunt Jujie almost walked in on them frolicking like devils in the spotless front room.

Roscoe, she could see now, was slicker than slick though. He knew Jujie a whole lot better than Jujie knew him. He knew her schedule, her rhythms, her cycles, her habits, her definite likes and dislikes, and he used this knowledge to manipulate matters so that, in spite of their unbelievable differences, open conflict and tension were kept to a minimum.

Angelina grew used to sitting half-terrified while her aunt delivered some flaming sermon about the evils of liquor and tobacco. Roscoe, his hat or cap pushed back on his balding head, face crinkled up, would sit patiently, chewing on a toothpick, say, and wait for her to come to the point and wind it up. Then he'd shake his head from side to side and say something like, "You know, Jujie, you really oughtta should get them people you work for to put up some money for you to build some kinda church and get you a congregation and start *rakin* in the bread. You can do it, I know you can! Hell . . . I mean, *heck,* you can just naturally preach. You a born preacher. I see Prophet Jones and Daddy Grace and them got them big-ass, I mean them big old cars and fine houses and servants to wait on em and stuff from preachin and here we sit in this raggedy coal-heated house scufflin like Mexicans—or whoever the hardest-scufflin people sposed to be—and cant even hardly keep our old struggle-buggy Plymouth in gas!"

Jujie'd give him her hardest, meanest stare which never failed to make Angelina's heart beat faster, but Roscoe—he'd stand up, cram his hands in his pockets, feeling for cigarettes, and carry right on. "I mean it, honeybunch, you can just naturally preach that jive, I mean, preach that gospel. Now, if you was to somehow get hold to you a church, even a little storefront kinda church, we could manage our money and rise up and get rich in no time and before you know it be done moved over there on Chicago Boulevard where all the resta the rich niggers breakin they neck movin to and set down in *style*!" Then he'd light up a cigarette, blow out a smoke ring or two to amuse Angelina, get himself a fresh beer from the refrigerator and that would be that.

In those days she could never understand how Aunt Jujie and Roscoe put up with one another. The hassling mustve gone on long before she'd come to stay with them. The pattern was simple. Theyd argue and squabble and then theyd be friends again. To keep token peace, Roscoe never lit a cigarette or took a drink on Sunday, never around the house at least, and he was very careful at all times about his language in Jujie's presence.

Angelina'd liked Roscoe because he was so easy to be with. In more ways than one he'd reminded her of her father. During that particular spell which lasted for well over two years, she only saw Daddy on weekends.

Aunt Jujie was like no one she'd ever seen before—a tough, high-strung little woman who seemed to live in a world all her own that, in retrospect, existed mostly inside her spooky head.

There were things about her though that Angelina'd found attractive.

For one thing, Jujie was—as Roscoe never tired of reminding them—a very moving talker, scarey to listen to at times; rather like those horror and monster movies that Angelina couldnt resist. Either she'd get Roscoe to take her to them or she'd watch them on TV. They got her all chilled up, gave her bad dreams and there'd be terrifying creatures lurking in her clothes closet or under the bed for weeks afterward—but she always went back for more. Being frightened could be fun. Sometimes.

Above all, she loved hearing Aunt Jujie talk about being able to float through the air like a ghost or spirit, or about being ridden by a witch in her dreams. That'd happened in Ajijic one morning, the day before she'd rung up Margo and found out about the telegram. She'd caught herself deep in a dream, wanting it to end but unable to move. If only she could wiggle a toe, a finger, hips, anything, everything wouldve been OK. Finally Watusi had turned over, mashing her shoulder, and she was home free. "When a witch be ridin you, any time a witch be ridin you," Jujie had said, "it mean somethin awful bout to take place."

It was this same human being nestled beside her in the automobile now who'd once shaken her awake in the middle of one distant night to say: "I got to tell *you* this, Angie, because you a little child and little childrens is more pure of spirit than we so-call grown folks, and it's a lotsa things yall more capable of understandin even though you might not even know this bout yourself. Last night, child, I rose up outta my body again . . ."

And now with the dumb car radio squalling up-to-the-minute Soul, they were roaring out into another kind of night—Roscoe behind the wheel—toward Greater Metropolitan Detroit as the deejay labeled it; toward the hospital and Daddy, but not without first stopping off and spending the night at her relatives' sad little house which at one point in time had been Angelina's headquarters for the whole world.

As they whizzed through what shouldve been familiar territory, she was having a hard time spotting anything that even remotely resembled a personal landmark. It had all changed so. Years ago she'd read an article in the *Free Press* that predicted what was going on now. Detroit, it said, would extend all the way to Ann Arbor within a very few years and O how those years had zipped by! Things really aint what they used to be, she mused, checking out Jujie's reaction to Roscoe's all but blazing cigar and the station he'd punched up on the radio.

Jujie didnt even so much as roll an eye his way. She sat right up next to her niece and told her, "Baby, it's really gon surprise you how this doggone town done changed!"

Angelina didnt really care about the doggone town. She wanted to know how Daddy was doing and what exactly had happened.

STORIES

It was the simplest of nights. Aunt Jujie made her a fat roastbeef sandwich with too much mayonnaise as usual and perked up a big pot of herb tea. The tea put her back in California for a spell, and the sandwich filled her groaning stomach. They sat, the three of them, around the familiar big oak table in the dining room. Angelina kept taking longer and longer glances at the Jesus calendars and knickknacks that Jujie displayed proudly and wondered what her Berkeley friends would make of the scene. There'd been a time when she moved among the kind of people who wouldve been delighted by these surroundings, even going so far as to acclaim them as ultimate kitsch. The few friends she had now would doubtless chalk it all up to bad taste, pure and outright. Who the hell cared?

"All right, darlin," Jujie began, "we'll tell you the way it went down with Matthew to the best of our understandin."

"Lemme tell it," Roscoe insisted. "I'm the one carried him over there to Herman Kiefer Hospital and got him checked in."

"OK, OK," Jujie agreed, "let Roscoe give you the general version and then I'll fill you in the nit-nat."

Roscoe took a deep sip of tea and breathed out a little too aspirately. Angelina'd watched him trek to the kitchen with his cup and figured—only because it was the kind of thing she mightve pulled—that he'd spiked it with a sprinkling of authentic booze. As a kid she remembered watching workmen coming home in cars at stoplights. Theyd have a pint milk bottle or cup of something with a rag or tissue wrapped around it and would take frowning sips from it till the light said go.

"Check this out," Roscoe said. "Matthew sittin up home one night, mindin his own business, aint studyin bout nothin but what's on the TV and all of a sudden somebody ring the doorbell, so he git up and answer it. Well, it's ten o'clock at night but he dont pay that much mind cause he kinda use to people droppin by late sometime. Ive even gone by there myself nine-thirty, ten, ten-thirty but never no later'n that unless it's some type of party or celebration or somethin goin on. Well, the way Matthew put it, he turn down the TV to go see who it was and wasnt too much thinkin bout peepin out long side the shade first to see who it was like he usually do. Say he open the door and it was two young Negroes standin up there talkin bout, 'Is Clarence home?' He say, 'Clarence who? Aint no Clarence live here.' They say, 'Well, Clarence Turner, dont he stay here no more?' He say, 'If he do it musta been way over ten years ago cause that's how long I ownin this house and livin in it myself. Yall must have the wrong address.' Matthew say he got to feelin kinda funny then cause he thought he recognized one of the boys—both of em teen-agers, you understand—from round the neighborhood except he had on one of them big old floppy sport caps like they use to wear back when I was a boy. I dont know whacha call em but I calls em them old bighead nigger caps, and the dude that's doin all the talkin he got his pulled down all cross his forehead so far until all Matthew can see is the nigger's eyes shinin out from under the bill kinda. Other nigger he just standin back chewin gum, got his hands jammed down in his coat pocket with his shades on and so—"

"Wait a minute, wait just a minute!" Jujie butted in, "if you gon tell the lie, let's get it right. You aint tellin it right."

"What I leave out?"

"Lem*me* tell it."

"All right, OK, Jujie, you tell it, you tell it! All I got to say bout that is you might can preach and get people all scared in they soul but you sure as heck cant tell no stories like I can."

"We'll see about that, Mr. Roscoe the Maestro. If it mean all that much to you I'll let you tell the story. I just wanna get in the part about how Matthew slipped up."

"Slipped up?"

"Yeah, the part about the gun."

"The gun? That's the part I was comin to, woman, before you started all that cacklin and carryin on and interruptin me! Look here, Angie—"

Angelina pulled herself back from all the directions in which her many minds had scattered. "I'm listening," she said automatically.

"Your daddy usually keep a gun packed and ready to shoot in the house. Matter of fact, he got two guns that I know bout. One he keep in a drawer by his bed and the othern downstairs in a overcoat pocket in the clothes closet near the front door. That the part you want me to get in, Jujie?"

Jujie nodded and folded her nightgowned arms.

"OK, so your daddy got suspicious about these two jokers and figured he'd just slam the door in they face and then reach round the corner in the closet for his pistol. Well, he kick at the door with one foot but before it shut both the niggers rush in and grab him like, talkin bout, 'Too late now, we gotcha, you old so-and-so'—well, I guess you got to know by now the expression they musta called him by. One of the young dudes, the one with the shades on, rassle Matthew down to the floor and ties him up with some rope he got in his pocket while the othern held a gun to his head and—"

Angelina was shaking by now. She felt a tension headache

spreading from her sinuses to her brain and down into her body. Her stomach felt as if it were being pricked and stabbed with pins. Why were all these guns and bad scenes suddenly messing up her life? Nauseous, she put her sandwich down.

"You all right?" Roscoe asked. "Dont you feel well?"

"I'm sorry," she barely whispered, "I just cant eat any more. I—"

"Now look what you gone and done," Jujie said. "You got the poor girl all upset."

"I was just runnin down to her what happened, that's all. I didnt mean nothin by it."

"Well, I reckon you done said enough. The poor child cant even finish her somethin-to-eat." She scooted her chair up close to Angelina's. "It's all right, darlin, it's all right. I know how you feel."

"Why did it have to happen to Daddy?" That choke was in her voice again. "Why him? He's never done . . . he aint never done anyone any harm."

"I know, I know," was all Jujie could say.

"Your dad's a good man, Angie. I dont know of too many that come anywhere near bein as good as he is. I didnt mean to get you all upset and jiggedy, honey."

"Your daddy can tell you all about it when you go see him in the hospital tomorrow," Jujie said. "He the one you oughtta should hear it from anyway. Wasnt nothin but a coupla these nickel and dime young hoodlums that Detroit is full of nowdays. Everytime you turn around look like somebody done hit somebody over the head and taken they money or somebody done shot and killed somebody or broke into they house and stole everything they figure they can sell."

"Yeah, it's a mess," said Roscoe, reviving his obnoxious cigar with a fresh light from a kitchen match.

"I done told you bout scratchin them doggone matches on the furniture, fool!"

"Sorry, Jujie, I guess I wasnt thinkin."

"That's what's the matter with the world today," Jujie went on, rising to remove Angelina's unfinished sandwich from the table. "Aint nobody thinkin. Aint nobody thinkin no more. Everybody drinkin and everybody stinkin but aint nobody thinkin!"

"Amen!" Roscoe shot back like a robot, dripping with cigar smoke.

"I read in the papers back in California where Detroit's now the homicide capital of the country. There're supposed to be more murders taking place here than anywhere else in the States."

"Wouldnt surprise me a drop," Aunt Jujie said, returning from the kitchen with a big glass of buttermilk which she set down in front of Angelina. "Drink this, baby, itll settle your stomach. It's a whole lotsa thievin *and* killin go on round this Detroit now. It aint never been no Garden of Eden, you wanna know the truth, but it's done got so here lately where you cant even walk down the street in broad daylight without worryin bout whether some dope fiend gon snatch your purse or knock you in the head. I was standin up here on Linwood and West Philadelphia little while back with a armload of grocery, tryna pick thru my purse for some bus change—and child, dont lemme get to tellin you bout how the buses is now—when some little joker, couldna been more'n ten, come zippin past me and snatched my pocketbook right out my hand! Got me so mad! Now, I'm a Christian woman, Angelina, you know that—least I try to be—but I aint gon lie. That snot-nose rascal got me so burnt up until if I'da had me some kinda hard-shootin pistol handy—and may the good Lord forgive me for even thinkin somethin like this much less sayin it—I'da shot the little nigger's brains out. Theyd still be pickin em up all up and down Linwood. I'da *blasted* him just like *that*!"

Jujie snapped her fingers so loudly and made such a face that Angelina felt she knew once and for all what living in Detroit must be like.

Roscoe said, "I can back up what Jujie sayin, Angie. Ever since them riots this town aint been right. Look like once they found out they could get away with anything even while the National Guard was lookin over they shoulder, these Negroes aint eased up since."

"Well, considering the racial pressures that were tearing Detroit apart," Angelina threw in—

"I know," said Jujie, "the Negroes was bein oppressed, mm*mmm,* so that give em the right to get rogue-ish, hunh?"

"It's that dope!" Roscoe concluded. "It's all that devilish dope that's got these people gangin up on one another. And I'll tell you somethin else—the polices and them *got* to be in on the deal or else they woulda been done broke it up by now. Course, since them riots, you cant get no police to come out to your house. After the niggers'd done stripped poor Matthew's house clean and taken off, wonder they didnt hurt him more'n they did, he got hisself loose and call the cops but they done got to the place now where they dont come out to your house— specially not to no colored neighborhood—less'n it's seven or eight squad cars full of em. Scared some of these youngbloods gon gang up and ambush em, you understand. And it's been plenty of that done took place too. Cant say I blame the police. I dont know what the world comin to. Tell you one thing though. You got to be on your toes ever minute. I always keeps me five or ten dollars tucked down in my wallet or pocket in case one of these punks stick me up. Way I figger is they gon *shonuff* hurt you they stop you and you aint got *nothin.* I always make sure my car doors is locked when I stop for a red light. It's some of these jitterbugs'll jump right up in your car and jam a gun to your head and say 'Take me to Palmer Park!' or to someplace where they can rob you. They done killed so many taxi drivers till you get in a cab now and you cant even hear the driver talk for all the bulletproof jive they done put up to separate the front seat from the back. I even read about some niggers that got in a cab, killed the driver, stuffed him in the trunk and drove around town pickin up fares and robbin em."

120

"Please!" said Angelina, exhausted, "I dont think I can take any more."

"Leave her alone," Jujie told Roscoe. "She just come here from way down in Mexico anyway. She need to rest."

WHO IS ANGELINA?

She sat by herself in the fluorescent waiting room, thinking about the time years ago when she'd slipped on a sliver of shower room soap at Durfee Junior High and cut her chin rather badly. The school nurse telephoned Daddy at work and he rushed right over in his post-office clothes and brought her here to Herman Kiefer Hospital where a good-natured Jewish doctor, using no anesthetic as she recalled, stitched up her chin while he hummed and half-sang snatches from "The Naughty Lady of Shady Lane." He'd even been so corny as to've told her, "A stitch in time saves nine, you know."

Oooo, that was long ago! She fingered the scar for the billionth time while she sat, legs crossed, reading, or rather, looking at a year-old issue of *Ebony*. The chubby black receptionist—who reminded her of Louetta Mae Barnes from Central High School—assured her that she'd be able to go in and see her father in about ten minutes.

It was early afternoon and raining outside. Aunt Jujie had driven the Pontiac to work out in Oak Park and Roscoe had arranged a ride with a job buddy to the Chrysler plant that morning and left Angelina the Buick. She was glad to be able to visit Daddy alone. She loved her aunt and uncle but she also loved being left to the privacy of her thoughts and emotions. That was the way she'd thought Mexico was going to be—a chance to lose herself in a whole lot of unpressured soul space—before Watusi turned up to charm her away from herself.

The receptionist kept looking at her and she kept looking at the receptionist. "How much longer now?" she asked when she saw by the clock that ten minutes had passed.

"Any minute now, Miss Green. Dont worry. It wont be too long. Theyre getting him ready for you."

She hadnt seen her father in almost three years. The last time had been in L.A. when he'd flown out for some sort of postal supervisors convention and she'd gone from Berkeley to spend the weekend with him there at the home of some cousins on the west side of town. His handsomeness and strength impressed her but he was growing bitter about the way his life had gone. He regretted everything then, it seemed—her mother's passing; the death of their firstborn, a son, Charles, who'd died a crib death in his tenth month; the fact that he hadnt taken full advantage of the GI bill and gone for a college degree; selling his land in Milan and moving to Detroit to undertake a civil-service career; having to farm Angelina out to his sister and her husband after his wife had died. She'd gone back to Berkeley with quite a headache, wishing there were some way she could warn Daddy not to count on her to make up for all the things that had gone wrong in his own life. "I'm depending on you," he'd told her one hot sunny noon as they walked around the La Brea Tar Pits. "It's no good thinking that way, Daddy" was what she'd wanted to tell him but, as usual, her heart got in the way.

"Miss Green, the nurse will show you in now."

Well, there he was. Even in the glare of overhead lighting, propped up with pillows, chest elaborately bandaged, surrounded by get-well gadgets and equipment and medicines in every form, he still looked handsome, the way she remembered him during her absences in California, Europe, Mexico.

His hair had gone completely gray. His jolly, broad face was thinning out, and his dark skin, the color of brown charcoal or burnt maple syrup, seemed a little pale—ashy, as Aunt Jujie had described him the night before.

She bent over his bed and hugged him cautiously. He held her to him for what mightve been an hour, touching his lips to her cheeks and forehead, pressing his face to hers until both their eyes were filling with tears.

"I knew you'd come," he said in the softest voice, "I knew you wouldnt let me down, Angel, I just knew it! I prayed to God for Him to send you to me. They told me you were in some foreign country and it wouldnt be possible to find you, but I just knew you'd come back and say some kind words to me if we could figure out how to get word to you about the condition I was in. You look so beautiful. The world must be treating you right."

"Daddy, I never was a world fan. You know that."

"I know that—and I know a little something else besides. I can remember back to when you were just five or six months old curled up in your tiny crib, and, just as sure as I'm laid up here now in this hospital bed, whenever I had a restless night—insomnia or something like that—or was worried about anything or my mind started working funny or getting depressed, you'd let out a cry in your sleep. I swear, Angel, you'd do it every time. At first it used to scare me. You'd do it with your mother and it scared her too. It was like you were tuned in to what we were thinking. It's always been kinda like that, hasn't it?"

A silence passed over them that seemed to stretch back through years, decades, centuries probably.

In the space of this giant silence—thirty seconds of wrist-watch time—she saw things in her father's face that she'd never seen before. His native calmness was there all right and she was happy being back in touch with it again, but there was something else mixed in with it this time. She could feel it

124

flowing from his entire body. It was hard to name, but it felt like the kind of anxiety she'd gone through when she was on the verge of having something good and new happen to her.

"What's life like out there where you call home now?"

"Pretty much like it's always been—peculiar."

"Peculiar?"

"I dont know how else to put it. The longer I stay out there on the west coast, the more I wonder what it was made me go there."

"Angel, I think we both know what carried you there. What I'd like to know is what in the devil's been *keepin* you there all this time? I mean, it's been years now, you know. Cant say I blame you much though. It's pretty bad around here now. I was thinking about you the night I got done in."

"What happened, Daddy?"

"I thought Jujie and Roscoe wouldve filled you in by now."

"They did but I wanna hear it from you—that is, if youre up to it."

"Not much to tell really. Coupla hoodlums forced their way into the house. One of em held a gun to my head while the other one tied me up. They got all they could. Worked pretty fast. Stereo, both TVs—the color set and the black and white—my shortwave radio, my movie camera and that expensive Polaroid I was carrying with me that time out in L.A. That's about all there was to steal really. They werent about to start hauling the furniture out. Too lazy, I guess. O yeah . . . they did go through all the drawers in the place and pocket a coupla rings and my Bulova watch. Come to think of it, they took the thirty-some-odd dollars I'd put in a desk drawer that I was saving up to buy you a birthday present with. They went thru my wallet lookin for credit cards but I keep all those hid away upstairs and only carry one with me if I intend to use it."

"Isnt it funny what they take?"

"How you mean, honey?"

"My place was broken into just before I left for Mexico.

They pretty much cleaned me out right down to all the change I'd been saving in a coffee can in the kitchen cupboard—came to about a hundred dollars, something like that."

"O, Angel, you didnt tell me about that! Do you know who did it?"

"Not for sure, I think it was a buncha kids who just moved into the block."

"Addicts?"

"I think so—if theyre the ones I think did it."

"That dope is pretty hard to get around. I guess you know that. Seems to be pretty much what the youngsters—and a lotta oldsters too—are involved with now here in this town. I even got behind these methadone programs cause I thought that might help break up the addiction some, and now, come to find out, methadone's just another form of dope. Now theyre stealing that and selling it on the street just like they do that heroin. I dont know what the answer is anymore, I really dont! We even have a problem with it with some of the employees, younger ones mostly, that work out at the post office now. They come in nodding and acting all slow and funny or else theyre half-sick a lot of the time. Either way they slow things down, and I'm the one supposed to be in charge of seeing that the efficiency's kept at a decent level. I dont know what I'm gonna do now. Right after the kids finished cleaning me out and were leaving with the last of the goods, I managed to stick my foot out and trip one of em, the one with the gun. It was a mistake, I know. He was hopped up on something, so all he did was get up off the floor and pull the trigger. The bullet grazed a lamp and shattered it on one side, but he took another shot and this time the bullet got me in the chest. I thought I was dead."

"What on earth saved you?" she asked, wincing and squeezing his hand so tightly she thought her own fingers might break.

"Doctors say I'm lucky. The gun was low caliber, first of all, and second of all, the little bullet cut through my right lung—not the left where the heart is—but for some miraculous reason it didnt collapse. Like, the bullet opened it up but they were able to do surgery on it and do some patching to keep it from caving in like a punctured balloon."

"Whew!" she sighed and threw her arms around him. "Daddy, I love you, I love you, I love you!"

"It isnt over yet," he groaned.

"Medication time," the nurse chimed. She reminded Angelina of Carol Petersen, a Wisconsin Swede she'd been at Michigan with. How she used to envy Carol's low, throaty voice!

"How long did they say you'd be here?" she asked him.

"They never said."

"We never said because we didnt know," the plump blonde nurse informed them, consulting her clipboard. "Couple more weeks is what the doctors're saying now. Mr. Green's recovering just fine, just fine, arent you now? OK, you know the routine, just roll up your sleeve and relax."

Up until a year ago, Angelina had hated the sight of needles. It was then, right around the time that her affair with Larry had gone sour, that she submitted herself to a series of painful gum operations. Peridontics they called it—and since she was working on a job that provided medical insurance which included dental work, she decided to get her mouth fixed. Before each session in the chair, some nurse would lead her into a darkened little room and have her lie down for her shot. Demerol was what they were serving. One gentle poke and Angelina would sail out of her stupid body and into the simple trembling tree leaves that rustled against one another in rainy light outside the window of that Berkeley dental building.

Now, watching the shiny hypodermic in the snowy-fingered hand of this friendly nurse prick a vein at the edge of her daddy's dark bicep, she identified visibly with the process being set in motion. She understood why legislation against drugs was useless.

She knew all too intimately why theyd both been robbed. If getting through days depended on Demerol, she'd steal too, but she doubted that she could actually rob anyone. Or could she? What would stop her if she craved that bright high feeling enough? All her life she'd been rummaging around in time looking for some version of this bliss she'd heard and read so much about. Was she so unique? Wasnt everybody really looking for the same thing? Call it happiness. Call it joy. Call it peace. Call it contentment. Call it whatever you wanted. She called it ecstasy—a joyous feeling of total release. She wanted to rise up out of herself and go zooming above the stupid-ass world like some giggly old saint who knew that nothing short of ecstasy mattered anyway. Was this what she sought in a man? Was this the kind of freedom she was looking for when she drifted away from this very town to become a wanderer like so many of her old friends had done? Well, a few of them had found what theyd been looking for in the form of some chemical like Demerol that positively dazzled the bloodstream. She'd tried a few of the so-called psychedelic drugs back when that was the hip thing to do. She liked them. LSD, peyote, mescalin—they all made her feel pretty special and wise. She liked what they did with time. Time was her drug really. She had a few visions, a handful of backyard Berkeley revelations, but mostly she learned that she didnt really need that kind of voyage. It was too dramatic. It always overwhelmed her. It wasnt her way. She was already too close to that edge, that edge being what she liked to think of as an exquisitely thin line separating the everyday Now-I-Have-to-Find-a-Job part of herself from the part that was absolutely unkillable. The whole time she'd been walking across San Francisco through that nighttime chill to somehow leap from the Golden Gate, some other guarded, secret part of herself had been whispering: *As good as life's been to you and just because things didnt quite work out with Larry, you must be crazy, really crazy to do this. You go around feeling sorry for yourself and yet all the while youre floating around in skies you havent even bothered to explore yet . . .*

The change in Daddy was instantaneous. Medication was morphine, the nurse had told her, and he seemed thoroughly relaxed, as relaxed as she'd been under Demerol. The dentist couldve cut her tongue out or simply tapped at her gums with a velvet wrench; she wouldnt have known the difference.

She wanted to ask him hundreds, thousands of questions that living out west and thinking back east had occasioned, but the nurse, the comic-book nurse, told her she'd have to be winding it up soon, that some staff doctors would be coming in shortly to inspect her father.

Daddy, what was the weather like the day I was born? Why did you and Mama have me? What was it that first attracted you to Mama? Why did you give up playing music? What possessed you to move from Georgia to Michigan and why that little racist town Milan and all that farming stuff? Why'd you pick the post office to work at for the rest of your life? Was I strange as a little girl? Do you love me as much as Mama did? Do you still love Mama? Do you still love me now that Ive been away for so long? Why'd you name me what you did? Did my name have any special significance to you and Mama? What was it? Who is Angelina?

All she really said was, "How do you feel?"

"Feel pretty good considering . . ."

"Considering what?"

"Considering I couldve been dead and gone and your last memories of me couldve been as a corpse in a casket instead of your old man recovering in a hospital bed. You gonna come see me again tomorrow?"

"I'll be here. I *will* be here."

For the first time all afternoon he took a slow, blinking look at the TV set at the other end of the room. It had been at the foot of the bed all along, way up high on some ingeniously designed pedestal, grinding out images with the sound turned off. The news was on.

"It's funny when youre sick like I am," he said. "What's coming in over the television sure doesnt make much sense. They could be playing anything. The news looks like cartoons, 'Meet the Press' looks like 'Laugh-In,' and the soap operas look kinda like these religious stories they play on Sunday morning or that stuff they run on educational TV. I mean, it all looks about the same to me. Everything they flash up there just looks dumb—and I'm a TV watcher! You know?"

She knew.

THE OLD WORLD

As long as she was going to be in town for a while and it was the weekend, she decided to look up a couple of old friends—Louetta Mae Barnes and Renée Appel. They'd all been at Central together. She hadn't seen Louetta since then, since high school, but Renée had spent some time at Michigan before transferring to Columbia in her junior year. They'd even lunched once or twice together during Angelina's New York period (eighteen months of hell and a hard way to go), and Renée had told her that she was tired of reading manuscripts for a Madison Avenue publisher and wanted to get back to her roots, Detroit, and get married. Angelina wished her luck. Months later she got a letter from Renée explaining how she'd married, gotten pregnant, and was now Renée Appel Heinz. The letter, in orange ink, had been signed: "Collegiately yours, RAH."

A couple of phone calls was all it took to locate the two of them. She remembered Louetta's parents' phone number from all the times she'd dialed it in high school. Fascinated in the tenth grade by the fact that they could dial the letters W-E-A-T-H-E-R and get the weather report, recorded of course, they'd set about translating their own home numbers into neat alphabetized codes. Angelina spelled hers out to read TOODLES. Louetta's became TOPPLED. Since they didnt live far from one another, their exchanges were the same and spellable variations were limited. Angelina had set out to formulate some grand, outrageous combination of letters but had to settle for what she could get. So had Louetta.

As for Renée's whereabouts, all she did was look in the telephone directory and find her listed simply and conveniently under her married name.

It was Sunday in the old world, Angelina's Detroit world. It was raining and Angelina was curled up on the sofa by the living room window watching it pour down onto a street she no longer knew. Most of the houses seemed familiar. A few had been painted and fixed up but most of them had fallen into disrepair. The very style of them fascinated her—large two-storied A-frame structures built mostly in the teens and twenties but lacking the solid, stately charm of the brownstones and brick-based homes and mansions that black people lived in just a mile away in the center of the city's thriving northwest district where she'd gone to school at Central High; main streets with names like Linwood, Dexter, Boston Boulevard, Chicago Boulevard, Oakman, Claremount, Twelfth; side streets ranging from privileged to bourgeois to working class to lumpen—Ewald Circle, Glynn Court, Tuxedo, Atkinson, Gladstone, West Philadelphia.

To live under this same roof as Jujie and Roscoe had been doing for longer than she could remember, for well over twenty years, was sad turning into unthinkable.

She toyed around with pictures of herself going through those changes but none of them made it. To eat and sleep, get up pissed, go to work, come back shot, blink at the paper, gaze at the TV, make some kind of Ford factory love (if they ever even did that) within these very walls of a paid-for house sagging with blues and grease and filled with department store and Woolworth furnishings, pictures of ghosts, framed greeting cards, knickknacks and bric-à-brac, coupon dinnerware, calendar Christs and *Condensed Reader's Digests*, would drive her off the Ambassador Bridge on the way to Canada.

She grinned at the Californian in her and it grinned back. People just didnt chain themselves down that way anymore, not the people she knew at least. She could relate far faster to white-washed single-storied plastic housing stacked on hillsides off the freeway on the way to San Francisco Airport than she could to this "serious" real housing surrounding her now which was more than sturdily built.

She flashed on her cluttered address book back in Berkeley. Her California friends kept her scratching out streets and numbers, but the people she'd known from back east stayed right there in the book where she'd left them.

While she was watching the sky fill up with light, she got the feeling that something was watching her. Easing her head around, theatrically, she saw Uncle Roscoe, legs crossed, in robe and slippers on a chair across the room. His stare had been tickling her bones.

"Checkin it out, hunh?" he whispered.

"Hunh?" she blurted out, cooling it instantly. "You scared me!"

"Didnt mean to. I been settin up here checkin you checkin it out."

"Checking what out?"

"Checkin *us* out. That's what you doin, aint it? It's like, you been all cross the country and foolin round the world and now you done bout got to the place where start start and finish finish—or'm I sposed to say where start begin and finish end?"

She stared at this man.

"Pretty little thing like you musta seen a whole lotta good times with that sweet disposition of yours. I got somethin to tell you."

"What?"

"*Shhhh* . . . It's a surprise, so I dont want you blabbin it to Jujie."

She stared at her uncle.

"It's been a long time . . . wait a minute." He walked over and plopped down beside her, continuing in a voice so low that she thought he might break out a plan to blow up the sun. "It's been maybe five years since me and your auntee been on a real vacation. Last time was when I hit on a horse out here at Northfield Downs for five hundred dollars and we went up to Canada and goodtimed for a week one Thanksgivin. Well, now I'mo take her on a trip back down in Georgia and Alabama but she dont know this."

"Tell me something, Unc," she said suddenly. "It seems to me that Aunt Jujie's really changed since Ive been away. I mean—"

"I know what you gon ask me."

"Well, it is kinda weird, you know, seeing her tolerate soul music in the house and not getting on you about smoking and even using a cuss word herself every now and then. It didnt used to be like that."

"I know it didnt, I know it didnt. Listen . . ." He lowered his voice another decibel. "I'll tell you somethin bout your auntee. Now, she a good woman and she a regular church sister and all like that—fact, she'll be gettin up tuhreckly to get herself fixed up and haul us both off to Holiness Church over here on Grand River. Unless one of us is sick, it aint hardly a Sunday go by that we aint there—but, like, as the years roll on, she done cooled down a bit bout all this sanctified stuff—and aint nobody happier bout it than me."

"What happened?"

"Time, Angie. Time is what happen. The same thing that put you out there gon bring you back in. I hear people on the radio and over the TV talkin bout space capsule and time capsule but lemme tell you somethin, young woman. This thing we goin thru here down on *this* earth aint nothing *but* a time capsule—a time machine, you wanna know the truth. Jujie got to the place where she couldnt get along all that good with the other church sisters and all the resta her old sanctified friends. She so sanctified until didnt too many of *them* wanna be around her no more. Took her a long time to get the message but finally she start easin off and loosenin up a little taste. She stop bein so strict with me and started enjoyin herself a little more. Angie, no lie, Jujie use to could shake em down with the best of em when it came to goodtimin and cabaretin and cuttin the fool and carryin on. When we first met back here durin the War, we was almost as bad as these young people is now talkin bout doin they thing. We wasnt into nothin but doin our thing shonuff, child!"

They both had to turn to watch a Pinto with a Camaro hot on its tail roar past at sixty miles per hour. Both cars skidded to near stops at the corner stop sign and blasted off again.

"Niggers crazy," said Roscoe matter-of-factly. "Use to be you could get a little peace and quiet on Sunday mornin but now these Negroes is out all times of the day and night all week long jepodizin folkses lives. You talk about them long walks you use to takin out there in California—*hunh!*—the way these people with they cars is now, you aint gon hardly catch *me* out there hoofin it! I read here in the *Free Press* the other day bout some nigger that drove his Mercury right up into some bakery store window. Just crashed into all the glass, cakes and bread and cookies and glass flyin every which way. Man what own the place was either a Pollack gentleman or an Eye-talian fella, say it got him so mad he was ready to go on out and get him a gun and shoot every nigger he finds head off! He didnt exactly put it like that over the news but I could tell that's bout how he felt and I told Jujie, you can ask her, said I didnt blame him one bit."

"This is really some awful stuff to be talking about on Sunday morning, Uncle Roscoe."

"I know it is but what, I mean, the main thing I wanted you to know was we gon be gone from here startin tomorrow for bout a week. You gon have the place all to yourself. Wont that be nice? I talked Jujie into takin a week out and I'mo use up the resta my sick time I got comin this year and we gon drive back down-home and just relax ourself."

"Yall hear that?" It was Jujie's voice sailing down to them from upstairs. "The way these damn hoodlums be's squeakin these streets nowadays you'd think Judgment Day was just around the corner—and it probly is!"

"Every Sunday seems like Judgment Day to me," Angelina told Roscoe.

"Me too, Angie, you aint just runnin your mouth! But, see, like, I'm a whole lot older'n you are and pretty soon it's gon get to the place where it's a lotsa Judgment Days—Sunday, Monday, Tuesday, Wednesday . . . Fact of business, I dont really get to feelin even halfway right till long about Thursday. Thursday through Saturday—now, them's my days if you just got to pick days."

She'd risen before dawn because she couldnt sleep. She kept picturing her father the way she liked to remember him—jovial and full of energy—and the way he was now. It worried her.

How nice it would be to have him back in good health and to be back in Berkeley, curled up in her own simple bed next to this same watery window, deep into her own kind of understandable craziness.

EAST COAST GHOSTS

"Angelina!" Louetta cried, peeping around the edge of the door before undoing the chain and opening up completely. "Angelina Green! I dont believe it!"

They lunged for one another, colliding in a frenzy of hugs and groans and laughter.

"Ooooo, girl, you sure have put on weight."

"I'm not as skinny as I used to be, that's for sure."

"I should talk. I'm the one need to lose some. I keep tellin everybody. One of these days I'm gonna get off some of this weight and cut out all this eatin and smokin. I mean it too. Come on in, girl, and gimme your coat. Make yourself at home."

Angelina tripped over something and, looking down, saw her feet entangled in a net of plastic string that led to a large mechanical lion, also plastic, flopped on its side in the middle of the living room floor.

"Sorry. Dont pay it no mind, Angie. That's Jomo's new toy that Ernest picked up for him yesterday. Ernest say it's educational. He go in for that sort of thing. I'd just as soon have him play with pots and pans and cardboard boxes."

Angelina spotted a menacing-looking baby crawling toward her from the kitchen. "Is this little Jomo? How old is he?"

"Nope," said Louetta, "this is Ahmed and he's thirteen months and look just like his daddy. Look like Ernie just hauled off and *spit* him out. When you meet Ernest youll see what I mean."

"Was he any at Central back in the old days?"

"Ernest? Naw. Ernest went to Northwestern. He was kind of a track star, made all-city. He graduated and went into the Army around the same time we were just enterin Central. He's a pretty good old man—slick but good. Jomo, I told you bout pushin Ahmed down. Stop that! He's littler than you are and he's just learnin to walk. Now, go back over there and give him a hug-hug and tell him you sorry! Excuse me, Angie."

Ahmed, flat on his back, continued to squall. Jomo, who was going on three, paid his mother no mind. He walked over to Angelina and stood staring meanly up at her. Like most kids, most toddlers anyway, he made her nervous. She wanted Louetta to do something, but all Louetta did was pick the younger child up and dry his eyes by wiping them against her own cheeks. Jomo, tight-lipped and sullen, continued to stare.

Just as she was wishing she'd accepted Jujie's invitation to attend Sunday morning service at Holiness Church, a dog, a wire-haired terrier pup, wobbled into the room. Now she really was ready to wilt. This was all she needed. She couldnt help flashing on W. C. Fields's "Any man who hates children and dogs cant be all bad."

Louetta bent down, took Jomo by the shoulders and shook him. "Look here, Jomo. I want you and Ahmed to go back into your own room to play and take Black Pride with you, hear?"

"Black Pride?"

"That's the dog. Isnt he a little charmer? We just got him a few weeks ago. The kids love him."

"But . . . Black Pride?"

Louetta reached out her hefty arm and patted Angelina's waist. "Girl, I can see you aint changed a drop. You still scared of things you havent been around too much. Black Pride the puppy's name. Ernest named him."

"Did he name the two boys too?"

"Yeah, how'd you guess? I think he pretty good at namin things myself. He figured, well, if they can name a doggone horse Black Beauty, then why cant we name a dog Black Pride. We all just crazy bout Pride—that's what we call him for short here round the house sometime."

Angelina gave the terrier a deep hurry-up glance. She had to admit it was cute. In fact, it reminded her of Ahmed, Louetta's younger son. Were someone to put a razor to her throat and say choose a dog, she'd probably choose a terrier. There was something friendly and intelligent about them.

"What you doin with yourself these days?" Louetta asked in the kitchen over instant Sanka where Sunday funnies and newsprint brightened the table.

Angelina leaned forward, barely avoiding resting her elbow in a puddle of grape jelly. "Do you wanna know the truth or should I just give it to you in general?"

Chubby Louetta, her broad forehead moist from the heat in the apartment, which was considerable, smiled a smile that took Angelina back into another decade when theyd still been children together. How awful life had been then. The problem was that they didnt know anything but thought they knew everything. For the moment she was glad to be twenty-six instead of sixteen. Life was tough but childhood was tougher. She wouldnt want to go through all those changes again—the first time you find out how terrifying the world can be: boys, men, the stupidity of most of the girls she knew who thought that to fall in love was to automatically become a slave to habits older than lust itself.

"I'm at the end of my rope, Louetta," she said. "I'm like that dude used to sing in the song, one of Roscoe's old records, where he says, 'I'm too old for the orphanage, too young for the old folks home'—if you can get to that."

139

"Angie, I got to it four or five years ago. Life aint nothin but one damn thing after another."

"But it's even more complicated than that, Louetta."

"Child, you aint changed a bit. I said it before and I'll say it again. You always were more into that thinkin too much about life than I was. I think it's a mistake when you get to worryin about shit all that much."

Angelina didnt remember Louetta as ever being this literal. She wouldve come on this way herself more of the time if her proper head didn't always get in the way. "It's more than just worrying about shit," she lied, "it's more about trying to figure out if any of it's worth it."

"Oooo, girl, you sound to me like you been hangin out round these schools too long. I never knew you to be like this. You were always the one that was gon go out here and do your thing and never take no for an answer. I always figured if anybody outta that class was gon succeed, you were it."

"I dont even know what success is anymore, Lou. I wish we'd kept in touch. I used to write a lotta letters but I cant seem to get into it much anymore."

"Know what you mean. I'm the same way myself. There've been times, a lot of em, when I thought about you though. Remember all the good times we use to have? Remember that night at the roller rink, the Arcadia, when we first met those two dudes . . ."

Angelina noticed that precious twinkle coming back into Louetta's eye. Her face, despite the Afro hairdo and new weight, was suddenly a decade younger. "How can I ever forget Henry and Archie? Are you kidding?"

"I still think about em too sometime. I even saw Archie back here musta been long around in August. I remember it was hot and I was headed into J.C. Penney to buy me some sandals and there was Archie comin out."

"What's he doing now?"

"Told me he was fixin to go back to Wayne State to get a teachin certificate, but you know Archie."

"Unfortunately, I do know Archie—all too well."

"I know, honey. He the only man I know that do what I call spontaneous lyin. Now, what I mean by that is: most men will lie. A man'll lie a whole lot faster than a woman will—and this just my personal opinion, you know—and think nothin of it. But Archie, Archie'll be sittin up talkin with you and laughin and jokin and carryin on and then, out the clear blue sky, he'll up and say somethin like, 'I met a man today who had three eyes.'"

A twinkle came into Angelina's eye as well although she had trouble controlling her emotions on the subject of Archie, the first boy she'd fallen head over heels unchecked in love with, but Louetta had his number and she had to laugh.

"Archie," Louetta went on, "told me he'd been sellin wigs over on West Grand Boulevard and doin all right but the grind was gettin him down and he wanted to get into somethin that was more challengin. But you know what I heard from Poochie—remember Poochie?—Mildred Valentine with her crazy self? Poochie told me she know for a fact that Archie in the numbers. She say he runnin a wig shop all right with this other dude, forget his name, but they really in the numbers and knockin down all kindsa bread."

"Well, all I know is that's one Negro put me through more changes than I ever thought I'd go through again. Actually, when I think about it now, he was just a young boy and I was really a young girl. I was so scared I was pregnant that summer . . . You remember, dont you?"

"I sure do, but you werent."

"But I thought I was. Missed my period and just knew Dad and Barbara could read my mind anyway. I used to read in books about where women would beat their stomachs with pillows, overexercise, swallow all kinds of things and even . . . even use darning needles to get rid of it. O, Lou, I went through hell."

"But you went out and got yourself fitted for a diaphragm

141

after that, didnt you? I'm the one talked you into it, remember? Whatever happened to Barbara anyway? That's the woman your dad used to live with, right?"

"Lived with? I guess that's a way of putting it. They were practically married. I dont think Dad wouldve ever been happy being married to anyone but Mama again. He told me at the hospital the other day that Barbara got sick of waiting and he got sick of waiting, so she took off and went back to Ohio and married some man she knew before she met Dad. He works for some government office in Cleveland. Theyre doing all right, I guess. I sure liked her. She had a sense of humor and she was always good to me."

"Do you like livin out there in California?"

"I sure like the weather. I dont know about the rest of it yet. It's kind of crazy. I mean, it's more than kind of crazy. Youve got all these people and all that mild weather and no seasons really and your brain operates funny. You go around trying to figure out where you fit in and come to find out there're all these other people wandering around trying to figure out where *they* fit in. Pretty soon you start doing things, silly things, like going on health food trips or taking up akido or astrology or anything to make sure you do fit in someplace. Does that sound dumb?"

"Nope. I been keepin up with it over TV and places and it sound to me like California's just another country. *Another Country*. You read that novel by George Baldwin?"

"James Baldwin?"

"George, James, whatever it is. I went to night school, you know, up here at this community college. I decided it was time for me to get down and find out what all this black jive was about so I took a black literature course from this dude that I dont think liked black people too much. He kept rappin bout how one day we was gon produce a Shakespeare or a Thomas Dylan or somebody. Kept puttin the books he had us readin up against some cracker's book. All the white people sat up in front but I sat in back so I could get a good look at the nigger and

142

make out what he was sayin. He come on so loud until it hurt my ears to be around him."

Angelina had dozed and acted her way through too many literature classes to want to talk about books. Her thoughts were on all the simple things she and Louetta did when they were girls together. How long ago it all seemed now. In California her sense of the past had been different. Louetta, Renée, Central High, Henry (Louetta's boyfriend of a year, famous for his fabulous record collection), Archie, ah that Archie, star basketball player and the only black kid to go out for the swim team and make it big in diving and free-style competitions.

"What does Ernest do?" she asked to change the subject.

"He work at the post office now but next week he'll be takin the civil service test for the police force."

"He really wants to do that? I mean, you know, be a cop?"

"What's wrong with that? The pay's good. Maybe I oughtta explain. Ernest isnt interested in bein a patrolman, directin traffic or anything like that. He got his bachelor degree in sociology at U. of D. this summer, and what he wanna do is get a position with the public relations division of the police department. Sure beats bein a social worker. I dont know how it is out there in California but these social workers round here been catchin natural hell. It's a lot of em messed up on that dope and methadone worst than the people they suppose to be workin with. How long you gon be—"

They both jumped at the sound of shattering glass, the squeals of children and dog barks from the next room.

"How long you gon be in town?" Louetta went on anyway as she got up to investigate.

"Dont know. Depends on how fast Dad recovers, I guess."

"That's right, that's right." Louetta's voice trailed behind her as she left the room. "Sorry to hear bout that, Angie. Musta been Ernest told me bout how he got robbed and shot up and everything. Sounded pretty bad. He really likes your father. They work out the same post office, the big one downtown. Jomo! *Uhhhhh,* Jomo! I know you the one behind all this devilment and I'mo get your daddy to spank your little boodie good when he get in."

Angelina wasnt sure what to do so she rose too and followed Louetta to the scene of the crime.

The floor was showered with pieces of lamp and lightbulb. Ahmed was crying. Jomo was whimpering. Black Pride was barking his hairy head off.

All Louetta did was lift both children in her arms and deposit them outside the room. Pride scampered out, yowling.

Both women got down on their hands and knees and picked up fragments and chunks until their eyes watered.

Angelina giggled.

"What's so funny?"

"Nothing. I was just thinking about the time we walked into the boys' lavatory by mistake over at school and they were all in there smoking and looking all suspicious and beady-eyed and we swore we'd never have children if we could help it because there were enough fools stumbling around through the world already without our adding to it. Remember?"

"Sure, I remember. What I wanna know is how'd you manage to keep your halfa the bargain? I guess I just didnt have the opportunity or sense enough to become a beatnik like you did. You always were kinda on the independent side. Shhhiiit, these damn younguns bout to drive me outta my mind!"

Renée Appel Heinz, her thick red hair newly done up Afro-style, enormous gold rings looped through her ears, looked almost resplendent in her floor-length dress as she led Angelina from the study to the little room toward the back of the house that she called her studio.

So she was painting now. Angelina wanted to paint once. She'd even gone so far as to take a life-drawing class at Berkeley Adult School one quarter. The models had posed a problem. To begin with, she couldnt draw hands and feet and no amount of practice seemed to help her overcome this inability. For another thing, one of the models, a truculent and masculine-featured woman named Deirdre had approached and hit on her in a most aggressive fashion. Upset, she'd abandoned the class before it was over and contented herself with sketching on napkins and in art-store notebooks which she showed no one.

"I want you to see what Ive been working on lately," Renée said. She'd maintained her figure, Angelina noticed, which had always been thin and shapely. Standing five-foot-four to Angelina's five-nine, she'd always made Angelina feel like some kind of a horse, a pony at least.

The sudden smell of oil paints, turpentine and charcoal excited Angelina. She entered the little bedroom that had been converted into a miniature workplace, thinking about the first time she'd eaten paste in first grade and the sweet early fragrances of crayon and colored chalk. She could almost taste the greens and magentas, the yellows, the oranges and reds, the pinks, vanilla whites and chocolatey browns. To paint a landscape that she could eat—*that* would be a trip!

The kids—Kelly, a girl, age five, and Solomon, the boy, age two and one-half—were neatly asleep in their beds. The fat maid on her way out had given Angelina a look that chilled her to the bone. "You Auntie Tom," it seemed to say, "what the fuck you doin hangin round here with this white woman I work for? What's your angle? What's your excuse?"

Most of the paintings Renée pulled out to show her were simple still lifes; colorful tightly framed renderings of books, vases, wine bottles, bowls of fruit at rest beside candles on tables. A few of them were charmingly done. Angelina loved the way Renée used color—lushly, extravagantly. This was the way she wouldve painted herself. "I love your colors!"

"You do? Thanks. These are mostly early things. I mean, like, stuff I turned out last year. I'm into a different sort of phase now—browns and blacks and whites and grays. I'll show you what I mean."

She undraped a stack of larger canvases and clicked on another lamp to brighten the room. "These're some landscapes and portraits Ive been doing lately, winter-type scenes."

There was one that struck Angelina almost immediately. It was a painting of a snowy tree-lined suburban street, possibly the same one Renée lived in right here in Oak Park. The leafless trees, dark brown turning black, their gaunt branches stiff with icy snow, made her think of the silvery little trees with their tortuously gnarled El Greco limbs that made her do double takes around Chapala and Jocotepec—the "tragicomic bougainvillaea" she'd called them in a note she'd written to herself one evening but which she'd promptly crumpled into a ball and tossed into one of Watusi's carefully built hearth fires.

Watusi. She wanted to see him again very much, but not before she'd put herself back together again.

"Lately Ive been doing a lot of portraits. Dont ask me why. It's just something I slipped into. People's faces, their bodies, the way they carry themselves—theyre really little universes, you know."

"I know," Angelina smiled, "Ive gotten lost in a few of those universes as you call them."

"Here's one I did of Kelly and Solomon a few weeks ago. Actually it started out with them sitting for me but you can imagine about how long that lasted, so I ended up working from Polaroid snapshots. What do you think?"

Angelina, who hated being put on the spot this way, barely had a chance to glance at the kids' pink painted faces with their sad blue eyes before Renée buried the canvas and flashed another one on her.

"This is Alex, their father, the way he looked maybe, say, a couple of years ago. I did it from memory."

"He's—well—kinda handsome."

"A regular movie star, isnt he? That's his problem. Actually he doesnt really look like that anymore. He's been letting himself go all to hell since we broke up—it frightens me sometimes. Never was much of a drinker, thank God for that, but he's been smoking an awful lot of grass and this summer this new chick he's with turned him on to coke and acid, so he's been doing a lot of that too. Angie, he looks awful and his brain's dissolving fast but to hear him tell it he's never felt better."

Angelina watched Renée's face take on an expression she remembered from another world, another epoch when theyd stayed up all night preparing for an Art History final at Ann Arbor. Renée had been on amphetamine but Angelina had stuck to black coffee. They both turned up for the exam looking like refugees from the Land of Oz. Renée had said to Angelina as they piled into the exam room: "Well, if I blow this one, I'm switching my major to Fizz Ed"—and then that look had taken over; an intense contraction of facial muscles that seemed to signal the end of some world whose realness she'd never been convinced of anyway.

"Who was the black dude?"

"The black dude?"

"That last portrait you let me get a glimpse of before you snatched it back like you did all the others . . ."

"Oh, yeah, you mean Steve. He's a beautiful man. Do you remember Derek, the guy at Michigan we both had a crush on but he was going with—"

"Eileen."

"Right. Well, Steve reminds me of Derek, in a funny kinda way, but I never really got over Derek. He was such a good artist. I thought he deserved someone better than Eileen. She was such a bitch with her stuck-up Bloomfield Hills ways. They finally got married I hear. It didnt last but about a year. They moved to New York so she could get away from her folks. They hated Derek, him being from a poor family and at Michigan on a scholarship and all that and their fancy daughter taking up with the likes of him . . . Steve reminds me of him. We met at a party right here in this house that Alex gave for his office staff. Steve was working for Alex at the time, doing graphs, I think. Alex was heading up a deal called Computerized Curricula Incorporated—C.C.I.—and they were designing a what you might call teaching-machine program for kids in Harlem. Can you imagine that? I mean, white wasp males, for the most part, organizing a teaching program for Harlem junior high students? Anyway, Steve and I got to be good friends and, you know, well, I guess I leaned on him a lot during those last rocky months when Alex and I were breaking up and—well, to answer your question, he's a good friend."

"Do you still see each other?"

Renée took a long sip of sparkling burgundy and with another hand rubbed her flat belly. "I never could fool you could I, Angie? Youre worse than my mother. Yes, we see each other fairly regularly. He's at Ann Arbor now getting an M.A. so I spend a lot of time around there mostly at his place on the weekends. Alex takes the kids or sometimes theyre with my mother. She lives just a few blocks from here. He's a beautiful cat. I really wish you could meet him."

"Is the divorce final yet?"

"As of last month, yes."

"How does it feel being single again?"

"About the same as when I was married except I have more time to get into my painting and think about things. It's hard on the kids though."

"It isnt hard on you?"

"It's hard on me, I cant deny that. It's hard on me but loneliness is something I'm getting to kinda dig. I know that probably sounds funny but it's true. My head goes haywire at times and there're even times of the month when I want to go to where Alex is and be with him and tell him, 'Let's try it one more time' but I know I'd be wasting my time. Theyre really so different, Alex and Steve. Alex loved me, I suppose, in his own tit for tat organized way. I still love him in a way you—well, in a way maybe you would understand, you being you. Steve I can get lost in. He's that vast. He's a real old-time lover."

By the time they were down to rolling joints, the bubbly wine having given out, Angelina had lost all sense of time, place and circumstance.

"Sorry to hear about your father."

"O yeah. I was with him today for a couple hours. He'll be OK. I'm convinced of that. He's looking better all the time. I expect he'll be home soon."

A BRIGHT
WARM WIND

And so, as always when the going got rough, Angelina fell back into time and silence. She'd never in her life been hard or tough but, like the trees in Asian proverbs, she too could learn how to bend with the wind.

The beautiful thing about time, she was coming to believe, was that it never stands still. As for silence, her old friend of friends, she knew it could be counted on to express what words could not.

Even the house had a story to tell. Take, for example, all that chewed-out gum she used to stick, on retiring, to bottom edges of the bed frame in her little room at Jujie's and Roscoe's. Well, running her fingers along there now, she could feel that much of it was still intact; hardened into wood-like lumps to become, in fact, as much a part of the old room as venetian-blind dust, sneezy curtains and images she fancied in the peeling walls.

It was the silence embedded in this grimy pink paint that spoke to her like waves to fish. She loved swimming in oceans of time the same way Watusi loved yawning.

Being in this big house alone wasnt at all like being in her toy

Berkeley cottage. A motel or hotel room wouldve been easier to relax in and ignore.

Larry'd loved motels. If there was extra money, theyd check into one just for the hell of it—even the Flamingo once, just blocks from where they lived—because impersonal, temporary settings turned poor Larry on. At bottom, she liked it too. You hang your clothes over chairbacks and door corners, click on the free TV, color if youre lucky, shower for an hour, break the paper band on a sterilized glass, fix up a drink and leap with a scrunch onto an antiseptic bed to lounge around forever, thinking gibberish, scanning newsprint or cutting into the middle of some quaint pulp war novel left behind in a bedside drawer atop the regulation Bible—or even read, for the pure joy of it, Ecclesiastes or The Song of Songs, her favorite Old Testament story poems. From time to time you glance up at some fawning, hairsprayed newscaster or talk-show host.

Motel-flavored emptiness was so much easier for her to withstand than this sad old room that was coming at her now, a room that too many years ago had been her only real world.

As moments grew into hours and hours grew into days, her thoughts began to put on weight. It irritated her that she was spending as much time thinking about Larry and Watusi as she did her father.

Holding on for dear life at times, she'd practically spent two years mothering and clinging to Larry, and only a handful of unscheduled days with Watusi.

Larry was a mess, a real brooder, the last one to get a joke and certainly not the kind of guy to laugh at himself for even a moment. She enjoyed Watusi's sense of humor and, though she was loathe to admit it, his sneaky way of being paternal.

What was it about Larry, besides his sexiness which was irresistible, that had captivated her for so long? Was it his gentleness, his intensity and devotion to whatever he believed in at the moment? He'd often said he believed in her. Or was it simply that he made her feel needed?

Watusi, for sure, was some other kind of nut; not at all like herself. Even in his silliness he was strong and assertive in a way that she could never be. She liked to think of him napping off an afternoon tequila high with earphones slipped down to his shoulders, a new Miles Davis LP having who knows what effect on his dreams, one hand at his crotch (a habit she detested), his giant mouth with its precious gold fillings wide open for the public to examine. Nevertheless he'd made her feel a little new again like an earlier Angelina who could keep life's hassles at a distance while she involved herself with pleasurable specifics: where to start looking for a new job or a new room, which friendships to continue, which boyfriends to drop, which party to go to and what to wear, what good grass or cheap coke to buy, and—going back even further—which male teacher to manipulate for an A.

"Your dad's much better," the blonde nurse with the pretty voice told her as they walked toward his room for the thirtieth time. "Dont quote me on this but I'm pretty sure we'll be releasing him in just a few days."

"O, Mrs. Washington, that's wonderful news!"

"There you go again with that Mrs. Washington stuff. How many times do I have to remind you Nancy is my name?"

Angelina had tried to remember to call the nurse by her first name but the last name had made almost as sharp an impression as that voice she loved so. She'd never met a white person named Washington before and would've been willing to bet anything that the nurse's husband was a spook.

"When you say a few days," she asked, "how many days do you mean?"

"We'd release him today if his breathing was what the doctors thought it should be. There're some complications and they want to keep him around for observation another week."

It was now almost two o'clock. She'd spent most of the morning reading around in *Human Personality and Its Survival of Bodily Death*, a fascinating book on reincarnation that Renée had laid on her. It amused her that she'd avoided mystical literature, spooky stuff, as Margo called it, the whole time she'd been in California, and now, stranded in hardbop do-or-die Detroit, she found herself gobbling up yoga, Zen and occult books as if by doctor's prescription. Over the course of several weeks, she'd read many of the classics, including most of the Edgar Cayce books, Alan Watts, Kahlil Gibran, and the powerful *Autobiography of a Yogi* by Paramahansa Yogananda. Another part of the day she'd devoted to housecleaning in preparation for Jujie and Roscoe's return.

Dad, for the first time in his life, was growing a mustache. She'd always wanted him to but it'd taken sickbed confinement to soften him up.

"How do you think it looks?" he asked her, smoothing his hairy upper lip with a finger.

"You know Ive been after you to grow one for years now. What made you decide to finally do it?"

Dad looked distinguished with his gray sideburns and salt and pepper kinks fluffed out. He was getting fat and she could see that the smile and frown marks indented in his oily brown face were going to be permanent.

"I always wanted to grow a mustache," he confessed, "but I didnt wanna do it while it was just the style. I never did go in for styles. Ive seen a whole lot more of em than you have. People seem to thrive on what the style is and my kick is to kinda, you know, stay outta style, just a little bit. I always liked sideburns, for instance, but I sure wasnt about to grow em back in the days when everybody, including the President, was letting theirs grow. Same thing with mustaches. I use to sport one back when I was a youngster coming along—had me a little toothbrush-style mustache going, but then Hitler came in with his little squared-off mustache and I up and cut mine off. I strictly believe in that individuality and that's what I tried to raise you on. Your mother was the same way."

"Do you still think of her?" she asked for the first time in years.

Her father's eyes looked away from hers to take in a few

moments of ghostly nonsense radiating from the TV screen. "The Newlyweds" was on. Some silly black couple, probably from Newark or New Haven, was busy putting lots of razzmatazz into the kind of showbiz bickering expected—and no doubt demanded—of contestants. Angelina wondered how they picked the husbands and wives this program featured.

Dad blinked, his smile quivering. "Do I still ever think about Lizbeth? Is that what you asked me?"

As if by cue, everything in the room grew silent, including the TV while the young, necktied colored guy on screen pondered a question worth fifteen points about his wife's sleeping habits. One part of Angelina detested him and all the petty-bourgeois nonsense he and his wife stood for. Another part of her was pulling for him to score higher than his competitors, the white guys. The most important part of herself was attuned to her father, awaiting whatever he'd have to say about her mother, his wife, the missing link.

"I think about her all the time. There isnt a day that goes by that I dont remember how we met, all the stuff we went through together. After she came down with cancer of the stomach around the time you were ten years old, from then on out life was nothing but hell for both of us. I'd never gone in much for religion up to then. My father, your granddad, Big Daddy, use to preach a little bit back downhome, so I grew up with Jesus, if you know what I mean. I knew all about the cat, a whole lot more than these little wet-behind-the-ears youngsters that never spent a day in church or read a line of gospel in their lives. I'm hardly what you'd call a religious fanatic, Angie, but after what I went through with your mother I did start to believe in a higher power, some kinda God or spirit or whatever you wanna call it that's bigger and more beautiful than anything we know in this world."

"But you hardly ever went to church," said Angie, "and you never really pushed me to go. Aunt Jujie had to practically drag you off to service the few times I remember you going."

"Well, see, there you go. It's like I was just saying. I never could get with what the going style's supposed to be. Going to church is a style the same as just eating vegetables or not wearing a hat. Later for that! I'm for the real thing which is being for real, if you get me, like, religion is for real—you can feel it and it works for you from the minute you wake up till the minute you lie down at night and all through your dreams if youre living right—but people get religion mixed up with churches and causes and that's where I get my hat. That secret little thing that gives you the power to go on living when everything else says 'Forget it and die!'—that's what I'm talking about. Take communism. Well, to me that's a kinda religion. It's something people can believe in that's bigger than they are. I'd have to say it's the same with making a lotta money, capitalism. Or take something like blackness. There're a whole lotta people who go at this business of being black like it's a religion. All people need religion. It's just a matter of what they choose to believe in. Of course you probably know more about all this than I do since youve been to college and all that. That one year I spent taking night courses taught me a lot and I'd give anything for a degree. I'm still gonna get back and finish up one of these days, God willing. But that's something else again. Youve been trained in this stuff, Angie, to study things. You got a masters degree in it. That was both Lizbeth's and my plan—to see you through college so somebody in the family'd be educated."

"I know that, Daddy, I know the faith youve put in me and Ive really tried to—"

She watched him reach out and stop her words by touching his fingers to her lips, but the feel of it is what she remembered; her own father's unfamiliar hand at her mouth.

"You dont have to explain anything to me," he said. "My old man made plans for me too, lots of em, but we have to lead our own lives the way *we* see it. I know your life's more complicated than anything I couldve ever foreseen. The world's a whole lot different from what it was back when me and Lizbeth'd sit around drinking coffee and carrying on after you'd been put to bed. While we were busy working out the future, the present sneaked up on us."

Angelina sighed. "Whatre you gonna do now, Dad?"

"Sit here and talk with you till you leave and then have my medicine and take a nap."

"No, that's not what I meant. Whatre you gonna do after youre released from this hospital?"

"You think theyll ever let me go?"

"Your condition's improved. You cant stay here forever. Itll probably be a while before you can go back to work. Where'll you stay? Who'll look after you?"

"I'll stay in my own home. Where else would I stay? All the years I been working to get that place paid off! I dont wanna be a burden to anyone. I'll stay in my own place and I'll look after myself."

A thousand thoughts, every one of them as lucid as starlight, came out in the sky of her mind, but all she could say was: "I know what youre thinking."

"O yeah?" yawned her father, scratching his head. "What'm I thinking?"

"Youre thinking that . . . that maybe I should—"

Frowning and smiling at the same time, he shook his head from side to side and touched the soft fist she didn't know she'd made. Like the speeded up flowering of a rosebud on film, her tensed fingers uncurled themselves.

"Angie," he said in his lowest voice. "Sweetheart, quit fretting and worrying. There's really nothing to get upset about. One thing at a time, one thing at a time. That's how I'm planning to live my life now—one day at a time, from hour to hour. That's all anybody can ask for—that one minute that leads into the next minute. I meant it when I said I believe in a higher power now. I'll be taken care of, dont worry about that. I know my being down's done caused you a lotta grief. I'm so happy you could even find the time to drop what you were doing and come out here to see me. I thank God for that. I'm not asking any more than that. Youve been beautiful. So many people have been good to me. Jujie and Roscoe, the people I work with, old friends from way back and even some of the folks from the neighborhood. I'll get looked after and done for if it's necessary."

"I know my place is here with you, Dad."

"What book you read that in or is that a line from some movie?"

"You pick some funny things to joke about. I'm serious. I mean, you know where I stand back in Berkeley by now. Why shouldnt I forget about everything else and stay on here with you?"

"I can think of one very important reason. Youve got your whole life to live and Ive pretty much lived mine out."

"Dad, please dont talk like that. I love you. I'm your daughter, your only child."

"Maybe so but the world isnt anything to play with and youve got a lotta things to work out before the dark days come."

The dark days? That's all she needed. These *were* the dark days as far as she was concerned. What could he mean? She asked him.

"Days when it looks as if life's got no meaning, no reason to it at all. You smoke a cigarette and hope there's a meaning. You sip on a drink. You sniff a little cocaine like I used to do snuff—that's what the children're doing nowadays, isnt it?—and you hope itll make life mean a little more. You make love to somebody and wonder if that's it. You make a little extra money and pat yourself on the back and wonder if that's it. You even kinda worship your children and try to be close to em and wonder if that's what it's all about. What you end up doing is getting down on your knees praying that life's still got some kinda meaning."

"Ann Arbor."

"Hunh?"

"You dropped that on me back in Ann Arbor one night."

"I did?"

"Ive never forgotten."

"Well, I'm surprised because back in those days when you were up there at college, I was living on the edge. I was leading a sort of life that I'm not too proud of now, lotta funny things going on."

"Really, Daddy? I'dve never known."

"Wouldntve known myself except it all caught up with me."

"I love you."

"I think you oughtta forget about Larry, forget about that job youre tryna get, forget about all the stuff you lost when your place got robbed, forget about now and forget about me. Go back home. This isnt your home anymore. Forget about everything but basics and I'll leave it up to you to figure out what *basics* means."

A bright warm wind blew through her. It stirred the dusty corner of herself that was nothing but guilt and shadow.

A WHOLE
NEW WAVE

Touching bottom, her ears popped and she let herself go, turning a slow somersault for the joy of it. The cool pull of the water resisting her motions was delicious.

Jacques-Yves Cousteau, deep-sea divers—she understood a little why the ocean mustve attracted them so. There was no solitude like underwater solitude and she didnt need a mission to get into it. Given the chance to begin again, she'd go into marine biology without so much as batting an eye. If she ever got back to California, she was going to look into one of those scuba-diving courses advertised during intermission at the drive-ins she and Larry used to go to.

Surfacing, she swam to where Renée sat at poolside, splashing the water with her tanned December legs.

"How was it down there?"

The words floated on the air and soaked through Angelina's swimcap. "It was great," she spluttered, water up her nose, not really able yet to hear herself.

"You shouldve been coming here with me all along," said Renée. "It's the only escape from Detroit."

I need to get away from more than just Detroit, she thought, pulling herself up out of the water and squishing down next to Renée. "Like, thanks."

"Like, youre welcome. Like, what took you so long to accept my invitation?"

Sun was shining on the snowy ice and brightening the shopping center's holiday stage set as they swerved and chugged through afternoon traffic to queue up at the expressway entrance. They sang along with the tune coming out of the car radio—*Dom / Dom / Dommmmmmmm . . . TA DAHHHHHH . . . TA DOMMMMMMM!*—Strauss's "Also Sprach Zarathustra," theme from the movie *2001: A Space Odyssey.*

"Alex and I used to make love to this," Renée said airily and a little too smugly.

So what? Over the weeks, Angelina had grown used to Renée coming right out with just about anything. Margo was a little like that too. It was one of those things about people who'd been through analysis that set her nerves on edge. Everyone she knew who'd had their head shrunk would tell you just about anything about themselves, no matter how private or inconsequential, and whether you wanted to hear it or not.

"That's nice," she told Renée, "but so what?"

Renée rolled down her foggy side window to check oncoming traffic before racing out onto the mad expressway. Once they were safely established in the slow lane, signaling left for a faster go of it, Renée cocked her head Angelina's way and asked, "What was that?"

"I said so what."

"So what about what?"

"So what if you and Alex used to make love to this music?"

"I dont understand."

"There's nothing to understand. I could be telling you things me and my man used to do to music, but I dont."

Renée, darkening, turned down the radio and shot Angelina a quick, hard glance. "So what's that supposed to mean?"

159

"Means I'm not in any mood to hear about your private love life."

"Are you mad with me or something? Have I said anything to offend you?"

"No, not especially." Angelina sat fidgeting with her hands, noticing how ashy her skin color had turned from swimming at Renée's membership health gym.

"Ive never known you to be this way before, Angie." A complicated minute dragged by, during which Renée shrewdly manipulated the Pinto to avoid being creamed by a gigantic black Cadillac crammed with slick-looking, nattily dressed white men straight out of *Paris Match.*

"Ive never known myself to be this way before."

"Did you enjoy yourself at the gym?"

"Loved every minute of it, couldn't you tell? I could swim and exercise forever and never worry about a damn thing. I'm really glad you kept after me to go."

Renée flashed a smile that Angelina knew was forced. "I'll call you in a couple of days to find out if youre feeling better. I worry about you, Angie."

"I worry about you too. I'm OK. When you come out to California, I'll take you down to Big Sur. Theyve got mineral baths there, hot springs, youll love them. We can have dinner at this place called Nepenthe. It's a treat and a half."

It was too late to change tunes and Angelina knew it. She also knew why she'd said what she had and was glad when Renée deposited her at the Clairmount exit off the John Lodge Expressway.

"Sure you wanna hassle those buses the rest of the way? I can drive you home in five or ten minutes."

"Ive got a little shopping to do around here and the sun's so pretty I thought I'd get out and enjoy a little of it."

"As you like," Renée said.

As I like, Angelina thought as she climbed out with her shopping bag, glancing back at Renée who sat all but gawking at the scene around her while the engine hummed.

"Renée, is there something the matter?"

"No, no . . . I was checking the intersection out. It's hard to believe I grew up around here."

"You did?"

"Sure did. Started school right across the street there at Crossman Elementary, and this is the corner where the store used to be where I scored all that penny candy thatll keep me in the dentist's chair for the rest of my life."

"History," sighed Angelina.

"History, hell!" Renée shrugged. "Duke Ellington wrote a song about it before we were born."

" 'Things Aint What They Used To Be'?"

"Things aint what they used to be. Angie, let's do this again when you feel in the mood. Youre still one of my favorite people, you know. Think about it."

"I'll call you." Angelina watched the words turn to steam in the frosty air as she shivered and gestured good-bye.

Renée, as she sped off, had no way of knowing that this was the beginning of a whole new wave.

DREAMING ON CREDIT

Dear Curtis,

I don't really know why I'm writing you again now. Maybe it's because I don't feel at home here and you're back in the only place where I do feel at ease anymore. Forgive me if I sound stupid at times. The truth is that I feel stupid pretty much all the time lately. Something's happening to me that's completely new and I'm trying to roll with the changes. I hope you'll understand.

Your riddle still messes with me. There are nights when I flash on it just before falling asleep and think I've got it solved. I love that time, that twilit instant between wakefulness and sleep when everything's so much clearer than it is when you're wide awake. A lot of my life's been worked out while in that state. I'll float with a thought, get warmly down into it, comfortable, you know, and then laugh out loud or groan or something, as I've done while pondering your riddle, and suddenly wake up with my mind a total blank, unable, for the life of me, to figure out what in the world could've been so funny.

When I was a little girl, I once took sick with fever and kept picturing myself on top of a giant wheel. The wheel would go round as I ran along its edge. I'd be trying to arrive at a certain point along that edge, a point which I alone knew about but, try as I did, I never could make it. I'd get hypnotized in real life, outside the vision, afraid that my mother or father might rush in and say something to melt the sweet web I'd woven around my consciousness. At least that's the way I remember it now.

What does all this mean? Not a hell of a lot, I suppose. I just want you to know that your riddle often crosses my mind at a time of day that's precious to me.

May I venture a guess? Do all the things you mention—a nye of pheasants, a lepe of leopards, etc.—share in common the fact that they're categorized and lumped into man-made groupings and unto themselves are something else? Is language itself the barrier you're pointing out? Or, again, am I still sounding hopelessly dumb?

I'm back from Mexico. My dad got caught up in a violent burglary. He's been hospitalized but is better now. I've been here trying to stick out his recovery. Now that he's home again, I feel relieved but I still worry about him. I feel guilty of course. I feel as if I'm all he's got and he deserves so much more. I love him and yet at the same time I can't wait to get back to Berkeley to pick up my raggedy life where I left it hanging, flapping like some tattered garment hung out on a clothesline. I feel I'm at some kind of crossroads. I can go either this way or that. I can keep on being passive and taking whatever shit the world's dealing out and continue to get messed around at every turn, or I can do a turn-around and do a little dishing out myself.

All I'm getting at is this: I'm tired of myself the way I've been. I plan to start exercising a bit of my own free will. I'm going to start telling people off when I don't approve of the jive they lay on me. I'm going to try doing away with a lot of my own bad habits—and I've got some stupid habits that need to be changed!

I've been getting into mysticism lately, the Eastern variety, and so much of what the yogis and Buddhists are putting out is stuff I can really relate to. I plan to get into meditation, change my way of eating and sleeping, try to live one hour at a time and see if that helps me feel better.

You know that old blues lyric that goes: "Cried last night/and I cried the night before/Cried last night/and I cried the night before/I'm gonna change my way of living/so I won't have to cry no more"? Well, that's my attitude now and I expect to be running into a whole lot of friction from here on out. In fact, I've already been upsetting a few of my relatives and friends around here. I'm calling everybody on their bullshit regardless of who they are! It'll probably cost me some so-called friendships but I no longer care about that. It occurs to me that I've been stumbling around down here in the world going on three decades now and with damn little to show for it. I want to be me, whatever that ultimately turns out to be or mean. That's what I most admire about you. You're simply you. You're Curtis for-real and right up front with it.

Spent Thanksgiving with my Uncle Roscoe and Aunt Jujie. They think I'm weird and I think they're weirder. Aunt Jujie's religious but not so much as she used to be. Uncle Roscoe's more far out than anybody you'd ever care to run into on Telegraph Avenue at two in the morning. He doesn't dye his hair green or wear funky clothes or an earring or a bone through his nose, but he and Jujie, despite the fact that they both work hard steady jobs and dream new Cadillacs, are about as peculiar as they come. I've been coming right out and criticizing them lately—not their life-style or anything like that but simply not letting them run over me or intimidate me like they've done so easily in the past. I've learned quite a lot. The same goes for my father. He's a wonderful man but I'm getting on his case too. It's fascinating really. I can't help wondering why I was quiet and super polite for so long.

Being by myself, instead of in the company of familiar people who've adjusted to my idiosyncrasies and personal problems, has meant so much. Everyone nowadays is busy digging for roots. Well, I know my roots. I know them well and it doesn't make a damn bit of difference when it comes to making sense of who I am and why I make the kinds of mistakes I do. In the end, I've discovered, it all comes down to being in competition with yourself. You can't even begin to get into that kind of thinking until you've been off alone for a while with lots of time to mull things over.

Time's the biggest problem (or asset) I've got. What used to take months to make itself clear now only takes weeks. I feel older than old, and if the world ended tonight I'd feel that I died a merciful death.

Christmas, for example, hangs sadly in the air even though we just did Thanksgiving. Aunt Jujie, just back from a surprise trip down south, prepared one of those ridiculous holiday dinners that would make a health-food nut (and that's what I've been becoming for some time now) flinch. The way these traditional Afro-Americans eat! She thinks nothing of serving at the same meal turkey, dressing, rice, mashed potatoes, creamed corn (fried of course), rolls, macaroni and cheese, gravy, cornbread, bread pudding, sweet potato pie, cake, and, naturally, some greens, beans and peas on the side to lend a little color to the starchy main dishes. Try breaking out a little crunchy granola in a setting like that and listen to them holler at you about birdseed and selling out to white folks. I'm not so sure that all those chitlins, hamhocks, hog maws, pigsfeet, spareribs and cooking with lard—soulfood so-called—isn't contributing more toward bringing about black genocide, as the phrasemongers would have it, than Sickle Cell Anemia.

Back when I was in high school they started putting up Christmas decorations right after Thanksgiving but now they get into it around Halloween. Next year it wouldn't surprise me if the stores started hanging out their Yuletide trimmings right after Labor Day. I get very depressed, as I guess everyone does, around this time of year. I'll survive it, I know, and, if all goes well with Dad, head back west where I know myself better.

Have a good holiday and take care of yourself.

Affectionately,
Angelina

PS: I've outlined all these resolutions with New Years just around the corner. Maybe I'm only dreaming on credit, but it's been nice being able to collect my California unemployment benefits right here in Detroit.

SOFT CITY
GALLOP

She clung to his arm, to the thick woolen sleeve, and from time to time she'd lean her head against his shoulder as they crunched through the new snow. She hadnt been this close to a man in public since Mexico, Watusi, those heartbreaking strolls through Chapala and Jocotepec. And more than ever she missed California where she'd first learned to air out her mind by going for long walks everywhere.

"I'm really gonna miss all this," he said.

"Now, Dad, surely youre capable of walking by yourself down here to the store and back. I think youre doing fine, just fine."

"That's not what I mean. Sure, I can go walking on my own now, but it wont be the same after youre gone. I'm just gonna miss doing it with you."

The late morning air was fun to breathe even though it stung her nostrils. The sunlight seemed so clean-smelling and was shining down on the dirt of the world with such sympathetic clarity that she didnt really mind being bundled up against the cold like an old-time explorer on a polar expedition.

They were getting to the point where words werent always

necessary. Glances, especially smiling ones, and gestures were often enough.

A very lanky young man, bareheaded, in red ski parka and dark glasses, his hair done up in elaborate cornrow braids, slipped and slid past them as he struggled to keep up with the Great Dane on a leash who'd just broken into a soft city gallop.

Angelina and her father glanced at one another and snickered.

"I know that boy," he said.

"Well, why didnt he speak to you?"

"He hardly ever speaks to anybody anymore. Used to be the paperboy on the block, a real nice kid, then he went and started stealing cars, got on dope, did some time in juvenile and now dont seem to have too much to say. Him and that dog is a mess! He used to hang out with those two jokers I suspect are the ones that stuck me up."

"Have you seen them around the neighborhood since youve been back home?"

"Nope. I been looking for em but I reckon they had sense enough to get on off the scene."

"What would you do if you saw them?"

"I dont know."

"Dont you know their families?"

"They live a few blocks from here but I really dont know all the people in the neighborhood."

"Would you turn them in if you recognized them on the street?"

"When I first went in the hospital I used to think a lot about doing them real harm, like, shooting one of them in the chest like they did me. I prayed to God the whole time I was laid up to take that evil thought outta my head. He did. I dont want revenge. All I want now is peace of mind. I got to looking back at all the wrong low-down things I pulled on people and figured that anything bad that happens to me I got it coming. Those boys'll get theirs somewhere down the line."

She couldn't imagine her father ever doing anyone wrong,

168

yet all the rest of the way to the store she searched her own heart for evidence of wrong past actions and found plenty.

All they bought was milk, bread, cigarettes, coffee and *Essence*. The proprietor, a black white-haired man not long up from Alabama kept telling her father how good it was to have him back on his feet again and what a fine devoted daughter he had.

Angelina wanted to tell the man what a pig he was for charging so much for his merchandise. For weeks now she'd been keeping her mouth shut out of respect for Dad who seemed to like the man.

The fat uniformed security guard put on his tight-lipped smile, leering at her as he always did, but kept that one hand at his pistol as his eyes followed them around the store.

"For crying out loud," she told the owner quietly as he was making change, "everyday we come in here your prices have gone up a few cents. Now youre asking a dime more for a loaf of bread than they ask at the A&P. This isnt a rich neighborhood, you know. Is it costing you that much to pay that doggone guard's salary?"

Mr. Grocer grinned. "Yeah, it's rough, aint it? I know how you feel, Miss Angelina. But it's the overhead. The big stores, the big *white* stores, they can charge less cause they deal in a bigger quantity than us little black businessmens. They set up for the real big turnover. Times is hard, I know, and I'm just tryna squeak by myself. I do good to break even some weeks. But believe me, I know how you feel and I'm with you. I keep tellin the wholesalers they prices is too high and the poor people in the community gon have a hard time meetin em, but you know how it is. You cant fight City Hall all the time. I do the best I can. Now, have you checked out some of the specials we runnin this week? We got a first rate buy on toothpicks, can milk, paper napkins and ketchup."

"All I know is we'd starve to death if we had to do all our grocery shopping here." Peeking back over her shoulder, she threw the rent-a-cop her surliest glance and raised her voice for the hell of it. "There're some expenses you could probably do away with that would help in lowering your prices."

"You might be right, Miss Angelina, and then again you might be wrong. Look at it this way. I'm operatin at a disadvantage to start with. My biggest overhead is rent, utilities, bookkeepin and labor. If I fire Leroy there, then the crime factor gon go up and the people gon start stealin me blind."

"By the people, you mean the community, right?"

"All right, OK, call it what you want to but I got to have Leroy walkin round here checkin everybody out. He kinda act as a deterrent to thievin, you know. Whatcha gon do? It's really the guvmint you fightin, you wanna get down to natural facts. The durn democrats gon always get you in a war and the durn republicans gon always get you in a depression some kinda way. Well, the way I look at it you cant win no how. I stays at war with the people in the grocery business and that's what keep me depressed. How you gon win? You tell *me*."

Later! she thought. It was like a quiet race. They made their tiny purchases quickly and unspectacularly, striving to attract as little attention as possible. One false move, she thought, and that Afro-American cretin with the pistol on his hip would probably shoot them down in cold blood.

What stuck in her mind all the way home—besides the feeling of being on the verge of a showdown wherever she went in a city like Detroit—was the rudely handwritten sign on gray cardboard taped to the back of the store's cash register:

THIEF WILL BE PERSECUTED

"That place makes me nervous," she told her father when they were back on the sidewalk again, thankful to be in the wind.

He'd been quiet during the change she'd put him through back in the store. She wondered what he'd actually been thinking.

"Yeah, it's like that everyplace you go now," he said. "If I had it to do all over again, and knowing what I know now, I'da never left the south in the first place. While I was getting well, I read around in a few black-history books, you know, and now that I been contemplating it pretty deep I'm coming to the conclusion that this up-north urban migration pattern's about the worst thing to ever happen to Negroes—excuse me—I mean, black people, African-Americans or whatever they wanna call themselves, since Middle Passage back in slave times. I dont know if we'll ever survive it."

They didn't have to say much again after that.

It wasnt the talk that moved her.

It was the walk.

GETTING OVER

With Dad asleep, dishes done, the whole downstairs picked up finally according to her own arbitrary sense of neatness, she could slip down into his basement workroom and get in a little meditation.

There, seated upright in a straight-backed wooden chair with a pillow to cushion her bottom, she strained in the dim light to achieve that state of tranquillity through a technique she was studying from a book.

Ignoring the plane saws and drill saws and sawdust and coils of shaved wood and the smell of varnish, she sat breathing rhythmically and lightly, concentrating on her third eye until the roar of the furnace started up.

Over the nights she'd come to realize how distracting everyday life really was. She was always sending energy out as she looked at things, listened, touched, tasted and smelled. She even viewed the process of thinking as a negative drain. With meditation, however, the emphasis was on turning energy inward, revitalizing rather than devitalizing her energy reserve.

Renée told her that she'd once joined a meditation group at Wayne State but had given it up because, try as she did, she could never manage the hour a day required to make headway. Angelina had no such excuse. With no permanent household to maintain, no children, nothing pressing, no situation she couldnt walk away from, what else was there to do but give it a try?

Minutes flashed by like unwatched TV programs. Eyes half-closed, attention centered between her brows, she fought off drowsiness and the temptation to dream. It was disenchanting to learn that meditation, far from being a passive activity, was at least as demanding as learning to concentrate.

She thought about all the textbooks she'd forced herself to read in high school and at college.

She thought about all the basic routines she'd struggled to master on all the dumb jobs she'd ever held.

She thought about Berkeley where the rent on her cottage was way past due. Would Montego put her out? Would he understand and give her an extension if she phoned and explained? Was Margo still picking up the mail regularly? Would burglars stage a comeback and carry off the rest of her pitiful belongings? Did she still stand a chance of getting the teaching position at the alternative school?

What was going to happen to Dad? Yesterday his boss called about the possibility of his returning to work on a provisional basis, working a couple of hours each day just to break himself back in again slowly. Dad was crazy for the idea but she had her doubts. Was she wrong in encouraging him to wait until after Christmas? The two holiday seasons she'd worked sorting mail twelve hours a day at Oakland's Bayshore Annex had, of course, influenced her opinion. That was all she really knew firsthand of post-office blues but she'd been left with some severe impressions.

She focused in on Dad's recent loss of weight, his low-keyed disposition and perpetual new smile.

Larry.

Watusi.

Curtis's leopards, lions, pheasants and Indians.

Ernest, Louetta's husband's hostility toward her when she

discussed old times with Louetta or any other subject he knew little or nothing about.

Mexican afternoons.

Faces of children on the school playground near Dad's house a few days ago when she strolled by and glimpsed them snowballing one another with a vengeance.

Uncle Roscoe, a little more than respectably drunk, limp on the couch after Thanksgiving dinner, eyes all lids, restless with a harmless erection which he half tried to hide by crossing and re-crossing his trousered legs sprinkled with ashes and table crumbs.

She fought to keep this invasion of images from fogging up her inner screen. Electrical blankness of mind was what she was after. The trick, as she interpreted her readings, was to concentrate persistently with an eye to shutting out all outside and inside interference until the blood cooled and consciousness shifted gears.

Attention tied to her breath, she imagined she was a soft string made of energy unknotting itself with each stream of air flowing outward, growing longer with air taken in. If air was space, then space was only a place. She knew exactly where she wanted to be and fought off, with a yawn, her impatience to arrive there.

In . . . out—

In . . . out—

This was what it was all about—

SAILING AWAY

For the first time in her life, she felt the windows of her loneliness opening wide to the world. There was nothing she wanted to leave unframed.

It had been weeks since she'd been around people she could freely act crazy with or get drunk or stoned with. There was always Renée but, when all was said and done, Renée was more of an intellectual than Angelina, always had been. Renée was the kind of person who, even when she was doing something really screwy or foolish never could relax and simply roll with it or enjoy it for what it was. There was always that self-conscious portion of herself that was painfully aware of what the rest of her was up to and which had to express it in some clever analytical statement or, worse yet, a syllogism—like her need to paint and to afterwards explain the paintings; why she did them and where she was at mentally and emotionally in each instance. Had analysis made her this way? Renée thought so, but Angelina'd never known a time when Renée had been any different.

Angelina had been into this kind of obsessive introspection around the time she graduated from college. Years of bumping around in the world had cured her and convinced her of its uselessness.

Of all the people from her fading past, it was Louetta who came closest to approximating the spirit of what she liked most about the Margos, the Larrys, the Curtises, the Watusis, the Scoot and Tanya Harpers and even the Tolby Crawfords, Sra. Ruizes and Madame Lolas from another now.

Dad, Aunt Jujie and Uncle Roscoe came very close to being approachable, but there was still too much of a blood and umbilical connection for her to experience them wholly and without reservations.

The truth was that, most of all, she loved open-hearted vulnerable strangers for whom she wasnt strictly obliged to feel anything.

The Christmas onslaught always brought out these supple little insights in her, tinged, as usual, when she got off down into herself, with just enough blueness to neutralize the big hurt.

Sitting in the movies with Louetta, a far cry from old times, Angelina's mind rolled on—

Dad's well enough to get around by himself now. I can do my Simone de Beauvoir thing and stick around like a dutiful daughter or else I can gracefully pack my bags, hug everybody and be back in Berkeley by New Years. It'd be nice to go back to Mexico right this minute and stick out the Yuletide hype down there where children actually sing in the streets and Christmas is still a simple Christian celebration the minute you get outta Mexico City. If I ever get rich I'll never spend another December in the States for as long as I live. Jujie's rushing around trying to make everybody happy, up to her neck in Mastercharge and Bankamericard—theyve got both and cant afford either! Uncle Roscoe's out juicing and comes in so spaced out you cant even talk to him most of the time. Dad is sad with his magazines and TV shows, listening to them squeal on "Let's Make a Deal." Wish I could introduce him to a sweet, rich lady who'd kiss his forehead every morning and take him for long country rides in her new Rolls Royce. No, he probably wouldnt like that. Better to set him back up on a simple farm in Milan with green corn coming along nicely, tomatoes expanding, rides into town for groceries and little brown bags of hot roasted peanuts sold from a carnival-looking truck at roadside, quiet squeeze of twilight dwindling the presence of old mid-century cars junked in rusty fields, neo-pickaninny and neo-redneck brats cluttering up the landscape with watermelon rinds, Coke and beer cans, cigarette butts and unsmokable roaches, twang of transistors, hundreds strong, beamed in to the latest *oooooo*. That's what Dad was really all about. I'd remake the whole world for him if it would make it easier for me to go back home again. America's out there in the trees and in the breeze and all I wanna do's to step off to one side, do my meditation, swim up for air for moments at a time and be able to dive back down and know I'm in this world too but really not *of* it. Why do I go on trying to find happiness in a man? Why should I keep on trying to make something of myself when I dont really even know myself? Why this need to get high, stay stoned, when I should be concentrating on getting straight for now and for future lives? If life's worth living at all it's worth living to the fullest, and peace of mind is all you can really count on. Is this what the gypsy was trying to tell me that sad afternoon in Menlo Park? Am I finally headed down that secret path she was talking about? Then why am I wasting my time at this silly movie with Louetta and striving so hard to enjoy it again?

The movie was *Putney Swope*, a film she'd caught years ago in San Francisco with Larry and enjoyed so much that theyd checked it out again when it hit the drive-ins. In the film, a Blood by the name of Putney Swope is quixotically elected board chairman of a faltering Madison Avenue advertising agency. He immediately changes the agency name to Truth and Soul, kicks out all but a token portion of the white board members, replaces them with blacks and proceeds to solicit accounts from advertisers who dont mind having their products hawked and spoofed by campaign executives whose notions of marketing appeal are farcically rooted in neo-black sensibility. It was really an outrageous light comedy from the impossibly romantic 1960s that Angelina'd giggled through twice and thought Louetta might dig.

They viewed it in a little so-called art theater on a downtown back street which Angelina used to bus to alone and secretly in high school days to live out a bit of her intellectual fantasy life that she couldnt have possibly shared with friends who hadnt read the same books she had or heard the same music or touched the same paintings. Louetta had been one of those excluded.

"I liked the Arab," Louetta said when they were finally settled at a table in the Esquire Delicatessen on Dexter where Ernest, Louetta's husband, was to join them briefly.

"What was it about him you liked?"

"I liked the way he came off," Louetta said politely, knifing more mustard onto her kosher cornbeef sandwich.

The Esquire, under another name, had formerly been run by Jews who light-years ago had sold out to the schvartzes, the Afros.

"The Arab seemed more for real to me than a lotta the other people in the flick. He talked that talk, you know what I mean? He actually reminded me of Ernest the way he kept gettin so excited about stuff and carryin on. I kinda liked the little skinny white boy too, you know, Sonny, the one that kept exposin himself every chance he got. It's people like that, I guess, but I dont know any. I got to admit I really didnt understand the part about the midget, the one they call the President, and his old lady—I'm afraid all that was over my head but I'm glad you got me out of the house to see this thing, Angie. How in the world did you ever hear about a movie like that in the first place?"

"In a place like Berkeley, you hear about everything, Lou. It was just something that was playing around and me and Larry drove over to San Francisco to check it out. We used to see a lotta movies together. I even acted in a movie once."

178

"Oh yeah?" Louetta's mouth was crammed with sandwich, so Angelina knew it was her turn to dribble the conversational ball. While she was figuring out what to say next about the storyless movie that Seishi, Margo's ex-husband, had shot, Ernest magically appeared and dragged a chair up beside them.

"Pretties, pretties, what it is, what it is!"

"Hi, baby."

"What's happening, Ernest?"

"It's a full moon hangin out there tonight and the natives—and I'm one of em—is restless all right."

"Well, I guess I must be one of em too," Angelina said quickly with a little laugh that clicked on something deep down inside her, "cause I feel like letting my hair down."

"You do?" said Ernest. "About how far?"

"About, maybe say, O, two inches and a half. Is that enough?"

Louetta sniggled and told Ernest, "You oughtta gone to this picture *Putney Swope* me and Angie just finished seein."

"Was it good?"

"Honey, I aint never seen nothin like that before as long as I been patronizin these movie theaters. They got some niggers in there—"

"Who in it?"

"Aint nobody in it I ever heard tell of before except that dude that sing so good, that Ronnie Dyson, you know the one we seen on that program 'Soul' that you so crazy about. Other than that," Louetta smacked on, still polishing off her sandwich, "it was just a mess, that's all! They got a nigger in there that put me in the mind of you."

Ernest looked hurt. "How you mean, Lou? I mean, it aint too many niggers—and I know just about every kinda nigger allowable by now—sad niggers, bad niggers, smart niggers, art niggers, homosexual niggers, intellectual niggers, jump-up niggers, pop-art niggers, psychedelic niggers, scientific niggers, black niggers, white niggers, pretty niggers, saditty niggers, doctor niggers, lawyer niggers, all-American niggers, Chinese

179

niggers, niggers on parade, niggers on parole, athletic niggers, pathetic niggers, niggers that—"

"Stop him," cried Louetta, reaching toward Angelina, "you dont know this man like I do! He fixin to go into a thing that could hang us up here for hours!"

"Now, aint you somethin," Ernest shot back coolly, iridescent in his broad-brimmed leather hat and leather coat buttoned up just enough to allow a triangle of shocking red shirt to shine through. Angelina liked his big 1910 mustache. "You and Angie can sit up round the house all day long and talk yall's stuff for twelve hours straight and soon as I get off into one of my own little perceptive listings of the species Afro-Americanus, then here you come woofin bout how I'm gon hang yall up for hours. That's just how come I'm ready to go out and agitate for men's liberation. We the ones need to be uplifted from the yoke of oppression."

"Ernest, we love you," said Angelina, "but I'm not too sure I understand what youre talking about."

Ernest flashed his fabulous grin, the grin Louetta'd said would win him the vice-presidency should he ever take a notion to run for it.

"Yall know exactly what I'm talkin bout," he said, "but you just dont wanna admit it. I'm talkin bout freedom. Freedom! Do you hear me? Now, you take Mao, Mr. Mao Tse-tung. He was a baaaadddd man and didnt take no shit off white folks but just look at what happen. One day Mr. Average Chinaman's wife got to lookin at all these cars and washin machines and hair dryers and things in a magazine somebody'd snuck in from the United States and next thing you know here come good old Chairman Mao—scared them honkie Russians, sposed to be his buddies, bout to whup up on him in the first place—suddenly he up there shakin hands and laughin and jokin with the leader of the paper tiger devils he been bad-rappin and puttin out adverse propaganda against for years. Now how you explain that? How you gon explain it? Yall so smart. How you explain that jive?"

"Ernest," asked Louetta, "have you been drinkin?"

"What's that got to do with it?"

"Just answer yes or no—have you been drinkin?"

Angelina was looking for an opening that would allow her to change the subject completely. The China she'd been living in of late in her head was Buddhist and Taoist. She wanted so much to be free of this fluttering distraction known as the world which she secretly loved too much for her own good. She was thinking of the elegant sixty-year-old lady who'd taught her ancient Chinese lit at the University of Michigan years ago, an Oxford-trained scholar, the first person to make her understand how it was possible to be simple and profound at the same time.

"What you think about all these so-called black movies they been puttin out lately?" Ernest asked.

"Wait a minute," Louetta said, "I asked you a question you aint answered yet. Have you or have you not been drinkin?"

"I was addressin Angie."

"Now I'm addressin you—yes or no?"

"Forget it, Lou, it's no big thing. Ernie's in a good mood. That's all that counts, really. I wouldn't mind having a few drinks myself if I weren't on—"

"If you werent what?" Ernest wanted to know.

"Aw, leave her alone and answer my question, Negro!"

"If I werent on the wagon."

"What you doin on the wagon and how long you been on it?"

"Ernest, that is none of your business and now I *know* you done had a few. I can tell just by the way you actin. You cant fool me. You been off with Herman someplace either drinkin that whiskey or else smokin pot—one!—I *know* you!"

"When I went into meditation, I decided to stop drinking and getting high off artificial stimulants for a while just to see—"

"Meditation?" The thin Afro-wigged Diana Ross-looking waitress was waiting to take Ernest's order but he ignored her. "I been hearin all kindsa talk about this meditation from all over the place. There was even a piece in *Ebony* a while back about a black family that went into it. Now, what is it exactly and what does it do for you?"

"Ernest, the young lady here wanna know if you wanna order anything."

"It's all right, sister, I can come back if he hasnt made up his mind yet."

"That wont be necessary," Louetta said while her husband and Angelina were yakking away. "Bring him a cornbeef, same as mine, and a strong cup of coffee, no cream, no sugar."

"Meditation's the art of getting back down into yourself," Angelina was saying. "It's a science really but, really, when you get right down to it there isnt much difference between science and art and religion if the ultimate goal is the pursuit of truth. Truth has got to be one thing and one thing only dont care how you go about getting at it."

"OK, all right. What I wanna know is what do you personally get outta goin through all this jive—deprivin yourself of a beer or a joint or a man, whatever, just to prove a point?"

"The point is I'm not just proving a point. It's all a matter of what you want." Angelina slowed down, measuring her words carefully. The whole idea of putting into words what didnt seem to need to be put into words made her cautious. "It's just something I'm into for right now," she said finally. "Next month maybe I'll be into something else."

"Well, excuse *me*, ladies, excuuuuse me! I'm just a poor American Negro out here tryna piece together a little information. I didn't mean to—"

"Aw, quit runnin your mouth, Ernest!"

"If it helps you to know," Angelina said firmly, "meditation's a way of relieving tension, physical and emotional. It makes me feel calmer than tranquilizers or anything else Ive tried."

"Well, all right, *all right* then," Ernest said. "You know anything about hypnotism, Angie?"

"No, not really. Why?"

"It's a dude at work—Reggie—say he know how to hypno-

182

tize people. He say he hypnotize himself all the time, say it helps him with his studies and stuff. I'd like to try it."

"What you want him to hypmatize you to do, Ernest?"

"Want him to hypnotize me into thinkin I'm white. I figure that with that type of mentality and arrogance I can get damn near anything I want, heh heh!"

Both women sat smiling, watching Ernest laugh.

"Didnt I tell you," Louetta said, nudging Angelina. "Aint he just like that doggone Arab in *Putney Swope*?"

"He shoulda hypnotized your mama," she mumbled way down under her breath.

"What was that?"

"I said the picture shoulda been in cinerama."

Louetta didnt understand but Angelina changed the subject by sneaking a peek at her watch and shrugging very dramatically. She had sense enough to know better than to get into a signifying scene with a sober friend's half-drunk husband.

She wanted the hands of her watch to spin her away from this irritating city softly into next year.

CHRISTMAS EVE:
THREE VIEWS

1/

As he came toward her, she thought for one raw moment that he looked a little like Uncle Mac from Milan days who wasnt really her uncle but who liked to have kids call him that. He'd drop by Saturdays, a pal of her dad's, ground down from a whole week of laboring and odd-jobbing it on neighboring farms, still in his workclothes but fresh out of the barbershop, smelling of aftershave and Lucky Tiger hair tonic, shoes shined, a pint of Teacher's Cream Scotch in one pocket, a handful of twenty-five-cent cigars in the other—as happy as he ever got.

She loved Uncle Mac when she was ten but this joker, despite the momentary resemblance, gave her the creeps. He was bonier, more haggard. Everything about him, she slowly noticed, seemed raggedy and menacing. His greasy slouch hat looked dated and ludicrous. His whole face looked bloodshot and he needed a lot more than just a shave.

He hovered over her in the aisle of the half-crowded bus, weaving and rocking on his feet. She was so afraid he was going to collapse on top of her that she grew petrified and tried to stare straight ahead right past him.

"Look here, sister—"

Granddaughter would've been more like it.

"Look here—"

Against her very best judgment, she looked. "Are you speaking to me?"

"Well, yeah, uh—" He was wearing a pair of those overalls with a hundred pockets. The boys back in Milan used to call them happyjacks. He reached into a random pocket and brought out a cellophane-wrapped wedge of cheese. "You wanna buy this?"

If she wanted a triangle of cheese, she was certainly capable of buying it at the supermarket herself. Who did he think she was anyway? "No, thank you."

"See what it say here," he muttered on, holding the cheese right up to her face. "It say one dollar and twenty-nine cent. This aint no Velveeta or some old flabby-ass bullshit cheese. This the real thing, sister. This some of that good expensive cheese. Tell you what. I'll let you have it for fifty cent. Fifty cent!"

"No, thank you."

Two junior flip teen-age diddybops across the aisle were taking in the scene and snickering, their transistor radio blaring.

The bum scratched his head and made the cheese disappear into one of the pockets, then he crashed down sideways in the seat in front of hers and glanced up toward the front of the bus where most of the dopey passengers were crowded.

Now she wished to God she'd taken a seat up there too, close to the driver and right by the door. A couple of pony-tailed white boys and a mannish-looking woman in a graying ducktail hairdo occupied seats in front of the teen-agers but none of them seemed to notice or care that she was being hassled.

Just as she was working up the nerve to simply rise and change seats, the old man went down into another pocket and drew out a carton of Eve cigarettes.

"How bout some smokes, sister? These them pretty cigarettes with the pictures all over em. I know you dig em. Gimme a dollar and they yours. A dollar, you hear me? Last I heard tell of, cigarettes was sellin for close to four dollars a carton."

"I dont smoke, thank you. Maybe one of the other passengers might be interested."

The creep was obviously annoyed by now. He shoved the carton away and, looking disgusted and hateful, cleared his throat. The grin he managed was thin and pitiful. "Sister, I really dont know how to say this. I aint had much schoolin or nothin like that—but you fixin to get on my nerves. Now, I'mo hit you with one more offer and then we gon have to really get down to takin care of natchal business!"

This time he reached inside the overalls, down under the bib, and extracted a shiny wrapped red moist steak.

Angelina could see at a glance that it was sirloin with a $7.95 price label.

"Now, you might not go for cheese and you might not go for tobacco," said the bum whose breath by now was ruining what little holiday spirit she had left, "but I know you like steak and here what I'mo do. I'mo drop this big thick juicy suhloin steak on you for what you might lay out for a decent quarter-pound cheeseburger. I'mo let you have this choice piece of meat for a dollar. You hear me, baby? One dollar. Now, I want you to think about this one before you go turnin me down. Here, feel it."

She didnt want to do any such thing but he plopped the warm meat right smack in her lap just as she'd begun to pretend to be weighing the matter, mulling over his offer. In reality she was thinking of screaming for help for all the good it'd do.

"Take this jive and shove it up your—" Something stopped her. She didnt need this kind of harassment. If she'd had Scoot's .32 she wouldve whipped it out and aimed for the biggest target, the chest. The meditative side of her said: No, no, Angelina, this is only the world and the world is only a stupid dream in the mind of God. The man's a fellow sufferer. He needs love now more than ever. You should take pity on him. He could be a lost brother or father or cousin or lover from some other life youve bungled through. Cool it, control it, but, for heavensake, dont blow it!

"I cant dig you," the man said, blinking his eyes goofily. "I know your type. You think you better'n me."

"I think you got a helluva lotta nerve!"

"I dont give a fuck what you think. Gimme a dollar, ho! Gimme fifty cent, a quarter, anything! I need some dope! I dont mean that. I aint one of them goddam junkies you read about in the paper. I'm a respectable ex-soldier colored man. I fought hard in the war before you was even born just like my nephews and them did over in Asia so you can ride around doin your little shoppin and shit." His voice softened. His eyes grew watery. "I just need me a drink, one of them po boy's of Ripple or somethin so I can be happy, fulla that Christmas cheer like . . . like all the resta these silly motherfuckers round here bouncin up and down. I aint gon hurt you, sister. I aint that cold-hearted!"

2/

It was supposed to be the beautiful time. All the bright and winking lights said so. All the charity sidewalk Santas with their hands held out said so. All the sad people pushing and shoving—about to spend a winter's worth of earnings on merchandise that grew tackier by the year—said so. Even the tired Yuletide music that yawned from shops and loudspeakers said so.

For Dad she bought a comfortable-looking turtleneck sweater in a rich shade of burgundy. For Aunt Jujie she bought a nice pair of house slippers; for Uncle Roscoe a quart of Wild Turkey; for Louetta a boxed gift edition of "Motown's Greatest Hits"; for Ernest some cologne and aftershave.

In the women's wear section of J. L. Hudson's, where she couldnt help browsing just to see what kinds of items werent available on the Coast, she couldnt stop thinking about what she might buy her mother if she were still here among the alleged living. She'd last bought her a cheap costume bracelet and Mom had loved it and kissed her for months afterwards.

The toy department was another one she couldnt walk past without thinking, as she always did at this time of year, of her unborn child, a miscarriage, who wouldve been going on two by now. Larry'd wanted a boy. She'd wanted a boy too. How great it mightve been to have a child to care for and do for and grow with and age with. Even if she'd ended up like Margo or Renée or all the other husbandless women she knew saddled with children to raise, it still mightve made all the difference in the world. Or was she only dreaming again?

It was supposed to be the beautiful time—national wish-fulfillment time. If Sunday was the day of rest, then Christmas was a time of peace and, for all the time she'd spent learning all about the world, she still couldnt abide by either of them. She and her mother had been in complete agreement. Neither of them liked holidays.

"You know what, Mama," she'd told her by the window, staring out at snowy Milan fields one Christmas Eve a thousand years ago. "I dont really like holidays."

"I'm with you," her mother had answered, a good year before she'd died. "Give me the regular days when anything that happens is money in your pocket because you dont be expecting anything in the first place."

Mama, where are you? she thought again as her spinal column tingled and her lower abdominal tract grew glad at the picture of her mother being safe in heaven dead.

If, as the preachers and psychics said, with God all things were possible, she'd wrap herself in an irresistible package—not unlike the ones she struggled with on her way home—and have it sent air mail special delivery into eternity.

Love is a funny-time disease. She wanted to hug everybody in the car—Dad, Aunt Jujie, Uncle Roscoe—as they cruised the neighborhood, checking out all the decorations. It was something they did every twenty-fourth of December. Jujie'd fixed a light supper and now here they were, maintaining tradition, and here was every house trying to outdo the one next door with elaborate displays of the Christmas spirit.

"O isnt that beautiful!" Jujie sighed, pointing out one conspicuously modest exhibit all done up in blue lights from picture-windowed tree to damn near life-size plastic replicas of Santa & Co. gracing the lawn. Sure enough, there was Rudolph leading the herd, his nose lit up in neon red—the only light that wasnt blue. "Wonder how they get his nose to light up like that, Roscoe?"

"Aint no big thing, sweetnin. They screw a red lightbulb into his nostrils and run a wire from it plugged in a socket. Detroit Edison sure must dig on Christmas cause people's electric bills must double. I know ours do."

Once at a party in San Francisco, Angelina'd met the young woman whose father and uncle created "Rudolph the Red-nosed Reindeer." She was a warm, lovely person and here it was Christmas on the sad, sad earth where the sight of simple Rudolph was making her father's sister happy. Well, that was something. She caught herself going mushy inside, sappy, surrounded by winter and smoke, like a maple tree that needed tapping. All her Christmases, laid out gaily end to end, still might one of these days amount to a good Halloween or Fourth of July or Memorial Day.

"Remember that time we drove out to Grosse Pointe to look at the rich white folks' decorations?" Roscoe said, very much into his role as driver.

"Yeah," said Dad, "it was obscene."

"Obscene?" said Jujie.

"Obscene," said Angelina, clinging to Dad's arm.

"What you know about it?" Roscoe asked. "You werent even there."

"O I just know. I been around rich white people, a lot of em. That's my one big prejudice. Ive been to school with em, Ive worked with em, Ive even been in their homes. Theyre really hung up on being rich and a lot of em never get over it. Theyre slaves to their wealth in the same way that poor people are slaves to their poverty."

"Talk it, talk it, talk it!" said Jujie.

"There's nothing really wrong with being wealthy," she went on, "so long as you arent attached to it. As a matter of fact, a rich man who isnt attached to his belongings and power is better off than a poor man who lives in a hovel and is very much hung up on what few possessions he owns."

"Aint it the truth," said Jujie.

"You sure can talk that talk when you want to, Angie," Roscoe said. "Maybe you oughtta been a preacher too."

Sad-eyed Dad gave his daughter a hug and said, "I didnt send my daughter off to college for nothing, but the stuff she's talking now I dont think she learned in any college."

"No, no," said Jujie, still gawking at the scenery, "Angie always did have a mind of her own. She one of us, a Georgian. I was talkin to a lady from Detroit the other day and she was tellin me her youngest girl was bout to marry some man from someplace way back up in Georgia. I told her, said, 'Girl, your child bout to really set herself free now, marryin a Georgian! Georgians and Mississippians the smartest people in the world.'"

"Thank you for lettin us Mississippi people in on the deal," said Roscoe.

"Well, the Seventeen done did it again," said Dad as they passed a large brick house.

"Yeah, them people is somethin," said Jujie. "They got seventeen kids—*seventeen*, Angie!—and they still manage to scrimp up and strain and put out a pretty good Christmas show. I love em. They so quiet and nice and aint none of they children even been arrested for nothin or been on dope or welfare. They good Christians. You oughtta talk to a few of em before you go back out to California. It's one of em, they oldest boy, Leonard, he teach school out here in Ecorse and he done read just about every kinda book that's ever been wrote. He the one schooled me on stuff like the origins of black militancy—Martin Delaney, Harriet Tubman and folks that go way back in our history—and Pan-Africanism and—"

"Dont care what you say," said Roscoe, "yall aint gon trick me back over there runnin round the jungle with a rag tied round my butt duckin all them lions and tigers and things!"

Angelina, who was laughing, fell up against her Dad whose laughter, like hers, was melting into Jujie's and Roscoe's.

"Oooo, lookit what the Baxters done come up with this year!" Jujie cried with one wave of her hand. "They the last white people in the block. Aint no tellin how they kids gon turn out if they dont move out soon. I dont understand em but they sure do turn out some pretty Christmas designs. They quality white folks too and right in tune with the community. I keep wonderin how come they aint moved out yet."

"They crazy," said Roscoe, headed for home. "They belong out there in Berkeley with Angelina but aint nobody told em yet. Angie, maybe you better talk to *them* too right after you get through seein the Seventeen."

All it was was Christmas Eve in the United States of America.

CHRISTMAS CHANGES

She wanted to know her mother, move inside her body again, see how her mind worked, feel the beating of her heart as it pumped warm blood into her fingertips and up to her brain that swam in images, impressions, sensations and language. What did it mean to her when she pronounced the word "work," the word "love," the word "God"?

Was Mama as passive as she was? Was it true that black women were long-suffering and strong? Memory was hard to trust anymore. She wanted to feel and experience events—and everything was an event, a change, an unfolding of process—directly and intensely.

Every time the preacher pronounced the name of Jesus, she wanted to see the man, stand in his presence, take that closer walk with him, sniff the air around him.

She'd risen and meditated in her room before she and Dad had driven to Jujie's and Roscoe's for breakfast. Something had clicked and kept clicking. You werent supposed to be able to learn the science of meditation from a book but her mind and senses that morning felt deep and camera clear.

There they were, the four of them, attending morning

services at Holiness Church which wasnt at all like Glide Memorial, San Francisco's nondenominational house of worship which wasnt at all like being in church. The congregation here seemed cool and undesperate. No one was out to prove anything. She hadnt been inside a regular church since high school.

Dad simply sat, straight-backed, hands in his lap; dignified in his dark business suit, blue shirt and fat black tie. Angelina had never seen him looking so peaceful and contained, but there was no telling where his mind really was. He was here more out of respect for Jujie than out of any need to be preached to. She couldnt wait to see him in the new sweater she'd bought.

Roscoe had a certain little smile he could work up for special occasions on a moment's notice. It was a vague, passive, noncommittal smile that seemed to say in a pronounced stage whisper: *Well, here I am, yall. I aint gon rock the boat dont care what happen but please dont get the idea that just cause I'm up here smilin mean I'mo go for everything that's comin at me.* Arms folded, Jujie at his side, he rocked his head in time to the sermon and music and strained to look appreciative even when he suppressed a yawn.

"It's the spirit of Christ, the Son of God, that we have to return to," the preacher was saying, warming up into song. "It's the spirit of Christ that gives us strength to endure the trials and tribulations of everyday life. It was the spirit of Christ that ran the money changers out of the temple. It was the spirit of Christ that made the blind to see, that made the deaf to hear, that made the cripple to chuck away their crutches for good and walk upright under the sun. It was the spirit of Christ that filled Martin Luther King, Jr.—God rest his soul—and gave him the strength and the courage to walk unafraid along the paths and byways of this sinful Babylon, this sinful society we are living in right now. It was the Christian spirit that moved him to utter those unforgettable words that still resound and will always resound in the hearts and souls of righteous-thinking men and women everywhere—'I have a dream!' "

"Amen!" shouted Jujie, setting off a volley of spirited *amens, hallelujahs, wells,* and *yes-SUHs* that popped the congregational air like strings of firecrackers.

For Angelina, who felt herself to be above such rhetoric-induced emotionalism, it was like wandering into a political or football rally or rock or jazz festival by mistake and catching herself being moved to tears, against her will, drawn in by the spirit of the crowd. She tried to look on detached at the spectacle and fought blending in with the congregation.

The passing of collection plates made her grin as she flashed on one of comedian Flip Wilson's routines about Reverend Leroy's Church of What's Happening Now and the novel she'd read by Ishmael Reed that satirized, among other things, a certain Church of the Holy Mouth.

But it wasnt like that. It had never been like that. Sure, there were a lot of bad memories, a few of them frightening, that gave her a headache when the word church was mentioned but it wasnt until today that she realized how much she'd enjoyed the sense of well-being and communality that those ritualized sessions had provided.

The youngish minister, dapper in his stylish new clothes, was probably a rascal who owned a Porsche and was building a second home with church funds. He probably even went with the cute lead singer or the chic choir director, but he knew what he was doing—filling a need and filling it well. This particular preacher, who looked a little like screen actor Billy Dee Williams, was respected around town for his outspoken stand on political issues involving the community.

She still had no trouble re-living the post-Sabbath whipping Mama had given her after one of the good church sisters saw her and Estelle Jordan palming a bit of spare change for themselves from the collection plate as it shot their way. Theyd been doing that for months. It was more of a prank than anything else. They were just getting to the money before the preacher did. But Mama, who didnt see it quite that way, called it "homemade sin" and whipped her for almost scandalizing the family name.

194

She sat up straight like Dad and Roscoe and leaned back, trying to be cool without comfort of shades but, by the time the choir got going and the preacher had hit his long-awaited stride, one part of her was examining half-heartedly the nature and meaning of religion while another part, a grander part, mystified, was shivering and grooving with the warmth she was feeling; the rawness of the moment; the indescribable sense of belonging—if only for an instant—to something that was vaster and deeper than herself, the four of them, the church, Christianity and religion itself.

"Right on!" she shouted instead of *amen*.

Dad and Roscoe shot her funny-looking glances.

Aunt Jujie just reached over and squeezed her hand hard.

HOURS

Alex Appel was even better looking in person than Renée's portrait of him. A big man, trim of build, in his mid thirties, his thick dark hair professionally coiffed, curled over his collar. He was simply but expensively dressed.

"Sweet little town that Berkeley," he was saying. "Spent a summer there once at U.C. as an undergrad. It was beautiful, beautiful. I really didnt get into studies that much but just being on the scene was great—hanging out around Telegraph Avenue with all the freaks and crazies who really werent all that weird back then come to think of it. I used to live in Robbie's, the Piccolo, really low-keyed fun places, and at night we'd drift from Telly down to that main drag in the flat part of town, forget the name . . ."

"San Pablo," said Angelina.

"Yeah, that's it. The Blind Lemon, the Steppenwolfe—any of those places hit home? Not too much happening—just a bunch of strange, lonely people hanging out, drinking beer and bad wine, nursing espresso, banging on guitars, maybe a little grass at parties here and there, a lot of casual romance going around. I used to pick a little five-string banjo, knew maybe around thirty tunes—double-thumbing, some Scruggs-style, all that stuff, which put me in tight with the folkies on the scene. Me and a couple other guys'd get together and knock ourselves out belting out tunes, nothing fancy, for all the beer and sandwiches some joint'd lay on us. Fun days, I tell you, it was kicks, man. Always wanted to go back but colleagues of mine who go to the Coast on business are always telling me what a bummer it is now."

"It's changed a lot," she said.

"How long've you lived out there? Seems to me that for years Renée was always threatening to split and join her friend Angelina out there in Berkeley. She was always talking about you, you know. In fact, she admired the hell out of your spirit of independence."

"Well, that's a laugh. I always figured Renée'd made the right choice. I dont know. Ive been through a lot lately. Once youve lived in the San Francisco Bay Area, it's kinda hard to adjust to anywhere else even though you realize that maybe youre just putting off the inevitable."

"The inevitable," he said. "Afraid I dont get you."

"It's kinda like that summer you spent there. I'd heard about San Francisco and how easygoing and cosmopolitan it was. I flew outta New York one morning, ended up in Berkeley, fell in love with it and stayed. That's all. I stayed. You left."

"But what do you mean when you say maybe youre just putting off the inevitable?"

"I mean, it's inevitable that you start thinking maybe Berkeley was just a stop after all. Youre supposed to learn from it what you can and move on, but there's a lot to learn. A friend of mine's mother who was visiting out there once called it a young people's town. I disagreed with her at the time because I thought she was being condescending but now I know that, being older, she could see things I wasnt able to see. Berkeley's a state of mind, an attitude, a pose, a style, a way of dealing with the real world by not dealing with it. There're days—late nights, I should say—when I actually see it as a ghetto, in the same way Orange County is a ghetto or Bloomfield Hills, with its own standards and dogma and code of ethics and prejudices."

"I'm from Bloomfield Hills and it's a state of mind all right," Samantha squealed. "I hear you, sister, rap on!"

Samantha was Alex's new companion whose high-pitched voice and what she had to say made Angelina want to dissolve into hot air. Straight off she'd pegged Sammi, as she preferred to be called, as one of those spoiled rich girls she'd known at college who was spending her life practicing up to be a sleaze, really working at it. She had all the attributes: bleached hair, too much makeup, studied bad manners and a foul mouth. She hadnt known until now that Sammi was from Bloomfield Hills but it didnt surprise her.

"I'm always telling people that a ghetto doesnt have to be black. You know that record 'The World Is a Ghetto'? Well, I grew up in that shit where everybody's ripping off the corporation or the government, fucking and sucking off everybody else and then getting indignant and almighty pompous when somebody gets caught doing it. Like, I'm as guilty as the next person when it comes to that bullshit but I dont go around pointing fingers. Live and let live. I'm down front with my shit. It's these hypocritical assholes in high-powered positions, like people in my own family, that I'm out to get. I believe in calling a spade a spade—no offense, sister, just a manner of speaking."

Theyd all been drinking and smoking strong grass that somebody'd said was straight from Cambodia, laced with opium. Angelina was probably the only unstoned guest at the party. She kept trotting back to the kitchen to fix herself a rum and Coke but all she really did was drop fresh ice into her glass and pour Coca-Cola over it. She'd made up her mind to get through the holidays without imbibing so much as a tumbler of beer. Because her will was geared to handle one day at a time, she'd already held out for ten straight days which was some kind of record achievement. Ah but that smoke clouding up the apartment air was so thick and omnipresent that, even though she passed up joints each time one was passed her way, she feared she might be getting a contact high.

She thought for a very long moment, lips tightening into the shallowest of grins. Then she looked Sammi right in those bloodshot blue eyes. "I too believe in calling an asshole an asshole," she said, catching Alex squirm out of the corners of her own tired eyes, "except where prick or cunt might be more appropriate."

The moment the words rolled off her tongue she regretted them. They tasted bad. It hurt to be speaking this way. It wouldve been better had she stayed back in Detroit and played chess with Dad and discussed in detail how he was going to get along under Jujie's and Roscoe's care once she was back on the Coast.

She understood why, as a seeker of something special, she'd have to keep her distance from the world for a while.

It had been Renée's idea to throw a New Year's Eve get-together in her boyfriend Steve's apartment and to invite her ex-husband Alex, Sammi, and all these people she didnt know and didnt want to know.

What a silly gathering. No one really knew anyone else but all wristwatches and timepieces had been set to jibe with one another which was all that mattered on December 31. How much of her life had been wasted at parties, vanity engagements, floating on a sea of drink underneath clouds of smoke? She knew the answer all too well and the thought of it made her queasy. Water and wind was what she needed with plenty of sky to contain it all.

"You aint gon meet nobody in a bar," Roscoe used to say, "but another drunk." By extension, she reasoned, you werent going to meet anyone at a party like this but another lonely person.

And loneliness, like dimmed lamplight, overshadowed everything—from the simple hors d'oeuvres to the restless guests.

She felt like Eleanor Rigby.

"Dont you remember me, Angelina?"

The face, especially the eyes, was so familiar she couldve drawn it in the dark, but there was no person she could readily attach it to. The aura surrounding him was peaceful and warm.

"Dont you remember those marvelous sessions we had over coffee in my studio and over at the Union—Lascaux, Botticelli, daVinci, Michelangelo, Hieronymus Bosch, Cézanne, Degas, Duchamp, Matisse, Picasso, Max Ernst, Hans Hoffman, Georgia O'Keeffe, Andrew Wyeth, Warhol and all those exquisite African primitives you were so fond of?"

Pictures of everything slid across her mind except whose face these gray eyes belonged to.

"Let me refresh your memory. You and Renée used to make special appointments to see me just before exam time to go over all the pictures that—"

She was picturing a loft crammed with paintings and prints and avalanches of books and records piled so high she was always afraid the floorboards were going to give way under the weight and send the whole scene crashing into apartments below. Theyd go up to his loft, a world really, on South State Street to get briefed on art masterpieces, she and Renée, and the whole place would be pulsing with the taped sound of crickets or electronic music which delighted her no end. He had a girlfriend, Israeli, a Sabra, pretty, who'd never say a word unless addressed directly. He always did most of the talking. He knew everything, but what was his name? It started with a D. David? Dennis? Darwin?

"Darryl," he said, "Darryl Dorough."

He still looked boyish but his hair was longer now, gracing his collar. She remembered it as being a lighter shade of brown than it was now. He'd grown a mustache, a handlebar, and sideburns. He also looked a few pounds heavier, but calm, so calm. Everything about him relaxed her and made her trust him at once.

"Whatre you doing here?" she asked.

"I'm still in the world, barely, but surviving."

They embraced one another for old times' sake. Her entire body untensed itself. Renée and Steve came over and got into the act. Steve, in his beach-ball Afro and technicolor clothes replete with stacked-heel shoes, looked quaint to Angelina. He was right in style but he still looked quaint. She could see him on some TV show, "Soul Train," say, shaking it down with the kids as he announced the next guest performer. Renée really went in for those movie-star types.

"I was just waiting to see how long it'd take before you two'd recognize one another," Renée said as she grabbed Steve's arm.

"This is one righteous honorary brother," said Steve who gave Darryl a theatrical hug with one arm, a gesture aimed as much at steadying himself as at acting out some pathetic show of friendship.

She didnt know what to make of Steve and Renée as a couple, but she was pretty sure by now that she didnt like Steve.

"I love this dude," he went on. "Darryl's a meditator and the last true humanitarian left in this wayward community of ours, bereft of conviviality."

"O my God!" groaned Angelina.

"Are you OK?" Renée asked sincerely.

She'd grown up hearing that whatever you did at the stroke of midnight on New Year's Eve was what you were going to be doing for the rest of the year. She prayed it wasn't so.

Someone had put on Billie Holiday, a refreshing change from the rancid acid rock that'd been pounding and screeching since she'd arrived. Did Steve actually go out and buy those records?

She hated being here so much that as soon as she and Darryl found a quiet corner of the dining room where they could breathe, she asked him if he had a car.

"Well, sure, but why? I thought we'd get a chance to talk. I mean, it's been years since—"

"Dont worry, we can talk but I'd really like to get out of here for a few minutes." With one hand, she fanned the air in front of her face.

"Smoke getting to you, hunh? I understand. I quit too."

There mustve been a dozen new people piled suddenly into the apartment which was already too crowded, too noisy, too smoggy. Two hours to go and already things were getting out of control. Couples danced and necked to the music. Fresh booze and dope were being passed out.

"We could go to my place, I suppose. It's quiet there."

"If you dont mind," she said. "I think I'd like that."

"Whatre you gonna tell your friends?"

"Wont tell em anything. I doubt theyll even miss me. If you wanna know the truth, I dont even care. Let me just get my coat and spruce up."

"Take your time."

She was hoping they could slip out without having to explain anything to Renée. Approaching the bathroom, she thought: I'm in luck. The door was cracked and the light on but there was no one waiting around to get in.

Safely inside, she looked up just in time to see Sammi licking Steve's upper lip and nostrils. Alex, Sammi, Steve and Renée— they were all in there, bunched in a huddle by the sink, arms around one another.

"Cant let none of it go to waste," Steve was saying. "How's it taste?"

"Bitter," said Sammi, her whole face puckering.

"O, I'm sorry," said Angelina. "I didnt think anyone was in here."

They all laughed.

"You could lock the door," said Alex, "and join us."

Renée had the tiny silver spoon under her nose now and was sniffing and clearing her throat. "Ahhhhh," she sighed, "this is good stuff."

"Some remarkable girl," Steve added, "if I may say so myself. You ever made coke, Angelina? This is some high quality shit. It will definitely put a shine on your forehead."

"I'm not in the mood," said Angelina.

"Relax, sister, relax," said Sammi whose plump bottom, like Renée's modest one, was being fondled by both men's hands. "What'd you come in here to do—pee? Well, go on and pee or whatever you gotta do. We'll turn our heads if it really bothers you."

They all laughed again.

"You really oughtta try some cocaine," Renée urged, "if youve never had it before."

"Ive had it and it's OK if youre ready for it, but I'm cool right now at the pace I'm moving at. You guys go on and knock yourselves out."

Backing out, she slammed the door shut behind her. She couldnt see any reason for giving them a third chance to laugh at her for the pure high hell of it.

No one, not even Renée, came running.

When the clock struck midnight, she and Darryl, having devoted less than one quiet hour to discussion of everything under the moon that really mattered, were seated on cushions, backs to one another, meditating in the silence of his East William Street apartment.

He, as it turned out, was much more into it than she was. For well over a year he'd been into T.M.—transcendental meditation. It had to be the calm vibrations he gave off, she realized, that attracted her to him at that horrible party. By day, he taught art history. By night, he was for real. This was all that mattered.

"I used to want to know everything," he told her afterwards on the freeway. "Now all I strive to know is what's a waste of time and what isnt."

"I learned the same thing when I was in love with that boy

from Atlanta I told you about, that rich brother, as they say, whose folks didnt think I had any background."

"Forget the stupid past," he said. "It's over and forgotten."

When he pulled into her father's driveway, she gave him a warm handshake and wished him the happy usual.

"Youll write me from California when you can find time?"

"I'll write."

"Cheer up, Angelina. The world's changing. I loved talking and meditating with you and finding out what we've both been up to, but the time'll come—you mark my sleepy words—when the world'll be such that we wont have to go sneaking out of consciousness-lowering parties to dabble at spiritual hobbies." He looked at his watch. She too could see. It was almost two o'clock. "Our hour's at hand."

His words made her blood tick. "Thank you, Darryl, and I'll write," she said again.

"And I'll read what you say and answer," he whispered, getting out to crunch through snow and open the other door for her.

BOOK FOUR

THE GLASS
SHATTERS

So home by the Pacific wasnt so different after all. There was still desolation to deal with, and ignorance and fear and sadness and being alone but, more importantly, for the time being anyway, there was the problem of getting back on her feet financially.

Something had happened to her in Detroit that she knew she wasnt going to be able to piece together for a long time to come. Maybe it all boiled down to the peaceful look on her father's face as she hugged and kissed and waved and stared after him good-bye.

Aunt Jujie was going to pray for her and she still put more than a little trust in prayer, her aunt's in particular.

Uncle Roscoe, bless his hokey old grabby heart, had even tried to slip her a French kiss on the sly at the airport departure lounge. She'd brushed him off with a niecely grin but had to give him credit for being tenacious and consistent over all those years that dovetailed into this embarrassing moment.

Fresh off the plane, delivered almost to her door by airport limousine, she lay on the mattress in her old cottage to which she now felt a stranger. She absolutely enjoyed feeling exhausted. The biggest delight of the moment was having a mound of unopened mail stacked up within arm's reach. Dozing softly, she slipped into a dream about standing at a gigantic picture window in a firelit room at dusk, watching snow swirl down upon a place that was neither Ann Arbor, Detroit, Mexico City nor Berkeley.

Two 3 o'clocks were enough for one day.

Slipping in and out of dreams, she lay thinking: What better way to spend a second afternoon dropped into your lap like money from heaven?

It took her three days to get around to being back in town officially.

Montego, the landlord, who was West Indian, was only too glad to extend credit to her for the back rent she owed. "You take your time, OK. I know youve been through a lot lately. I just hope you get that job. You deserve it."

"I hope so too," his wife Sara mumbled. She'd never been open to Angelina. "We've got a lot of bills to pay too, you know."

Montego was a checker at one of the Co-op markets in town and Sara, like Angelina's dad, was a postal worker. They had a twelve-year-old daughter to support and a younger son, a dwarf whose enlarged head matched his ten or so years but whose body and height was that of a five-year-old.

Both kids were fond of Angelina who played with them when she could find time and was in the mood. She knew that they each had problems she'd be hard put to cope with herself.

"I'll get the money to you, I promise. No matter what happens, you *will* get paid."

"I'm not worried," Montego assured her. "We're just happy to have you back with us alive and functioning. We were really upset about your place getting robbed. How's your father?"

"He's much better, thank you. I still feel a little guilty about having to leave him and come back here but, well, I think he's in good hands."

"You let us know if there's any way we can help out, OK?"

"Youve already helped out lots by not evicting me."

Throughout all this, their daughter Denise sat cross-legged on the living-room floor in front of "The Electric Company" while Alfred, their little boy, squirmed playfully in and out of Angelina's arms.

She wondered what she might have been like or still might be like as a mother.

She picked up her unemployment check and, for the first time in her life, applied for food stamps and got them. The unemployment lady asked her if she'd had much luck finding work back east. Angelina told her no but was glad to have been able to collect unemployment benefits while she was looking back there. The paranoiac in her always came out when she felt herself at the mercy of civil servants.

"I'm hoping something'll come through soon. God knows it's been some time."

"Relax," said the lady with a sudden twinkle in her eye. "Jobs are tight all over the Bay Area now, so we've had to extend benefit periods."

Coming out of the Bank of America on San Pablo at University Avenue where she'd gone to cash her check, she heard her name being called. "Angelina! Angelina Green, I'm over here!"

She looked across the street. It was Connie Moran, a woman she'd worked with at the botanical lab in Richmond. She crossed San Pablo to where Connie, all 250 pounds of her, stood waving an unopened umbrella in the air. It was one of those gray, tense come-rain–come-shine days.

"Connie, I dont believe it. I thought you'd moved back to New Jersey."

"I did—twice—but I'm back here now."

"Are you still married to, uh . . . I'm sorry but I forgot your husband's name?"

"David? Nah, we broke up a few years ago. He's in New York. Ive got the kids."

"Kids? What kids?"

"Two kids, both girls. I guess it's been longer than I'd thought since we've seen one another. So how've you been, Angie? Do you ever get back by the lab? I hear theyve torn it down or were thinking about tearing it down. So how've you been?"

Ho hum. She'd never really cared for Connie much. The woman talked too much. She remembered long one-way raps on the job as she stood by the autoclave, sterilizing glassware, or timed some sample being run through the centrifuge machine. Connie had a master's degree in chemistry. Angelina, who could never even learn valences in high school, was strictly a lab aide; a glorified dishwasher who got to wear a white coat too. When she wore it to the A&W Rootbeer stand on lunch breaks up the street, the halfwit counterman who had a crush on her would call her Dr. Green.

It all drifted back: racks of test tubes, flasks and beakers; the rubber gloves, that suffocating mask, that humiliating acid solution she bathed glassware in and had nightmares about. What a universe that damn gig had been, and what a memorable pain in the ass!

"I saw Zoltan buying some motor oil over at B.B.B. Discount a couple years ago. You remember him, dont you? The Hungarian who used to come in two hours late every morning with his white coat on so everybody'd think he'd been there all along? What a character! Remember the time Dr. Olson finally caught up with him and had him busted down from working as her special assistant to cleaning the rat cages for that weirdo Austrian, what was his name?"

"You mean that Somerset Maugham freak—Dr. Carlbach?"

"Yeah. He was always making passes at me."

"Carlbach made passes at anything that moved slower than three miles an hour. But Zoltan, I'll never forget Zoltan."

Connie's face went dreamy as Angelina remembered how

this portly lady and the professional refugee were always locking themselves up in the nematode room. She'd walked by and hear giggling.

"So tell me, Angelina, how've you been? Are you married yet? Did you ever go back and get your teaching certificate in French?"

"Yes, but it was in Spanish."

"Ah yes, Spanish. The girls and I were in Spain last year. We sure couldve used a . . . Hey! Hey, whatre you doing? Stop!—"

A lanky black teen-age boy had slipped up between them and was tugging at Connie's fat purse. It happened so quickly that it took Angelina a moment to actually tune in to what was taking place. Even at that she couldnt believe that anyone would be so brazen as to snatch a purse in broad daylight at an intersection as busy as this one.

"Stop!" Connie screamed. "Come back here, you bastard!"

The boy had the purse and was off up the block, zipping around pedestrians like a crafty quarterback running a field goal.

Without so much as blinking an eye, Angelina grabbed Connie's umbrella and took off after him.

People stopped in their tracks to stare.

The thief saw her coming and shot around a corner. It was a side street off San Pablo and there were few people on the sidewalk. She knew she should be out of breath by now but didnt have time to think about it. Feeling the weight of her own shoulder-strap purse banging at her ribs as she ran, she thought about Jujie, she thought about Daddy, she thought about Margo and all those creepy robberies in her recent past. She clutched Connie's umbrella and put every drop of energy she had into this chase. He couldnt get away, he just couldnt! She'd stay in behind him to the end of the world if she had to.

He shot across the street and barely missed getting slammed by a passing car.

She was right on his tail now. She could tell he was panicking. He hadnt expected all this—just another poor, oppressed brother

211

out to snatch some honkie's pocketbook to keep body and soul together in this capitalistic dog-eat-dog, racist-ass society . . . .

Somebody's bulldog, with a mouth full of teeth and a bellyful of bark, rushed down off a porch and began snapping at the young man's legs and feet.

This is it! Angelina thought, tears streaming down her cheeks. Her right side was beginning to hurt. *A few more steps and I'll have the sonofabitch!* The Arab from *Putney Swope* popped into her head. She was grinning and drooling as she heard him holler, "Your ass is mine, jim!"

Suddenly she got her second wind. Both she and the bulldog were on the trail now. She forgot about the pain in her side and the annoying banging of the purse at her ribs. *The asshole doesn't stand a chance!* Already she was waving the umbrella around, slashing the air, Samurai-style.

The joker slid momentarily as he sprinted smack into a pile of fresh dog waste. Angelina cut around it, thinking, *This is it!* But he managed to hold his balance although she could tell he was losing speed. She wanted to hurl the umbrella, pointed end forward, as if it were a spear but she held onto it, happy now that she'd worn flats and slacks instead of the heels and skirt she'd laid out the night before.

Something clicked. She focused on her third eye, that center of energy just above and between the eyebrows. Everything began to happen in slow motion the way it did whenever she was about to witness something dreadful—the accident in the car with Larry when he'd parked downhill on one of those impossible San Francisco streets. The emergency brake didnt work. The Volks began to roll down toward the car parked in front of it before she was safely on the sidewalk. The countdown began. It all happened in time-lapsed photography and played like a dream, like a movie, like now—

The thief zagged into a yard, the dog at his heels. She was out of her body, up above it all, watching the entity known as Angelina Green pursuing this youthful purse-snatcher. It was all so vivid, all so detailed. She even flashed on herself wondering why Connie wouldve picked such an ugly purse in the first place.

She was surprisingly calm as she watched him toss the plastic handbag, as though it were a football, out into the street before crashing into a child's tricycle parked beneath a loquat tree.

She saw his twitching mouth with missing teeth. She saw his frightened yellow eyes. She saw him throw his hands up in front of his face and heard him scream, "Sister, dont hit me! I was just jokin, I didnt mean nothin, I aint hurt nobody! Dont!"—

Centuries flowed by and came to a standstill.

She watched herself swing the umbrella down across his head as he scrambled to untangle his legs from the wheels of the overturned tricycle.

"Shit! Quit it!"

She whapped him in the belly, in the chest, across the thigh and finally in the face. She was crying again, blind with tears. "God, forgive me," she heard herself groan, but she couldnt stop hitting, poking, jabbing, stabbing.

The boy by now was on his knees, hunched over, arms wrapped tightly around his stomach, face in the grass. She hauled off and planted a clumsy kick at his rear but missed and banged her toe against the trunk of the tree. It hurt, O it hurt, but she immediately drew back her leg, this time the stronger one, the right one, and connected with a hard heel blow *thunk!* in his ass. The impact sent him tumbling forward and onto his back. Again his hands went up to protect his face. She rapped at his fingers and knuckles with swift criss-cross strokes, forcing them away. She was running out of strength. Her whole body was beginning to tremble but she wasnt collapsing yet.

Blap! Blam! Bip! Whop! . . . .

Again and again she brought the umbrella down across his face, striking the jaw, the chin, the tight-lipped mouth. His nose was bloody; his cheek cut open. His legs kicked out at her. She fell back against the tree, bounced and gave him one last solid crack, this time on the scalp as he struggled to get up.

He was sobbing. "Motherfuck you, bitch! You gittin me mad!"

She was fading back into herself now, descending; aware of being frightened.

Umbrella quivering at her side, her breath fading, she watched him finally pick himself up. *O no, O no, I'm not about to let you get away from me now, not behind all this!*

Their eyes met. He was scared too, very scared.

He pushed her. She wouldnt budge. Her adrenaline was pumping again. She pushed him back. He almost reeled over but caught his balance again and ran past her back out toward the sidewalk. The bulldog, who'd been yapping at a distance all this time—she had no way of knowing if a minute had passed or only an hour—rushed in doing what a riled-up bulldog does, forcing the youth to hedge and dodge and run in circles around the yard.

People were coming out onto porches.

"Owww, goddamit, my leg!" the boy shouted and, totally discombobulated, fell to the ground again.

Mustve twisted his ankle, Angelina not so much thought as knew by means of some crisis-induced telepathy, the ESP of violence.

The dog was on him like a buzzard. "Call this . . . motherfuckin . . . dog off!" he whimpered.

Men, women and little children were gathering to watch. One old man, armed with a baseball bat and a tire iron, hobbled into the yard and called the dog, whistling and hollering: "C'mon Freddy, c'mon now, here boy, here boy!"

Angelina was too exhausted to react any longer. Breath heavy, shaking, she dragged her feet across the grass past the excited spectators, most of them black or hippie, and picked up the damn purse which had landed at the curb.

The glass shattered.

She felt her mind click off just as the obnoxious gurgle of approaching sirens invaded her peace.

An elderly black woman came over and asked if she were

OK. She didnt answer. She sat on the curb, both purses in her lap, head in her hands, and cried and shook her head and cried some more.

Connie climbed out of one of the three police squad cars that had screeched to the scene. "That's him," she cried, red-faced, flanked by two brown-uniformed officers, hands at their guns. "That's him all right, and that's my friend Angelina, and that's my purse!"

"Pig scum!" some young man dressed in grimy bib overalls yelled out, a snot rag tied round his Pocahontas coiffure. "Get the fuck outta here and leave justice to the community!"

The cops—one sporting blond locks that trailed from the regulation hat to his shoulders; the other a generous Afro—ignored the remark as did most of the crowd. The pairs of cops in the accompanying cars were visibly cool but obviously ready for anything.

In an instant, the thief, face bloodied and swollen, was gathered up, handcuffed, pushed against the car with feet spread and frisked.

"Youre the witness," the young blond cop told Angelina. "It would help if you came along with us to the station and registered a statement."

Angelina nodded.

Connie asked why.

"Well, youre gonna press charges, arent you?"

Connie's face turned an even deeper shade of red. "Well . . . I dont know. I—"

"You mean behind all this," said Angelina, incredulous, "you arent going to press charges? This *is* the man. I stalked him down with *your* umbrella, and we can both identify him. I dont get it!"

"Could I speak with my friend alone for a moment?" Connie asked the officers.

"Sure," said the officer. "What can I say?"

The cops, guns drawn now, hustled the now alleged thief into

215

the squad car while Connie went over and spoke to Angelina in a low voice.

"Listen," she began, "I know you might think I'm crazy but . . . I mean, I do have my purse back. No harm's been done. After all, you know how much of a chance a poor black stands at the hands of—"

"I dont wanna hear it!" Angelina said loud enough for everyone to hear. "I dont wanna hear that bullshit, Connie. It took everything I had to catch up with this dude. You let him go and he'll be back out on the street pulling the same evil shit on somebody else just like *that*! Youve *got* to press charges."

"Put yourself in his place, Angie. His whole life'll be ruined. The prisons are already disproportionately filled up with blacks."

"Yeah and with rapists and murderers and people that would just as soon slash your throat as look at you. It's up to you, Connie. It's your choice to make. If you wanna press charges, I'll back you up but youre a damn fool if you decide not to. This simple-ass petty criminal next thing you know'll be publishing his letters and memoirs and screaming about police brutality and the black struggle and all he is, is a goddam punk, Connie, a nasty little *punk* that needs somebody to take a dukey stick and beat him all around his head like I just did, like—" She felt herself getting worked up again and fought to keep her voice down.

"Uncle Tom collaborationist!" the same dog-faced hippie who had edged his way to the front of the crowd shouted out, pointing a finger at Angelina.

All the cops tensed and were ready for action.

Angelina turned from Connie and faced the heckler, looking him dead in the eye. She knew she should ignore him but, since this was probably going to be one of her big days in the world, she looked him dead in the eye.

"Uncle Tom my ass, you dumb-ass white boy! Dont come giving *me* that chicken dudu about Uncle Tom collaborationist. This aint World War Two and you aint the goddam French

216

Resistance. I'm sicka you refugees from suburbia jumping up in my face with that Uncle Tom shit! There's a whole lotta people around here who work hard to stay poor and just because youre mad at your mommy and daddy because they gave you everything in the world except themselves now youre gonna move to Berkeley and talk all that ignorant horseshit and get a whole lotta black people's backs busted and heads split open in the name of the revolution—whatever the fuck that is!—so you can get your sick rocks off and score your expensive dope and then straighten up when you feel like it and take a bath and trim your mangy hair and put on a suit and go get some high-paying executive job or get your law degree and run for congress on the Peace and Love ticket, naturally. You put on a suit and you just another nice white boy. I dress up and get a fucking PhD and win the goddam Nobel Prize and I'm still a nigger, you square motherfucker, you . . . corny scavenger creep! Your old wrinkle-bellied mama's an Uncle Tom and your no-dick daddy's a . . . . Go back to Atherton and talk that shit! Go—"

The black cop walked over and placed his arms firmly around Angelina who had begun to shake all over again. "Take it easy, young lady," he whispered in her ear. "Take it easy, sister, or we might have to book you for assault."

Tentative applause broke out in the crowd.

"Asshole!" the young man muttered, his face red as Connie's as he slunk away.

"I'll press charges," Connie shouted finally. "I'll press charges, only let's just get the hell outta here!"

The arresting officers drove off with the suspect. Connie and Angelina rode to the station in one of the other cars. No one said a word for a long time.

"I suppose I should thank you," Connie mumbled at last.

"You dont have to thank me for anything," Angelina said. "Maybe I'm the one who oughtta be thankful."

"I dont understand."

"Youll never understand. Skip it."

The garble of the police radio eased their silences.

217

"I really didnt know you felt that way about things, Angie. I didnt even know you knew such language. I'm sorry."

"I try to stay outta situations that cause me to use such *language,* as you call it. I'm really an easy-going all-American girl but every now and then I have to get my nigger up."

THE OTHER END
OF DREAMS

In the reception room, waiting to be interviewed at last for the alternative-school teaching position, as comfortable as she could be in a plastic chair connected to other plastic chairs, she pored over a stack of the more interesting-looking mail that had gathered while she was away.

She was almost the same way about letters as she was about opening any kind of elaborately wrapped gift. She took her time. She liked to put it off until the moment was right for her to savor the envelope or package before leisurely proceeding to peek inside. Such momentary ritual lent mystery to everyday life.

There were several handsome Christmas cards from friends. It embarrassed her that she enjoyed receiving them so much because she never sent any herself. One bore a British Honduras postmark, a broad blue envelope with a gorgeous stamp and her name centered neatly in typescript that looked very vaguely familiar. But she didnt know anyone in British Honduras.

She worked her black teakwood letter opener gently along the seal. The card, charmingly designed, depicted a Nativity scene at which the three Magi were present. The stately head of

219

Balthazar, the black wise man, had been carefully circled in the same red ink that was used for the handwritten message:

Querida Angelina,
¿Qué pasó, guapa? ¿Qué ha sido de tí? No te llamaba aun pues no sabía tu número de teléfono. Lo busqué con la ayuda de la operadora aquí en la guía de Berkeley/Oakland pero no pude dar con él. ¿Dónde estas ahora—en Michigan o en California? ¡Escríbeme! No sabes tú, negrita, que te echo mucho de menos? Ayer me había propuesto aprovechar mi estancia aquí en esta linda Belize para mirar los escaparates en busca de regalos para tí. Me encantaba muchísimo cierto ópalo que ví durante la semana pasada en Mérida—nada del otro mundo, pero muy grato a primera vista. Sin embargo me dicen que los ópalos traen mala suerte. Por eso, te estoy mandando este checque personal para que compres con ello cualquiera cosa que deseas. La verdad es que por buen aviso que tuve acerca de cierto caballito listo al "racetrack" en Guadalajara, he ganado unos pocos pesos. Parece que siempre me aprovecho bien de tantas apuestas. ¡Pues cuidado! Pronto estaré en camino de San Francisco. En cuanto conteste a este mensaje, voy a llamarte por teléfono a tu casa. Te echo de menos, te echo de menos. ¿Por qué será? Hasta luego, Merry Christmas, Happy New Year.
Cariñosamente,
El Watusi

Dear Angelina,
What's happening, pretty? Whatever became of you? I never called because I didnt know your number. The operator looked it up in the Berkeley/Oakland directory but couldnt find it. Where you at—in Michigan or California? Write me! Sister, dont you know I miss you a whole lot? Yesterday I'd planned to take advantage of my stay here in lovely Belize by window shopping to find you a present. I was tripped out behind a certain opal I saw last week in Mérida—nothing far-out but a groove when you first check it out. Still, I'm told that opals are bad luck. So, I'm sending along this personal check for you to buy whatever you want. Truth is that thanks to a heavy tip on a hot little horse at the Guadalajara track, I picked up a few pesos. I always seem to come out OK on bets like that. But watch out! I'll be on my way to San Francisco pronto. Soon as you answer this note, I'll be ringing you up at home. I miss you. How come? Until then . . . .

It was signed "affectionately" and the check was for $300 American. Where in the world did he get all that money and, with all those kids to support, how could he afford to be so generous? Was he smuggling dope or what? Maybe he really only wanted to tie her up and make her feel indebted to him for the hell of it.

Come what may, it was an impressive chunk of money and, spread around strategically, would stave off quite a few creditors. She was prepared to pay it back five dollars at a time if it ever came to that.

"Surprised?" he asked, not batting an eye, reclined in his big leather chair, pipe in hand, jacketed in herringbone tweed with one of those big stylish bow ties that made her think of some giant vampire butterfly gracing his collar.

Yes, she *was* surprised, shocked really, but cool from get-go. If he was determined to keep his front up, she was willing to make the most of hers.

"Have a seat, Miss Green. Make yourself comfortable. Would you care for coffee?"

"No, thank you, I never drink it. It makes me nervous."

"I see. Very well. Ive been reading over your résumé. As you know, the person we'd originally hired to fill this position has taken seriously ill. It's going to be tough finding a replacement at this late date, but find one we must and *soon.*"

"Excuse me," she said, ignoring his smirk, "but I thought I was to be interviewed by a Mr. Galvez."

"That's correct, entirely correct except, I'm sorry to say, he's been kicked upstairs as of last week. You must have made the appointment some time ago. I'm the new man here, so to speak, but you neednt be ruffled or taken aback. I fully expect that youll do well."

He could hide everything but that persistent smirk which weakened his strained off-Broadway version of a man acting thoroughly relaxed.

"Your résumé, if you dont mind my saying so, is very promising."

"Well, I do enjoy teaching. I suppose you could say it's what I see as my calling."

How long was she going to be able to keep this jive up?

"Tell me," he said, leaning forward, leather-patched elbows touching the desk as he flipped through pages of the résumé she'd spent a week preparing and getting xeroxed in quadruplicate, "What do you see as the primary purpose of an alternative school such as the one we're about to open here in Oakland?"

Try as she did, she still found it difficult to see the man objectively, to think objectively or answer anything he asked objectively. If this were a jury trial she'd request that he be disqualified on grounds that he made her feel uneasy.

"My biggest complaint with contemporary education, as reflected in its practical application in the public school system, is that it tends to discourage rather than encourage the so-called culturally but actually economically deprived pupil or student. It's been my experience that—"

"Forgive me for interrupting you, Miss Green, but, if it isnt too much trouble, would you mind defining the term 'culturally deprived'? I mean, it's employed so often by our applicants."

Bastard! He knew what she meant and, tactically, it was a dumb point to belabor when there were doubtless so many riper ones waiting around the bend.

"To be blunt," she said, "we both must know by now that the term's a euphemism for the poor student whose parents work low-paying jobs or who're on welfare—namely the children of blacks, Chicanos, Filipinos, Native Americans, poor whites and the like who comprise a considerable proportion of the populace in our immediate community."

"Ah yes, I see. Very well, proceed."

Who the hell did he think he was—some senate investigator or somebody? Why couldnt they just talk plain English?

"Wait, I'm not finished. Let me give you an example of how

222

I see the term 'culturally deprived' being constantly misapplied, OK?"

The chubby Negro looked at his big expensive wristwatch as if she were a TV contestant on one of those silly quiz shows, trying to squeeze her answer in before the buzzer sounded.

"A child who speaks only nonstandard black dialect, say, is placed in a learning situation where he's expected to understand standard middle-class dialect with all of its implicit judgmental values and—"

"I dont think we need go into all that," he said, clearing his throat, "do you? I'm more interested in what you as a teacher of ah—" (he consulted the pages before him) "Spanish have to say about our alternative educational projects which, I might add, are presently undergoing severe budget cutbacks, owing to certain judgmental—as you would have it—values imposed upon us by the reigning powers that be, the federal government, to be explicit, which has determined that funds allotted for some of the bolder classroom experiments carried out in the Bay Area—the Berkeley all-black school, say—were unconstitutionally discriminatory. In a word, racist. There were those among us, of course, myself included, who objected vehemently, but, all factors considered, federal funds are federal funds and . . ."

She clicked off while he droned on, finding it more titillating, in a dismal sort of way, to dwell momentarily on the way he'd been dressed at the Harpers' party that Sunday night. A dashiki and an ascot, indeed! She wondered if he kept that big .44 magnum of his tucked away in a desk drawer. How in hell did he land this job in the first place when he was supposed to have had such a soft, well-paying civil-service gig?

"But I digress. Forgive me, Miss Green. Since you would be working with both black and Chicano youngsters as well as with whites, tell me how you as a language instructor would apply your skills to the alternative format?"

So what was she supposed to say? At which point was the vengeful side of him going to surface and sweep her away?

She cleared her throat. "Ive found that language learning affords the perfect opportunity for both teacher and student to participate in a bicultural milieu. We tend, as you know, to equate our own parochial values with what's universal and perfectly normal. The middle-class-oriented individual is no less guilty of this presumptuous way of thinking than the person of lower- or upper-class conditioning. By studying another language, which is really to say by studying another culture, it's possible to enter another world whose social and value concepts might vary from ours tremendously. We become more keenly and, I think, beneficially aware of the peculiarity of our own linguistic system which, as I've already implied, reflects the social setting of which it's a product."

"Yes . . ."

"So, if a language teacher is at all flexible and imaginative in his or her instructional approach, it's quite possible, I've found, to stimulate a student to examine any given society's attitudes and mores from a highly advantageous perspective."

"Yes, of course, of course. I couldnt agree more. Could you give me an example of how youve actually put this theoretical ideal into classroom practice, and what sort of success it has met with—if any?"

Ho hum, this bureaucratic simpleton with his styled hair was truly beginning to get on her nerves. Already her underarms were moist and her stomach was tightening. For the first morning in weeks, she'd overslept and skipped meditation, a grand misfortune which she now regretted.

"Take, for example, the idea generated by American society —the mainstream, if you will—that people of color are inferior to whites in all ways and whose popular image is far from being looked upon as positive or desirable. Well, I've gotten across to both black and white kids by bringing in poems and stories or musical recordings in which words such as 'negrita' or 'mulata' are employed in a decidedly positive, and, in instances, endearing, connotation. When a Latino uses the term *mi negrita,* for example, he does so admiringly. It means—"

224

"I'm perfectly capable of following you without recourse to translation, Miss Green. Ive studied a few languages myself."

O fuck you, Tolby Crawford! she thought, almost aloud, as she remembered the little oath Louetta used to lay—half-playfully, half-seriously—on people in high school: *Go to hell! Go directly to hell! Do not pass purgatory!*

"I also like to point out to my students," she continued, "such things as the way we look at basic life processes. The Navajo, to illustrate, do not say, as speakers of English and other Western European languages do, that someone has died. They say rather that death is taking place with such and such a person. This implies a concept of death as a natural and normal stage of existence inseparable from the process of living. Fascinating, dont you think?"

If she so wished, it would be easy to turn the tables on the Negro, but she needed a job and this was no time to play that particular game. In her mind, she'd given up from the moment she'd entered and laid eyes on him.

"Fascinating, indeed, indeed!" he chuckled self-consciously, caught off-guard.

She could picture him in top hat and tails, sporting a bonafide monocle, posturing beneath a wall-mounted lion's head, hoisting a few gins with colleagues before brushing up for supper at the club. The damn fool! George Orwell was right. The only two words a functionary needed to know were Yes and No; everything in between was apt to be bullshit!

"I must say, Miss Green, that you do have a great deal going for you, as they say"—(She wanted to stop him right there and ask, Like *who* says, Mr. Pootbutt, like *who* says?)—"and your training appears to be excellent in all respects." He retreated into the résumé again. "Hmmmm . . . B.A. from the University of Michigan, M.A. degree from Cal Berkeley, travel in Spain, Italy, France . . . two years with the Neighborhood Youth Corps both in Berkeley and San Francisco with, I might add, excellent recommendations, if I may say so. You're undeniably an attractive young woman."

225

Uh-uhhhh, here the nigger was getting fresh, shifting into his chauvinistic bag. Should she cut him short? Should she blow the whole interview? Ah, what the hell, say it!

"I think you have nice legs yourself, Mr. Crawford, if I may be so insouciant as to say so."

"I beg your pardon, Miss Green, I dont think I caught that." His eyes were narrowing as he took a deep breath. He'd heard her all right and it occurred to her that if he made things unpleasant she could actually put his ass in a lawsuit for coming on sexist while functioning in an official federally funded capacity.

"As I was saying, your qualifications appear to be impeccable and, whereas I cant promise you anything—I'll be interviewing quite a number of applicants over the next few days—I can safely state that I'm duly impressed with your enthusiasm and outlook."

"Thank you, Mr. Crawford."

"I take it you may still be reached at this same address and phone number?"

"That's correct."

If the joker got drunk and came out to her place or called her up and made any unsavory overtures, she'd sic Scoot Harper on his butt again.

"Thank you, Miss Green, thatll be all. Have a nice day . . . and again, let me reassure you that your application will be given every reasonable consideration."

They shook hands formally, laughably so. His thick paw was clammy with sweat and so was Angelina's.

"Miss Green," he called out in a soft voice when she'd reached the door. "I sincerely hope that youll be merciful with respect to any embarrassment we might have caused one another during past encounters. I've been through a great deal of soul-searching since that . . . well, you know the circumstance. You have my apologies and best wishes."

Even though his delivery was mechanical and doubtless premeditated, the words drifted straight to the heart and made

226

her feel cheap for being such an undercover bitch, however justifiably, the whole time she'd sat in that interview chair.

"Please forget it, Mr. Crawford," she said, not sure if she meant it, "I dont believe in harboring grudges. Thank you for your time."

There were moments when formality provided the perfect atmosphere for what needed to be said.

He smiled with relief.

She faked hers with a nod.

She wondered about the sincerity of his words. Had he actually learned anything and grown from that sad experience?

Had she?

REAL ON REAL

She was getting there, getting there, planted in peace upon her mattress in half-lotus position, everything around her tuned out except the delicate fragrance of incense.

Yesterday is tomorrow and tomorrow was now.

Past and present blend so movingly.

Flesh and blood, meat and vein, soft inner eye and brain, fur and enamel, tooth and nail, she is organism, fluid, air, electron, emptiness—

She leans forward. The room is blank. The light is pure white. The answer to a question that hasnt been asked and can never be asked is already yes. Her otherness is alive in this endless now—

Now light is green. Even the music she hears in her secret ear is green, the color of Earth from afar. Breezes from the barely cracked windows of her two eyes, almost closed, blow over and under and into the room of her body to the spot where soul lives—

Has an hour gone by, six hours, a week? She doesnt know. She's too far away from the warmth of the room and the sound of steadily falling sunshine to notice. It's better than being carefree underwater. She's bubbling with happiness and she's the bubble; the way she felt on that jet to Mexico except more so and more in control now; an ever-expanding ball of water and air stretching out for some sea vast enough to hold all the living joy she takes in with each renewed breath—

Darryl back in Ann Arbor had suggested that she join a formal meditation group such as the one he belonged to, explaining that mutual vibrations of a peaceful nature have a way of reinforcing one another.

She hadnt tried it yet and, as relaxed and vibrant as she felt now, saw little need to follow his suggestion.

Totally relieved of every bodily tension, she longed to attain the same state on a mental level. When she read of yogis who ascended to the stage known as *samadhi,* absolute transcendence of body, mind and their attendant ego, it sent glad shivers up her spine and filled her eyes with happy tears. Just knowing that there were real worlds beyond what most people perceive as being the only real world, reachable without the aid of narcotics that paralyzed the will, gave her more to live for than she'd ever known.

Later for a movement! She loved being moved all alone this way; ablutions performed, meditation attended to, stomach empty, her entire body tingling with energy in the familiar seclusion of a newly cleaned cottage.

A short time later, after she'd plugged the phone back in and thought forever over a large mug of hot herb tea, there was a knock at the door.

The shift from the world of meditation with its quietude and private light back into the public world of shrillness and shadow was becoming increasingly difficult, often painful to bring off, but she tried to manage it during the time it took to get from her tiny kitchen to the front door, a casually paced distance of some fifteen seconds.

Intuition, because she was beginning to depend on it again, was her ace. Observed in the spirit of common sense with a little practical action to back it up, it strengthened the will and freed imagination.

There stood Margo Tanaka with her two kids—Greg who was ten and Mitzi, her Eurasian daughter by Seishi, who was all of five—and, God, beaming there behind them in rain poncho and simple jeans was none other than Curtis himself whom Angelina had secretly dubbed the Riddler of Reality.

"Dont you think we'd make a handsome group portrait?" Margo said with a bold grin and shrug of the shoulders that told the history of her whole life. "We came to whisk you away with us to the warm, dry beaches of Santa Cruz, California, U.S.A. Too much tranquility and not enough hassle make Angie wise girl."

She hugged all of them and said, "It's so good to see everyone. I could use a little sea air for a change. Come inside while I get my bathing suit and stuff."

"Angelina," said Curtis, "youre more beautiful than ever. You seem to be glowing."

"I hope so," she told him as she snuggled up for a second hug. The scent of his aftershave delighted her.

"I wasnt sure if I'd ever see you again."

"We'll all see each other again and again," said Margo in her tie-dyed jeans and middy blouse.

"Mom, are we ever gonna get outta here?" asked Greg who was precocious but something of a grouch. "I thought you said we'd get there while the tide's still high so I can take some pictures of it."

"Dont be so impatient all the time," his mother said, taking quiet little Mitzi by the hand.

The water was icy cold and broke against the shore in gigantic waves. Greg was beside himself with glee as he skipped about snapping shots with his birthday camera.

The beach itself was warm enough, considering the time of year they were in.

Angelina dug her feet down into cool sand as she sat on one of the outspread blankets with Mitzi twisting in her lap.

"Angelina, do you know how big the ocean is?"

"No, not really."

"Well, I do." The little girl was simpering.

"Betcha dont either," said Curtis, pinching her cheek.

"Betcha I do too know."

"How much you wanna bet?"

"Uh, I bet a dime."

"Youre on, Mitzi. Now, how big is the ocean?"

"It's around this big," she sighed, stretching out her arms to form a large circle, then widening it. "Well, maybe it's just a little bit bigger. It depends on the day."

"What's the day got to do with it?" asked Curtis, winking at Margo who was lying close by on her stomach in bikini and dark glasses. Angelina thought Margo still had a pretty trim figure for a mother of two.

"Well," Mitzi said ponderingly, "sometimes on certain days the ocean's big, like today, you know. Other days it's kinda little. It all depends."

"Depends on what?"

"O cut it out, Curtis," Angelina said finally, "and pay the poor girl the dime you owe her."

They went for a stroll, Angelina and Curtis, along the beach down toward the reefs where a young couple sat drinking beer. Except for a weekday sprinkling of idlers and sunbathers, the beach was deserted.

"I got all your letters," Curtis began.

"Youre one hell of a letter writer yourself," she said. "I mustve read that first one you sent me in Mexico a hundred times."

"Dont know what made me do it. I just felt as if I had to get in touch with you. Youve been on my mind constantly."

"I was so happy to get your letter. I needed those good words. Are you still living over in the city?"

"Yeah, right there on Valencia Street in the Mission. I'll have my biz ad M.A. come June unless campus riots come back in style and they decide to shut the damn university down again."

They both laughed.

"Whatre your plans after that?"

"I really dont know. There're a couple of big companies with management training programs halfway interested in me but beyond that, I dont know. It isnt the best time to be starting out, you know."

"I know," she said, "the Great Society days are over, that's for sure."

"I'd really like to go into business on my own, eventually, once I can get on my feet."

"Like, what kind of business?"

"O, I dont know—maybe something that might benefit black and poor people."

"How about opening up a private mint where people could work manufacturing their own money and get to keep a percentage of what they produced for salary?"

"That's not a bad idea," he laughed, "but I'm serious."

"So am I."

They finally reached the rocks where the young couple by now was necking it up shamelessly. Pressed together, their mouths engaged, the boy's hands had slid down inside the bottom part of the girl's bathing suit while she kneaded his bottom with her own chubby hands. He wore his hair in a ponytail, a bead in one ear, and was blonder and tanner than the frizzy-haired girl who, as Angelina observed, with her shoulder tattoo and quivering flab, shouldnt be seen in a bikini.

"My, my," Curtis snickered, "aint white folks got no sense of shame?"

"You mean young folks," she whispered, "and we mustnt pass judgment on others."

She found it weird that she and Curtis should be so formal with one another when, only months ago, theyd been naked together and drunk in her bed and a lot more carefree than these kids.

They found a spot away from the couple where the early afternoon sun shone warmly.

"Well, so tell me, Curtis, whatever possessed you and Margo to stop by my place on impulse?"

"Impulse, nothing! I phoned her last night to ask about you and she told me you were back in town, so I suggested we all do the beach together today."

"But what if I hadnt been home?"

"But what if I hadnt called Margo?" He stretched out his long hard legs.

She was admiring his body's dark brown color and firmness; the sketchable face with its deepset eyes, angular cheekbones, and the pleasant disposition it mirrored.

"You see, my distant friend," he went on, embracing her playfully at the waist, "our whole being here's due to impulse. As you said in your last letter, 'We can only live one moment at a time,' or something like that. I'm glad you were home. We tried calling first but got no answer."

"I unplug the phone when I meditate."

"So you really went on into that like you said you were going to, hunh?"

"I'm trying."

They looked away from one another; swung their legs which dangled over the rock's edge. A gull glided by on the high blue air.

"Did you figure out my riddle yet?"

"No, and I wasnt going to even bring it up because I'm embarrassed."

"Embarrassed? Tsk, tsk. It was only for fun."

"Well . . ."

"Well, what?"

"Are you gonna tell me the answer? Ive given up."

"If I tell you the answer I might not ever get a chance to see you again because then you wont have any need for me."

He smiled.

She smiled.

The cinematic waves crashed in the distance, sweeping everything clean in their wake for the moment.

They stared into one another's eyes.

She knew she shouldnt be doing this. What was it about a man that always drew out the woman in her, the female ego she wanted to subdue? No, she thought. I cant, she thought. I wont get involved and all excited and lose this hard-earned spiritual high. We'll just be friends, soul mates.

"Angelina," he whispered.

She leaned into the kiss and right into his arms, and sat there and sat there while he held her and held her, coming down softly like sunshine.

THE SKIN
OF RAIN

She spent a few days getting her life back in order, paying bills, answering Watusi and all the other letters, getting her teeth cleaned, writing her father and phoning him too. He told her he was feeling better and was back on the job on a part-time basis. Jujie and Roscoe were coming by regularly. He missed her, of course, but understood, and would be very pleased if she'd give him a call whenever she could find the time.

The weekend rolled around on schedule. Curtis called. She hadnt heard from him since Santa Cruz. He wanted to drive over and take her to dinner. She declined with the vague and weary expectation that they might end up afterwards at her place and have to go through those changes again. It took too much out of her to be tempted that way. She wanted to leave their little sudden beach scene buried back there by the ocean in sand. This time she would be firm and discreet.

"Then how about dinner in the City tonight? We can go take in some music or whatever you feel like."

She felt like a fool which was nothing new. Live music was something she missed, maybe needed. Now that she thought about it, months had passed since she and Margo had gone to catch one of the New York avant-garde jazz groups at Mandrake's in Berkeley. In the name of freedom and liberation, the band had assailed them with an evening of screeches, growls and noise; uptight, psychotic, hostile city music, contemptuously formless. The audience was tense. Its effect on Angelina was such that she wanted to go out on the streets and stab somebody, anybody.

"That sounds pretty good," she told Curtis. "Do I get to pick which group we go to hear?"

"I wouldnt have it any other way. What time should I pick you up?"

"I'll take the bus."

"You have got to be jiving."

"No, I like taking the bus over. It gives me time to think about things."

"That's your trouble, you think too much. Is it OK if I pick you up at the terminal?"

"Slick."

"Wear something warm and bring an umbrella. It looks like it might rain over here."

"Over here too."

They had a Chinatown dinner, the works, from sweet and sour soup to fortune cookies. Curtis's skillfulness with chopsticks impressed her.

"Juliet Fong taught me how to use these things," he smiled, clicking the sticks together proudly for effect. "Took me a while to get the hang of it but after I had it down pat I used to come over here, order, break out my own personal set, and make a big production out of doing up a meal."

"Why all that?"

"Just to show some of these prejudiced people around here that gave me and Juliet a hard time that I could do their thing as well as they could. Americans sure are hard on each other, arent they?"

"Yes, we are. Did you run into the same kind of trouble with your Puerto Rican girlfriend?"

"Howd you know about her?"

"You wrote me about her. She didnt like Chicanos, remember?"

"Estrellita had too much splib in her, Afro blood, for people to even notice we werent supposed to be together. What's your fortune say?"

She read the tiny strip of paper aloud: "You will enjoy prosperity and tranquility in your new home."

"What new home?"

"Dont ask me. What's yours say?"

"It says, 'Dear Curtis—' " He threw his head back and broke up.

Angelina laughed too, enjoying the release. Maybe she was being too uptight about meditation and the pursuit of serenity. The last thing she wanted to become was dull and inflexible like most of the people she saw around her lately—dreary, cheerless hippies and straights, whites and off-whites, blacks and browns, oldsters and youngsters.

"Come on," she urged, "what's it really say?"

"Says, 'You know how to enjoy the simple pleasures life has to offer.' "

"Is that all?"

"That's it, I swear." He handed her the message. "Now what the hell kinda fortune is that supposed to be?"

"Uncle Tom fortunes. They know we arent interested in hearing any kinda jive that might get us upset."

"I think you might be right," he said, picking up the check and glancing at it solemnly. "I sure know I dont, not behind the way these prices keep going up every time I come in this joint."

It was nice to be in out of the rain, squeezed up next to other hungry listeners seated at little tables, soaking in the music; passionate sound that made so much more sense than words.

She drank it all in: sounds and silences, melody, harmony, beat and cacophony; the drummer's gravity, the bassist's professionalism, the pianist's brooding joyfulness, the responsible gaiety of the added percussionist who looked authoritative in his Big Apple cap and hip shades with lenses that grew darker or brighter according to light.

Most of all, she was hypnotized by the leader's exuberance and his musicianly spirit which was strongly emotional, wide-ranging and mischievous—Rahsaan Roland Kirk, blind composer of "The Inflated Tear," the poignant melody that expressed all too painfully her terror on the morning of the Harpers' big Sunday night bash. A multi-instrumentalist—saxophone, flute, clarinet, recorder, manzello, strich, siren, chimes—Kirk was famed for his ability to play a combination of woodwinds simultaneously and always with breathtaking skill and imagination.

Lively and receptive, the audience gathered at Keystone Korner was dominated by people in their earlier twenties. Here she sat growing old again.

Under the table, Curtis held her hand and did crazy things. He squeezed it, stroked it and tapped out rhythms on it, but when he placed it boldly and squarely against his thigh she snatched it back and poured wine with it, a libation she had no intention of sampling.

When he folded his hands, sat back in his chair and stared straight ahead at the bandstand, Angelina was hoping that the soothing current of musical vibration would clear the air between them and heal each of their passing wounds.

They headed for home in a downpour. Home was her cottage, not his place.

"I guess I really dont understand you after all," he said, breaking a silence that had lasted the span of the Bay Bridge.

She thought of the first time she'd made this crossing in a rush of philosophical excitement, expecting everything she'd failed to find in her lonely life back east to be waiting on the other side.

The downpour softened to a light drizzle.

"I think you do understand me, Curtis. I know you do. Your letters showed that. It's just . . . well, why cant people have deep feelings for one another, even love each other, without their bodies always getting in the way?"

She toyed with the handle of the damp umbrella and brushed raindrops from her face while she waited for the poet in him to come out and ease the sting of her own harsh words.

"Our bodies seem to have done OK on their own in the past, dont you think?"

Owch!

He took the University Avenue off-ramp into town. As they drove past gas stations, shops, restaurants, the Toulouse, she stared at a herd of desperate hitchhikers with their thumbs out and placards held up for SANTA CRUZ, VANCOUVER, BOSTON, NEW YORK. One hirsute yawner, his childlike wife plopped on the watery curb, cradling a baby in her arms, was waving a sign that read ANYWHERE!!!

"Tell me, does this meditation youre into call for your being off everything else in addition to booze, tobacco and bad food?"

"You mean, like, men?"

"Yeah, sex."

"Well, there's no regulation about it or anything like that," she sighed, glad that theyd finally gotten around to broaching the unsayable. "I just wanted to see if for once in my stupid life I could get into something and really do it the right way. If I make out, I come down, to put it bluntly. It's as simple as that."

"How long do you think youll be able to stay up?"

"I really dont know. Havent you ever been through anything like this before?"

"I quit smoking once—that was all it took, that one time. I never took it up again. O yeah, I cut out eating pork for about three years once, but I'm sure what youre going through must be on a tougher level. Does it make life easier for you?"

"In a way, yes, but in another way—well, I dont know yet. It's a day-to-day trip."

"You havent thought about taking any more walks across town to the Golden Gate, have you?"

"No, but I still havent forgotten how bad I felt then."

"Then meditation must be something that's good for you. Me, I dont think I could cut it, not at this point in my life anyway. I hear it's pretty good though if youve got the temperament for it. I just hope it doesnt end up making you unhappy by cutting you off completely from friends and close ties."

"I dont really think there're really enough of them for me to worry about."

"I think a lot about you and *of* you, if that makes sense, and Margo really loves you like a sister. I know that might not sound like much but considering this is California that's a pretty good average, I think."

She hugged him at the door. He was sweet and polite.

"Think youre gonna stay on here in Berserkeley?"

"Depends on whether or not I get that teaching job."

"If you do, let's keep in touch. If not, let me know where you are, OK?"

She kissed his cheek. "You dont hate me, do you?"

He held her very close, stroking her soft damp curls, and whispered a hot, maddening "Of course not!" in her ear.

"Youre such a tease," she said.

"Am I really? I hope you get the job. I'll give you a ring in a couple of weeks and find out how youre doing."

With a lump in her throat, she watched him turn, head up the rainy walkway, then pause and take a long look at her. "On second thought," he called out in a loud whisper, "maybe I'll just write. That way nothingll get in the way."

She motioned him off playfully with a sweep of her hands and rushed inside. Two cups of tea later and a peanut butter sandwich, she noticed that she hadnt taken her coat off yet and had left the umbrella in his Volkswagen.

ALL THE BRIGHT FOAM OF TALK

In the window of the Caffe Mediterraneum on Telegraph Avenue where she'd biked to charge a new dress and boots, Jack Jefferson and Bobby Lane were playing chess.

Like most of her friends, Angelina avoided the Avenue, detested it, and had long ago broken her habit—established during lonely grad school days—of stopping on her way home from class to peer inside the old coffee hangout (longtimers still called it the Piccolo) in the hope of spotting someone she knew and liked well enough to sit with and chat over cold Italian sodas or ice cream. Jack and Bobby had been among the handful of regulars who'd fascinated her back then when she was earnestly seeking that unnamable something she'd never found at home or in heartless New York. Their glittery rap both thrilled and intimidated her. She imagined the hundreds of thousands of man- and woman-hours spent under this roof, lingered away over drinks and toy food; yakked away glibly with practiced opinions on everything under the sun—politics, the economy, religion, sex, metaphysics, dope, literature, race, cinema, you name it.

"Have a seat, Angelina Green," Bobby Lane said, motioning

her over, "while I teach Jack Jefferson a lesson he wont ever forget."

Bobby deliberated conscientiously before moving a pawn forward one space.

Jack grinned and groaned as he slid his queen backward two diagonal spaces and yelled, "*Check!* You the one gon get taught a lesson. *Check!* And dont you go tryna pull nothin funny cause my main knight is ridin shotgun for Her Royal Majesty all up and down this militarized zone. I'm gonna do to you what Stalin done to Hitler and what Ho Chi Minh and Giap done to Sam over in Vietnam—trick your no-thinkin ass right up into some terrain you dont know nothin about and aint got no business invadin in the first goddam place! *Check!* Your queen is in bad trouble, chump! Rescue the bitch!"

Bobby Lane, the shorter and darker of the two, rubbed his chin with a faint grin as he rolled his sunglassed eyes at Jack Jefferson and Angelina, and glued them to the board again. "How you doin, Angie, haven't seen you around here in a long time."

"O, I been having my ups and downs. I didn't know you guys still came in here."

"Well, I can only speak for myself. I get down here maybe once or twice a month. Cant fight these thugs and thieves and tramps and freaks and junkies no more. I cant fight these dogs and I cant fight that dogshit." Bobby lifted a rook from its square, made a circle in the air and replaced it.

"Better not make *that* move, jim, cause if you do that's all she wrote. You lookin good, Angelina. Why dont you stop by the pad sometime?" Jack lowered his voice and bent toward her. "We got some of that good Thailand grass and I mean it will tie your tongue in a knot. Ask Margo about it."

"Has she tried it already?"

"Tried it? Hey, Bobby, you hear that? Has Margo tried it?"

"Jack had to drive that broad home the night she was over at my place cause she was scared to even get in that Toyota. That stuff wont only tie your tongue in knots, itll tie your whole head up into one of them—what you call them designs and things these hippies be round here makin outta string and knots? It's a chick up here on Saturday be sellin em out in fronta Cody's Bookstore . . ."

Jack Jefferson's eyes lit up. "Yeah, I seen that broad too and she is one fine, healthy-lookin stallion—Jewish broad, right?"

"Looks Armenian or Syrian to me."

"Well, you know, Semitic, got that dark beautiful blood and that cold jet black, long Delilah-lookin hair. I been meanin to hit on that chick."

"Samson the one had all the hair, Jack Jefferson, with your illiterate, ignorant self! All I wanna know's the name of that cord-work stuff. What's it called, Angie?"

"Macramé?"

"Macramé, that's it. This shit we got will knot your whole head up like some kinda macramé or somethin. You gotta try some and I guarantee you wont ever go back to this little weak windowsill jive they be dealin up and down the Avenue here."

"I havent been into smoking much of anything lately," Angelina said tactfully.

"Well, you look like you might need to soon," said Bobby. "I get up in the afternoon, have me a toke or two, work on my manuscript, study my French, and then take me somethin good to read off the bookshelf and head on over to San Francisco to punch in on the docks."

"Still a longshoreman, eh?" said Angelina. "This is about the longest Ive ever known you to hold down a job."

Jack Jefferson laughed. "Dont you know theyve just about automated those docks, baby? Bobby dont do anything but stand around all night watchin them *machines* load and unload that cargo. He just lay around on lunch breaks—I think the union got it so now that the men get three or four of em a shift, dont they?—readin and talkin that talk."

"Fuck you, Jack Jefferson."

"Nigger, are you gon move or admit defeat or surrender or what?"

"Whatcha reading these days, Bobby?" asked Angelina who was trying to decide whether to buy anything or not.

"I'm back into my ace, Faulkner, you know. Why dont you put your packages down and join us?"

"Dont you put them packages down," Jack squawked. "One of these nasty-lookin scavengers'll be on em like flies on manure."

Bobby Lane was snickering. "Your metaphors and similes are appallin, Jack Jefferson."

"Well, you know how it is," Jack shot back, winking at Angelina. "We dont all have time to lay back and peruse Faulkner. Anyway, I betcha if youda gone down there snoopin around his place, Faulkner woulda said, 'Git this nigger offa my plantation, this aint one of my niggers!' "

Angelina, as always when she found herself in their company, tried to keep a neutral face and stay out of Bobby's and Jack's hassle of long standing—an unpredictable mixture of good-natured ribbing and outright hostility and aggression—which she suspected might date back to years when she was seriously wondering if she was ever going to graduate from Milan Elementary. They had a sneaky way of involving outsiders in their teasing, but this time she planned to watch it every step of the way.

"Angie," Bobby said suddenly, "I was sorry to hear about all the bad luck you been goin through. Margo said you got ripped off and then had to fly outta Mexico back east to see your father. Is he OK?"

"Doing much better, thank you. I'm trying to get myself back together now."

"I know all about that," said Jack. "I been tryna get myself back together since 1959."

"Well," said Bobby, "if there's anything I can do—like, if you need some furniture or somethin or whatever was stolen that I got extras of, you welcome to borrow it."

"And this sucker got a whole warehouse crammed fulla shit, Angie, so you better take him up on this offer cause the stuff just

244

gon sit around and mildew and rust. Hey, you wanna buy a car? I'm sellin my car, the Oldsmobile, cheap."

"How cheap is cheap?"

"Mmmmm, a hundred dollars."

"Does it run?"

"Run your ass to the poor house," cracked Bobby. "You dont wanna even go near that old piece of car, Angelina, not with the energy crisis bein the way it is. I borrowed this fool's car one day to drive over to Sausalito and had to stop two times and put gas in it—on the way over and on the way back!"

"Dont listen to him, Angie. You know this sucker aint put but a dollar's worth of gas in at a time."

"Noooooo, no!" Bobby was moving his head from side to side with exaggerated emphasis. "I filled that mother all the way up myself until gasoline was spillin out all down the side of that raggedy vee-hickle, cost me somethin like ten dollars to make that trip not countin three quarts of oil which I threw in outta the kindness of my heart! Dont you let Jack Jefferson talk you into buyin that car, Angelina!"

Jack Jefferson was gloating over his big chess maneuver again, rubbing his hands, beaming from the forehead of his brown-bearded freckly face all the way down to his thick polo-shirted neck.

"I get around OK on my three-speed bike," she said defensively, "and the busses are still running, you know."

Jack said, "Yeah, I see you got your little bike chained up out there, tryna do your little European thing. I'm sorry but them doggone bikes dont always get it, baby—and dont you believe for one minute that a European aint gon run down and get him some kinda motorized wheels the minute he get hold to a few pounds or francs or marks or whatever the currency. The way the shit is goin now they gon pretty soon be able to buy Cadillacs and Lincolns insteada them little Fiats and things cause the world market done got this dollar by the throat and chokin the dudu outta it."

"Isnt it the truth," she said, relieved that the conversation was finally taking an impersonal turn. "I dont know what we're going to do. I applied for another teaching job and I'm scared to death the bottom's gonna fall out of the economy before I can get straight again."

"What economy?" said Bobby, pushing his chair back, his voice rising. "You aint seen nothin yet, Angie. Before this downward trend is over they gon be rationin pee water!"

"No lie," some Buffalo Bill-looking character at the next table commented as he closed his copy of *China Reconstructs* and tossed it on top of a *Zap Comix*. "I imagine itll be like Germany in the late twenties where you had to carry your money around in a backpack to lay out five thousand marks for a plate of sauerkraut and sausage."

"But what the hell can we do about it?" asked Angelina.

"All the hip people I know with bread say they gon invest in gold. I'm thinkin about it myself."

"Listen at Jack Jefferson, will you. This dude is runnin all up and down the west coast doin these heavy weldin jobs just so he can keep his rent paid, a few groceries in his icebox, go gamble in Reno or Vegas, and now he's gonna go out and buy gold. Do you know what gold is sellin for these days?"

"I read back in Detroit where it's supposed to go up to something like four or five hundred dollars an ounce over the next few years."

"Tell him, Angie. Now, can you see poor old sleepy-eyed Jack Jefferson with his big-foot self strainin up and draggin his little savins up to the man, talkin bout, 'I'll take half an ounce of gold please and a coupla grams of silver if you got any left'? Now, can you see that? Angelina Green, I been tellin yall all these years to get yall's little shit together cause the geopolitical situation was gonna get rough and this yankee dollar wasnt gon be excitin everybody like it use to. Americans are somethin else. You cant tell em shit! Sam is use to runnin up in somebody's frontyard, squeezin off a few rounds of ammo, stickin the flag up, buyin up a few puppets and toms and then wave that dollar in everybody's face and slippin a whole country in his ass pocket. But it dont work that way no more—noooo, no! It's a whole new day, baby. People gon be usin dollars like we use to do cardboard and newspapers back durin the Depression to cover up the holes in our shoes."

"So are you still going to Paris?" she asked.

"This nigger aint goin to no Paris, unless you mean Paris, Texas, or someplace he know a little somethin about."

"Jack Jefferson dont know what I'm up to," said Bobby, standing up. "Now, what he does know is how to talk a lotta old simplistic chicken hockey but—"

Jack doubled over with laughter and said, "Chicken hockey! That's pretty good. I havent heard that one since I left home in Mississippi."

"Angie, now, you know as well as I do Jack Jefferson aint never left home—be down there in Oakland at the Housewives Market every Saturday mornin when the trucks pull in lined up with all the other colored folk and Okies and Arkies waitin to buy greens, cornmeal, salt pork, chitlins, spareribs, grits, lard and all the resta that high cholesterol so-call soulfood kill your fat hardened arteries *dead!* White folks round here eatin wheat germ and yogurt and raw seaweed and shit, tryna get away from all that grease—and here niggers is lettin their old nappy hair grow out and tyin it up in pigtails, talkin bout soulfood, soulfood! Dont tell me nothin about our people!"

"Quit jivin, nigger, and move! I aint got all day!"

"Time out, Jack Jefferson, I gotta go upstairs and use the john. Angelina, keep your eye on this sucker while I'm gone. I got the board memorized but you just watch him, hear?"

"You goin upstairs you better get the key from Giovanni first."

"You mean theyre back into lockin up the toilets again?"

"With all these junkies and hypes around here, it's a wonder they dont just up and seal em off for good."

Buffalo Bill, who'd never see fifty again in this lifetime, got up with his magazines and limped past their table. He and Jack exchanged nods on his way out.

"That guy once told me he was a genius. He writes, makes films, paints, is an expert on opera, and even designs jewelry in his spare time."

"Have you ever seen any of his work?"

"Never seen a goddam thing. When he told me he was a genius, I just looked at him and said, 'Well, if you say so, Myron.' "

Angelina and Jack Jefferson had gone out together a few times. She loved him in a sisterly, friendly way, the same kind of affection she also reserved for Bobby. He was the kind of guy women felt easy being around as long as there was no pressure or threat of romance. One divorce had been enough for him. They visited one another two or three times a year and talked about their unscheduled lives over wine or smoke or over dinner in some simple restaurant such as La Fiesta up the street. Their relationship had always been open and honest.

"Have you seen Larry?" he asked in a different voice.

"No, you know I havent. I dont ever expect to again."

"Well, I have."

Her heart jumped but not as suddenly as it might have a few months ago. "Where?"

"Over in the City, Ghirardelli Square, comin outta Señor Pico's."

"How'd he look?"

"He looked funny—kinda sheepish, guilty, you know, or maybe I was just projectin my own idea of how he was supposed to be feelin. He was with a girl I know."

Angelina put everything she had into feigning indifference and wondered how Jack was receiving her act. "O? Do I know her?"

"Dont think so. Her name used to be Iola Fredrickson but now she runnin round callin herself Iola M'Bulu. She's a dancer. Anyway, she got a little money from the Neighborhood Arts

Program to get a dance workshop goin out in Hunter's Point."

"How do you know her?"

"She used to teach modern dance over at the Y and my ex-wife use to take from her. She was an OK girl then, good-lookin, intelligent, but now she done got liberated and all that rhetoric and goes around with a fancy cornrow in a native gown, says she's gonna get her nose pierced and wear a bob of some kind in it. Larry wasnt hip to me watchin but I saw him kinda flinch when she said that. Theyre both into a heavy African trip. In fact, theyre supposed to go to Kenya this summer."

"Is he working or are they both living off her grant?" It felt strange to feel the old bitterness welling up inside her again. She'd been so convinced that it had all been drained away.

"Now, I didnt ask em all that. I just wanted you to know I saw him. He's lost a little weight and looked preoccupied. I imagine that broad is gettin on his nerves. She sure got on mine with all that how-much-she-hate-white-people shit, and how black people, or, African-Americans, she calls em, oughtta get themselves unbrainwashed and come on back home to Africa. Talk about hateful! That bitch hate *everybody* from what I could tell the few minutes we talked—hates white women and black men more than anybody else though. My ex-old-lady was Irish, you know. She dont seem to hate the white man all that much but I believe she'd just as soon throw a sheet over her head and string a black man up and castrate him in a minute! Brrrr . . . she gave me the shivers."

"If theyre supposed to be so African and *with* the people and all that, then what in the hell were they doing in Ghirardelli Square eating at a place like Señor Pico's?"

"I guess they figured Mexican food was Third World or somethin. Angie, I dont know. My head hurts when I get to thinkin about these nig . . . I mean, African-Americans and see how fucked up and evil they can be."

"Well—" She couldnt think of any graceful way to ask it, so

she stuttered right out with it. "Well, did he act as if . . . I mean, did he make any mention of—"

"No, he didn't ask about you but I think he wanted to. He told me to say hello to everybody in Berkeley and that he'd be getting over here one of these days."

"O he did, did he? The nigger can just walk out on somebody like that with no explanation after two years and I couldnt even begin to add up how much money he cost me, not that I cared about it, and be just that cold-blooded about it, hunh? Jack, that is one sorry so-called Negro. If you run into him again, you can tell both him and his dancing African queen to kiss my spiteful dogged-around you-know-what!"

"I knew I shouldna told you but I had to. You understand, dont you?"

"I understand you, Jack, I really do. I'm glad to hear Larry's doing all right but I sure wish he'd get the fuck outta California and far away from me and stop messing with my life." Her tiny voice was quivering.

"But he isnt messin with your life anymore, is he? Angie, there probably isnt any man in the world that knows as much about this man and woman thing as I do—and I'll tell you, you make yourself suffer. Cant no other one person cause you to suffer if you make up your mind you dont want em too. People run some deep games on one another. Like, take that bitch Iola Lee Fredrickson—M'Bulu my ass!—she use to wouldnt go out with nothin *but* white dudes. There was nothin a ninion could do for her. Now here she come talkin all that sick black shit. So tell me, what kinda game is she runnin and who the hell is she supposed to be runnin it on? Aint runnin it on me cause I can see her shit is raggedy from in front. So who is she runnin it on?"

"Well, Larry must be goin for it."

"Larry just some nice light-skin dude—forgive me, Angie— that's goin along with the program. The bitch aint runnin that game on nobody but her own self and that's what a lotta these niggers round here hollerin and screamin and shit are up to. Iola dont come from no ghetto. She come from a nice respectable middle-class home like most of these white boys and a lotta these niggers round here on the scene do. Now what's she feelin so guilty about?"

Bobby Lane came back, overhead lights reflecting off his closely shaved head. He sat right down without saying a word and, as stone-faced as a fighter pilot, proceeded to stare at the chessboard. He lifted his king and pushed it forward through the air several squares before slamming it down triumphantly—blam!

"Now . . . Nowwwwww! Let's see you extricate your smug, arrogant tight-ass self outta this situation, Jack Jefferson! And dont say shit!"

Bobby flung his open hand out and Angelina slapped it and waved them both good-bye.

"Dont forget about that macramé," Bobby called behind her.

"I wont," she said, pleased to be able to tell the truth.

Out on the corner the Hare Krishna people were doing their thing, prancing and dancing to flutes and drums and the odor of strong incense.

A Negro with his head completely shaved—much more closely than Bobby's—except for a little bun in the middle toward the back, rushed up to her, his saffron costume rippling in the wind. He held up a copy of *Back to Godhead*, a lighted stick of incense and a collection cup.

For a moment, she stood frozen, even frightened by the spectacle. Who were these people anyway and what would they make of them in Calcutta?

The boy, whom she kept reclothing in her mind in varying styles of trousers, shirts and jackets, stared unblinkingly at her as he smiled and pushed the cup forward.

"Hey, I remember you," she said. "Sather Gate. Hubert. You used to be there all the time."

"I beg your pardon, my sister."

251

She wouldve sworn she remembered this same young man hanging around and heckling Hubert the Evangelist on campus all the time.

Finally she snapped back into her business-like self, dropped a quarter into the cup and biked off with the magazine and lighted incense, vaguely confused but not worried in the least.

WALLED IN
BY NIGHT

The landscape feels familiar but the time's all wrong. In a refreshing stirring of wind and light she sits relaxed in her long sleeveless dress, sky-blue, like the one she'd almost bought on the Avenue.

The moon's still up but the sun is rising and she doesnt want to miss a single moment. She yawns and stretches. Trees in the distance yawn back at her greenly, shaking their limbs, rattling their leaves. Each blade of grass is in touch with her and, like an ocean in repose, she can feel both the pull of the moon and unseen stars beyond.

Becoming aware of the place where she sits, which is smooth and cool, which is stone, she looks all around her and sees that it's a deserted amphitheater she's wandered into. Is it the Greek Theater on the U.C. campus? Seems larger somehow, more circular, stonier, the tiers of seats scrubbed spotless and descending more gracefully to the central arena: a bright open space, a perfectly trimmed circle of grass.

She looks down and watches the faraway woman, herself, who runs barefoot thru the dewy blades, who pulls off her garment and rolls around naked. She can feel the cool morning

253

wetness next to her body, while she laughs at herself from the stands.

Now it's twilight. Sun has receded but the night is still warm and the moon beams down like a spotlight.

One by one people are filing out into the arena. She doesnt recognize any of them. No, she knows them all but not by face and not by body. Theyre all wearing masks and their forms have been costumed. But she can feel who they are, every one of them.

She sees no musicians yet music surrounds her—a giddying mix of Roland Kirk, West African high-life, Bessie Smith blues, the Holiness Church choir; Japanese koto music, Django Reinhardt gypsy/jazz guitar crammed with intermittent surprises; a solo piano ripe with ragtime, drumbeats invoking the Spirit, the precious rattling of wind chimes to accompany tree leaves in their trembling.

She is drunk on this music, drunk on this feeling. Cradled in her arms is her two-year-old son who has fallen asleep, a smile on his tender face. She can read his thoughts. He is thinking: *This is the moment you must learn from and carry with you and tend as you would a delicate garden, for it blooms and blooms as you too will bloom in the thrill of its ceaseless becoming, Mama.*

She wants to dance. The chorus of friendly strangers gathered below can sense this and dance and sing for her. Still she cant resist slipping out of her body and joining them in the warm moonlight.

Now she's a spectator again. Someone has taken her hand in his, a man. She cant see him but he's there next to her—just as this entire amphitheater, walled in by night, is crowded with people she cannot see but whose presence and spirit she can feel brushing against her as soothingly as breezes and musical sound.

This is why I chose to be born through you, Mama. . . .

The colorful chorus has arranged itself in a semicircle. In brisk succession, each member steps into the center and, to music, delivers a little message which is read from a colored strip of paper plucked from a large crystalline vase formed in the shape of a fortune cookie.

Sra. Ruiz (*dressed as a dove in white mask and feathery costume*): I come in the spirit of la paz, Angelina, and to remind you that this peace will be found within when you are finding yourself able to laugh at yourself, ¿verdad? O yes, and why have you not yet contacted my son Mario as you have promised me that you would?

Uncle Roscoe (*got up in old clothes and a long-snouted mask as Br'er Fox*): Life aint nothin but livin, Angie, and the grave really isnt its goal. And for as long as *you* live dont you forget that!

Aunt Jujie (*in a brilliant red 1890s dress, complete with hat and parasol*): It says in the first book of Corinthians—chapter two, verse ten—"Treat the word of light not lightly." Now, I want you to think about that some and keep in mind that God helps them that help themselves, hear?

Louetta (*dressed as a pregnant tigress in maternity shift*): I'm ready to sit down now, Angie, and listen to the grass grow but it's somethin inside me wont let me be. Cant you feel somethin movin inside you too?

Ernest (*dressed in a day-glo policeman's uniform and the mask of a lion with bloodshot eyes*): I'm just tryna get over while the gettin over's good and look after things like my daddy said I should.

Madame Lola (*in peacock feathers and painted ancient Egyptian-like mask*): In dealing with weeds, firm resolution is necessary. Walking in the middle remains free of blame. But even sitting on a fence requires that you use common sense— otherwise, your stall could mean a fall . . . that's all.

Dad (*a dolphin with the head of a dark-faced, white-maned horse*): I stay outta style but not outta tune. You must go with God, go with the wind, but take your own time, your own time, your own time, sweetheart.

CURTIS (*dressed as a long-distance runner; his bare head crowned with laurel leaf*): The world is one long endless poem and my words only whisper to remind you again of true love which has never been tender.

THIEF (*in a bright gold robe and a Yaqui-like deer mask designed with a radiant smile*): Your teeth may glow and your eyes might shine, but, remember, I too am of the divine.

WATUSI (*a witch doctor/shaman with the head of a boar*): It aint whatcha do, it's the way how you do it—Chick Webb said that. It aint whatcha know, it's the way how you show it—I said that.

MARGO (*a butterfly with a huge orange head*): Youre lonely and I'm lonely. Cant we talk with one another? Cant we talk like in the old days, cant we talk like, cant we . . .

The air's collapsing around her. She wants to hold her baby close to her and kiss it but, looking down, she finds it's vanished. Her eyes scan the chorus to find Larry. She thinks she sees him in a magnificent African buuba and top hat, hands joined with Iola M'Bulu and Tolby Crawford but, no, it's her own mother who's made of pure ectoplasm, waving at her, cradling her, smiling and moving from side to side to the slow beat of drums, to a voice-flavored flute, Roland, it's Mexico, it's now, it's the whirr and rustle of wind chimes tinkling as the light dissolves, as she holds on, not wanting to leave, never wanting to leave, in a wash of white light, red, the greening of feeling, wind chimes growing louder, deafening her in a new dark place—in another skin—the other now. . . .

She reached for the ringing phone in darkness and knocked it from its cradle. Sitting up in bed, she snapped on the lamp. It was three in the morning. Her blood seemed to spin. It was like that night in Mexico City. She was still stumbling rudely out of a dream. Her head was lost. Somewhere out in the yard a solitary bird was singing in the rain, and a toy voice that drifted toward her from nowhere in space—

256

"Hello, hello. Angie, are you all right? Hello . . ."

"Hello," she yawned into the receiver. "Who is this?"

"Angie, it's me, Margo. Are you OK?"

"I guess you woke me up. I was halfway hoping you'd be somebody else. I was deep in a dream—I mean really deep off into it."

"Angie, I know it's late to be callin but I thought you might still be up."

"What's the matter?"

"Nothin. O—I know you must think Ive really flipped out this time but I need somebody to talk to."

"You mean, like, right now?"

"Right now. I cant sleep. I got some pills but I dont wanna drop any. I'd just like to come by for a little while and sit and talk. You wont even have to say all that much. I'll probably end up doin all the talkin. Please, Angie, you know I'm not in the habit of wakin people up in the middle of the night."

What could she say? She'd certainly used Margo often enough for a shrink.

"Come on over. I'll fix coffee—wait, I'm not even sure I have any."

"Dont worry about that. I'll bring somethin. I just have to be with somebody for a while."

Angelina's head, still vibrating from the dream, was now a painful tangle of somewhere and nowhere, maybe and never, and unconnectable points in-between.

Had she been dreaming or at sea in a trance? She'd never experienced anything quite so vivid. Was her astral body trying to tell her something?

THE OTHER NOW

"Ive had it, Angie," Margo was saying, "and I dont really know what to do."

They were sitting around the brightly lit kitchen, facing one another across a table. Margo had brought with her the remains of a half gallon of so-so burgundy and was mixing it with Fresca and lemon slices. She was also lighting up one Benson & Hedges off another and the smoke was giving Angelina a headache.

"I mean, Ive been around this goddam antsy little town off and on goin on a decade now and I dont think I can stand it anymore, all this grand paranoia. These people just dont wanna make it, that's all. They bitch about everything, put everything down, look down their noses at just about anything you wanna name. Theyre arrogant, petty, jealous, cheap, contemptuous, smug, bored and flat out fascist with a lotta their shit. I got to thinkin a few months ago, what the hell am I doin here? I believe in people doin their thing all right but the kinda thing theyre doin around here just isnt relatin to me lately. Am I makin sense or are you just sittin there lettin me prattle on about stuff youve already heard?"

Angelina had been thinking along similar lines for God

knows how long but found it hard to get worked up over it in a tiny suffocating kitchen at four in the morning. She got up to crack the back door and open windows.

"What you have is the Old Berkeley Fear Blues, Margo. I come down with em at least once or twice a week."

"Never heard em called that before, but you *do* know what I'm talkin about?"

"Sure. I was almost ready to stay down in Mexico with that guy I told you I met down there. That's how strongly I feel about it sometimes. I stay on the verge of letting it all go, giving it all up and just taking a bus or hitching a ride to the first destination that pops into my head."

"But I been doin that, honey. I take off and go to London or Paris and fuck around and if that doesnt get it I can backtrack to Mexico or go to Maui, whatever the hell my body says do. That's one thing about havin a little bread comin in and tucked away, you can buy a little free time and privacy. If I had to go back to workin a regular gig now, I dont know what I'd do, probably start shootin smack or somethin. I dont want nobody tellin me what to do anymore by danglin a paycheck over my head. A job just doesnt say that much to me. I suppose I could always marry again—somebody interestin, a fancy showbiz lawyer or another artist or somebody, but Ive had it with that marriage shit too—not in this sick, sexist, racist society! You sure you dont want a hit off this wine, Angie? I can mix you a really weak drink."

Angelina's nostrils were filled with smoke and the smell· of burgundy, a combination that wouldve made perfect olfactory sense a few months ago. She mightve even found it inviting. Now it annoyed her; made her feel unhealthy and wish that Margo would ease up.

"So what's really on your mind?" she asked. "Youve been here an hour giving me all the old rhetoric and generalizations we've run through before and you still havent told me what's really bugging you. Something mustve happened since I saw you last. What?"

Margo, who'd been slouching in her chair all this time, cigarette cupped in her hand, sat up straight and blinked. This was when Angelina noticed that she'd had her hair cut and restyled and that she was wearing mascara, eyeshadow and lipstick.

"When did you have your hair cut?"

"So you finally noticed, hunh? Coupla days ago." She turned her head. "How do you like it?"

"I think it's very becoming. Youve got beautiful red hair but now I can see how long it was getting. Makes you look younger styled this way and I think the bangs are flattering too. How come youre wearing makeup?"

Margo sighed, burped, and excused herself. "I was out with Leonard. You dont know him. He's a lawyer, frienda the lawyer who handled Seishi's settlement for me. OK dude, youngish, fortyish. He's very hip in that making it in San Francisco kinda way, you know. I like him, I guess, but he can be a real A-hole too. He's sexy and—well, Angie, he pulls down an awful lotta bread. Manages a coupla local bands on the side, jazz/rock, that I know're gonna make a fortune. To hear him tell it, everything he's touched has turned out to be the original pot of gold. And you wanna know what else? He's funny. I mean, funny ha-ha. He makes me laugh. It's been a long time since Ive gone out with anybody that's good-lookin, prosperous and that's got a little money to boot. You knew what Seishi was like—handsome, polite, loaded, reasonably adventurous because he wanted to be a big-time underground filmmaker of some kind but basically he put you to sleep, right? The sonofabitch was a high-class dullard. Booker was pretty as they come and talked all that fast, flashy spook bullshit and I use to actually have wet dreams behind just thinkin about the bastard, but he was silly and vain—like most people, I'd say—and didnt have a pot to piss in until I set his ass up. He wanted to get into TV or movies so bad it was a real downer bein around him. Now he's knockin down a coupla thou a week on TV down in L.A., struttin around in that new cop series. The joker sends me a few hundred every once in a while because he's got a conscience but in the write-ups Ive seen on him he's all-black now, got him some simple-minded chocolate mama starlet type and aint *never* had nothin to do with white folks—except take their money, cha cha cha! You didn't know Greg's father, my first old man, a KPFA liberal from way back—the kinda dude who couldnt relate to a black man unless he was a pimp, a thief, a hustler, a junkie or a convict. Had a Ph.D. in Comparative Lit, taught at big-time universities all over the country, and never once had anything good to say about his black colleagues except somethin he'd mumble, usually when he was drunk, about them bein part of what he called 'the emerging arts and intelligentsia.' Shook him up when he found out I was goin around with Booker. He use to tell me that when it came to black people he'd take Africans first and West Indians second—they were closer to the real thing—and after that came Afro-American women. He could relate to the plight of the strugglin black woman. All the black men who werent involved with what he called the movement—you know, hollerin and screamin and callin him a mother-fuckin honkie—he just didnt have time for. They were all toms. It blew my mind. Here I am comin from the South to begin with, and here this Northern so-called radical intellectual was tellin me essentially, if youll excuse my language, that a nigger wasnt shit. That's just the kinda stuff I was tryna get away from. You know, I was one of them typical Southron girls, brought up protected and middle class, a virgin until I was twenty, out to prove that not everybody from the South was the devil. I was determined to personally set the record straight for everybody even though I never did really believe people from up north—black or white—ever had what we call down there good sense. How fucked up can you get, hunh?"

Angelina felt sad. All this time she'd been knowing Margo, all this time theyd been hanging out together, leaning on one another, and they still had to go through these changes. The

American Racial Problem. Wouldnt they be better off talking about men or menstrual periods and letting old blood feuds run their course?

She stared into Margo's sleepy face—the big glassy eyes, wet and green, the color of grass in the dream she'd just left, pug nose, pouty lips, freckles, wrinkles that were beginning to form at the edges of those eyes, firm chin, long neck—and saw that she too had a dream. But what could it be? To be loved, to be happy (that pitiful man's dream on the bus at Christmas), to be free, free of herself, free of being Margo? If she had Margo's income, good looks—well, she really had no complaints in that department—and white skin, would she be lounging around, bitching and getting juiced? You never could tell. That was the problem, she just had no way of knowing.

"Anyway, Leonard—and I want you to meet him soon— Leonard and Ive been seein one another, no big thing, you know, and it's been gettin kinda good to me, if you know what I mean. So we go to this big dinner party tonight up in the Hills, acquaintances of his, pretty well-off people. Somebody breaks out some hash, some real good dope, and the next thing I know Leonard's disappeared. Where do I find him? He's upstairs in one of the bedrooms mushin it up with the hostess, this lawyer friend's wife. I hear his voice and peep in on em and he's lyin across the bed in the dark and she's down on her knees with her bleached blonde head workin up and down between his legs. Now, how do you think I felt when I caught that action?"

Angelina didnt want to comment, didnt want to react, but the picture Margo's words had sketched in her head brought a nervous little smile to her lips which she tried to counter with an understanding frown.

"Did you say anything?" she asked politely.

"Hell no! I got another couple to drive me straight home. I never wanted to see the bastard again. So I get home—the kids're spendin the night around the corner at some friends' house—and get pissed with myself for gettin so upset. What the hell did I expect? I mean, I'm supposed to be liberated and all that shit and Ive been in some pretty far-out scenes myself but that was a long time ago. I start drinkin vodka and switch to wine and pretty soon the bastard comes by, wants to know how come I left like that without tellin *him*. I go into a rage and throw wine all in the motherfucker's face and slap him a couple times and then break down cryin. He gets me to calm down and asks me what's the matter? I say, 'What the fuck do you think's the matter, asshole? You cut out from downstairs and I gotta look all over for you and there you are layin back grinnin in the dark while some bitch is goin down on you.' He said he thought we might be interested in swingin with them a little, swappin or somethin. I told him I might get stoned a lot and do a lotta freaky shit but I didnt play that no more because it only leads to a lotta complicated hard feelins and I'm tryna simplify my life. O, Angie, we went around and around with that kinda talk and he cut out feelin guilty about an hour before I called you, and now here I am still upset. Can you blame me?"

"No, how could I blame you, Margo? But I will say one thing, and I hope you wont get mad. I really cant say my life isnt complicated, because it *is* in its own quiet way, but since I stopped getting zonked and wiped out all the time Ive noticed I dont feel as pressured as I used to. I did manage to simplify things a little bit by cooling down and doing some thinking."

"Meditation. I see that happening to people who get off into meditatin. It must be all it's cracked up to be, hunh?"

"I can only speak for myself. There're mornings when I walk out that door feeling like I'm about to blow away. I feel just that high and light. There're other mornings when I just feel good, the way you do after youve had that first hot sip of tea and it flows into your stomach and warms you all over. I still have hassles to work out. I still get headaches. I still get fed up with everybody and everything and wanna go hide someplace. I'm just saying that the change Ive been going through makes things a lot more interesting probably because I myself feel more in control and on top of stuff."

"Ive been meanin to cut this shit out," Margo said softly, exhaling smoke to make room for a quick swallow of burgundy, "but I know I'd go nuts in no time. I like to drink. I like to get outta my head once in a while. Gives me another perspective."

"I do too. You know that. It's just that I got tired of running into myself coming around corners, always headed in the wrong direction. You wanna know how the suicide note I wrote started out? I can quote it to you. I know it by heart. It said, 'Well, what is there to say if you aren't really sure you mean it? I know emptiness and I know nothing. Are the two really so compatible as the mystics would have it?' You know, here I am about to fling myself off the Golden Gate and I'm into all that romantic bullshit about 'to be or not to be that is the question.' I cant even figure where my head mustve been at in those days."

"It wasnt all that long ago."

"Maybe not, but even if youre gonna do yourself in I think it oughtta be for some worthy cause, not just on some kinda self-pitying dare. I didnt even know what the hell to write, for crying out loud, and when I look back at those scribbles now, I wanna break out laughing because it sounds corny to me. That's how out of touch I was with my real self. On the other hand, now I'm into territory that frightens me sometimes. Like, just when you called I was having a dream—or a dream was having me, I still dont know which—that was the farthest out thing Ive ever been through. It was as real as we are sitting here now."

"What was it about?"

"I dont know. Just about everybody I know was in it, you included. Everybody was dressed in some kinda symbolic outfit—like, you were a butterfly and your whole head was orange and you kept talking about loneliness and getting together to talk and—" She paused, distracted by the wail of a distant siren.

"O my God, Angie! Stop it, youre makin me nervous. You mean I was actually sayin shit like that? That's just how I was feelin when I rang you up—lonely, stranded really . . . That really blows my mind. That's how come I stay away from heavy spooky stuff. My nervous system just cant take it. My mama use to fool around with it. She was into Christian Science. Those people must know somethin because you go to one of their meetins and theyre all pretty well-off. Mama use to say there were spiritual ways to attract material needs and attain worldly goals. I didnt wanna believe her but facts was facts. She use to go to a lotta those séances too after Dad died and would come back tellin us how she'd contacted him through some medium. I laughed at her but it still made me feel uneasy like that dream you just now told me about. One thing I'll never forget though. One night we're sittin around at dinner—Mama, my oldest brother Judd and my little sister Peggy—and Mama starts talkin in this really freaky voice, like an old lady or somebody. She says, 'Yall all turned out to be every drop as beautiful as I thought yall would.' All us kids looked at her real hard. My hair just about stood up on end. She was sittin there with this big grin on her face and her eyes, her eyes . . . oooo, I cant even tell you what her eyes was like—all half-shut and glazey and starin straight ahead. Judd, who wasnt scareda nothin, not even rattlesnakes or Old Man Lyle's hainted house, he commenced to turn dead white in the face. I was scared too but I still had enough nerve to pass my hand in fronta Mama's face and I swear, Angie, her eyes didnt move atall. We knew somethin was wrong. Then just like that, she snapped outta it."

"Did she remember what'd happened?"

"Naw, but I read up on it years later at college in a book about—what do they call it?—psychic somethin or other, and the man was sayin somethin about people that's dead can get in temporary possession of the minds and bodies of people that's still livin and say and do stuff through them. I wrote Mama about it and she said it was probably her own grandmama who'd lived long enough to see us born but died around the time Peggy was two. We're all just a year or so apart."

The cry of the siren wasnt so distant now. It seemed to be only houses away. Both women fell silent. Margo bolted down the last of her wine cooler and lit another cigarette.

The siren wound down at what sounded like Angelina's front door.

Margo, in her Mexican peasant dress, got up and pulled on Angelina's hand. "Angie, what on earth can that be? I'm scared. This is like it use to be back home when somethin sudden'd happen."

Angelina could see the gooseflesh of Margo's arms and felt uncomfortable herself. "We'd better go see what it is," she said. "Youre clean, arent you?"

"Got a coupla reds and a yellow or two but I can flush em down the toilet."

They rushed to the front window and pulled back the bamboo curtains but saw nothing but the dim reflection of red light against lemon-tree leaves in the direction of Montego's frontyard.

"Let's go around front and have a look," said Angelina. "Something tells me it isnt the cops."

They got there in time to see the parked ambulance with its motor running. Angelina's eyes filled instantly with tears as she watched two white-coated attendants carry a stretcher down the Harpers' front steps. The form on the stretcher was completely covered as they smoothly transported and slid it into the rear of the vehicle.

Scoot Harper was standing on the sidewalk with his arms tightly wrapped around Tanya who was in convulsions, sobbing and muttering—"O Lord God, forgive us please forgive us, Lord she didnt stand a chance, she didnt stand a chance, Lord have mercy . . . Lord *please* have mercy. . . ."

Angelina looked around for Etta Jean in the sad streetlight but didnt see her anywhere.

People in neighboring houses emerged from bedrooms and mattresses and stood around on porches, front steps, lawns and the sidewalk in robes, pajamas, blankets, street clothes, paying drowsy witness to the spectacle.

All the while a very thin rain dripped from a lightless sky.

266

Margo, whose makeup had begun to run, giving her the appearance of a dirty-faced child, took hold of Angelina's arm. "What the hell's goin on?" she whispered.

"Mama Lou is dead."

"Dead? You mean somebody's died?"

"Mama Lou is free."

"O my God. . . ."

Angelina wanted to cross over and say something to let Scoot and Tanya know how much she sympathized with them, but knew it would all come out sounding trite and insincere.

Anyway, this wasnt the time.

It wasnt Mama Lou she felt sorry for; it was the living, the half-dead, the ones she'd outlived and left suddenly behind.

Scoot managed an acknowledging nod in Angelina's direction before the unreal ambulance slipped very quickly and quietly away, before she and Margo walked reluctantly back to her cottage in the slow, slow, everlasting rain.

They sat saying nothing on pillows in the front room. Margo was well into her third straight cigarette before she began to doze and burn her fingers.

"If you wanna sleep here," Angelina said, shaking her, "Ive got a really good sleepingbag that the burglars overlooked."

"Nah, I can drive home. I'd like to wake up in my own place anyway." But she showed no sign of wanting to leave and made no effort to move. "Funny how when somethin like that goes down it makes all your little petty hassles seem like kid stuff, doesnt it?"

"She was almost ninety," Angelina said, nodding, and went into the kitchen. She poured herself a coffee mug of wine, drank it all down in one thoughtful gulp and poured out another without pausing.

She woke up in her clothes, her head fuzzy, the room filling slowly with dawn light. The nauseating smell of stale smoke was everywhere.

Margo, also clothed, was sprawled out upright, back to the wall, snoring away with her mouth wide open.

Her head was resting in Margo's lap.

They both had blankets around them.

TIME ON FIRE

One sunny afternoon at the end of the rainy season, she came home shot from a solid week of teaching. She still wasnt so sure that Tolby Crawford had done her any favor by not throwing a wrench in the works. Maybe this was his true revenge. She was so tired of uppity, lazy students and papers and colleagues that her messy old job at the lab in Richmond seemed, by comparison, like a breeze. If only it paid the kind of money she made at the alternative school, she'd sign back up in a minute and give her poor brain a rest.

She wasnt meditating as zealously as before and felt guiltier than ever about it, all the more since she'd given in to Darryl's Ann Arbor advice and joined a regular group—The Prana Society—to keep in touch with others who were embarked upon what was respectfully termed the Path.

At a sanctuary up on Grizzly Peak Boulevard in the Berkeley Hills, donated by a wealthy constituent, they convened every day of the week at 6:00 A.M. sharp. Gradually she'd begun to hit and miss, and now was down to a 50 percent attendance average. It was so nice to sleep in mornings, getting up just in time to make nine o'clock class. Besides, she was going out with Curtis every now and again and staying up well beyond bedtime. The bad old days and restless nights grew further and further away.

She came home, dying for a Friday shower and nap, saw the shiny black Bentley parked in front of Montego's, did an innocent double take, and continued, still very much into her graceful young teacher walk, on back toward her renovated cottage.

There on her doorstep sat Sylvester Poindexter Buchanan, blocking the entrance with a grin.

Elegance was hardly the word for it. How could she describe a man of indeterminate age who sat so affirmatively in the flip-flop world in a crisp new-looking pinstripe suit with a white boutonniere blossoming from the lapel, clutching a mixed bouquet of roses?

His hair was trimmed and he'd lost some weight, but his hugeness still overwhelmed her.

She wasnt sure what to do, how to approach him, what to say or not say. The smile on her face was pure and spontaneous as she dropped her valise and ran toward him. He hugged her so hard she thought he'd damage her rib cage.

"Baby, I told you I'd be gettin back to you, didn't I?"

"Yes, you did, you big nut, but that was about fifty years ago. What took you so long?"

"I got sidetracked. I'll tell you all about it. Here—let's carry these inside and put em in some water. The man that sold em to me didnt gimme no warranty."

"O, Watusi, theyre beautiful, beautiful!"

"I slipped my man here one," Watusi said, pointing toward Montego's midget son who was swinging in the backyard, a red rose in one hand. "Hope you dont mind. I was about to cut out and come back later but he kept tellin me you'd be gettin home any minute now."

While Watusi gathered up her valise and a stack of brightly

wrapped packages he'd brought, she unlocked the door she'd just painted bright blue and together they crossed the threshold.

He poured a fresh round of champagne—his third, her fourth—the one drink she couldnt turn down. She had changed into slacks and a comfortable blouse. He sat on the new used sofa with jacket off and sleeves rolled back. She thought he looked good in his yellow tie and shirt set off against the white walls she and Margo had spent a whole week re-doing.

"So that's how it went down, pretty. That's how come you aint heard from me. Them people had me comin and goin—slippin and slidin, peepin and hidin, like Little Richard say. I still dont know where Baxter is. He jumped bail in Florida and disappeared. My bet is he split to Switzerland where he keep all his bread stashed. I got a little taste tucked away there myself. But I dont think he stuck around over there. Baxter too slick, slicker than slick! We been workin together too long for me not to know that."

"Wait a minute, just a second!" she cried. "Youre coming at me too fast with all these details. *¡Momentito! Más despacio por favor*—just slow down please! Now, was this the first time you ever got into anything shady?"

"Damn straight. I may act crazy but I aint no fool. We were runnin a legitimate import-export operation—native arts, crafts, rugs, clothin, a few pre-Columbian artifacts on the side, jade, shit like that. I had a whole lotta chances to run grass and smack and wetbacks and all the rest of it but I wasnt about to get my ass thrown into one of them Mexican jails where they stick you so far back up in there until they have to pipe in tortillas and beans. That almost happen to a clown I use to hang out with when I first moved there—Chino, a slick little spook outta Spanish Harlem got in a traffic accident and come givin the police sass insteada cash. Only way he got out is I called the Russian Embassy—this was a long time ago—and told em one of my downtrodden black countrymen was havin a little legal trouble and the racist U.S. Embassy wouldnt help him out.

They got him out the next day. Times sure have changed, aint they? Now the Russians'd probly say, 'Let the motherfucker rot!' But he had to get his hat after that."

"But youve been making a living strictly on the up and up?" Angelina asked patiently, accustomed by now to Watusi's tendency to stray from the point.

"Yep, that's right, I swear. O maybe every once in a while we'd take a little commission off somethin we knew was a little sticky but Baxter got a degree in international law or somethin just as good from Columbia University. He knew where to draw the line and we was doin OK, so why blow it? But this diamond deal—O Lord, I tell you, them diamonds'll make a Catholic nun start gettin ideas! You read about them priests that's been caught smugglin heroin? This diamond deal was too good to pass up. You see that James Bond flick, *Diamonds Are Forever*? Well, that says it all."

"So, you were telling about how this Lebanese dude approached you in San Felipe. . . ."

"That's right, I was down there to look into a line of jewelry he was payin the natives to turn out. We got to drinkin mescal one night and I'm loose enough to start free associatin. So I'm lookin at that worm they put at the bottom of the mescal bottle—you know you spose to drink it all down till you get to the worm and that's considered the big prize. Aint no way in the world they gon get me to fool with that nasty worm, baby! But I'm lookin at this worm and talkin out my head and I say to this Arab, Dahoud was his name, that somebody could probly hide enough diamonds in that worm to get in a year's wortha leisure."

"Clever idea," she commented thoughtlessly.

"He thought so too but said it was really a small-time idea. But he had a friend just back from Sierra Leone with some semipolished cuts he wanted to get up to New York. I got to thinkin, well, Watusi, you been knockin yourself out for a long time now. This might be a way to get out the rat race and slow down for a few years, get your own business started. Already I was figurin I could maybe come back into the States at Nogales where they let you bring in up to a gallon's wortha booze for openers. I could declare the rest and pay duty on it. I know some people in Oaxaca in the mescal business I could get to re-seal bottles for me. But it still sounded small-time and I never liked puttin my neck out for peanuts."

She got up and put a Stevie Wonder album on the new stereo turntable. She only owned half a dozen LPs now and this was one of them.

"So," Watusi resumed, beating out a few licks bongo style on his thigh, "I get back to Jocotepec and damn if Baxter aint already heard about the diamonds—dont ask me how, the little joker know everything—and we both thinkin the same way. We decided to split the shipment but for the time bein to stay cool. One day I'm in this *refacciones* place gettin a mechanic to re-tool some parts for my old beat-up Karmann Ghia—bought it night after you left—when I flash on another idea. Tell you, Angie, I'm a genius when I feel like it! So I run it to Baxter and he say, 'Yeah, yeah, that's it, man! Lemme do some research and we'll get to work!' Now, that's how we got mixed up in the shit and you know the rest."

"No, I dont know the rest. You keep telling it backwards and inside-out. What was the brilliant idea you hit on?"

"I dont know if I oughtta be tellin you this. That's how Baxter got busted, tellin our shit to this dumb young Costa Rican broad he was runnin up to Mexico City to see cause her old man was rich and wanted to throw some bread into our company. He musta promised her one of them stones or somethin cause she damn sure knew about em and run straight to the pigs after she found out he was jivin a coupla other chicks on the side right there in the capital. O, I forgot to tell you, Baxter and her was supposed to get married but one of her thousand brothers saw him comin outta the Maria Isabel Hotel one night with Carmen, his other steady who'd worked with us on a jade deal. Lucky they didnt shoot him. Ive known it to happen. They dont play that foolin-around shit down there, not when you bout to marry into the family."

"So you hid the diamonds in your car in some kinda concealed compartment, right?"

273

"Naw, that's too crude and mickey mouse. We hid em in the bolts up under the cars."

"How'd you do that?"

"The only way you can. We drilled through the bolts, crammed em with diamonds, welded a thick strip of metal on top to cover the holes, got em lookin like theyd never been tampered with and went on bout our business."

"So how'd you get caught?"

"Do I look like I'm caught? Baxter the one fucked up and got me to backtrackin and duckin and dodgin and shit. He got all the way to New York in his old beat-up Mercedes, nothin fancy, delivered the shit and went to see his folks who're retired in Florida and from there was gonna fly back to Mexico. But while he was in Key West, the Mexican authorities, I guess you call em, had done sent out word to the people up here that he oughtta be picked up and investigated for smugglin. They had a tip. They tracked him down through gasoline credit cards, booked him, and let him out on twenty-five-thousand-dollars bail. That's when he flew the coop and aint been heard from since. I was just about to drive up and deliver my shit when Dahoud, who got a cousin that's some kinda special detective with the Mexico City police force, sent word to me that I was probly bein watched on accounta me and Baxter been in business together for so long. Now do you see?"

She nodded, bubbling, and sipped from her glass.

"So that got me to goin through them changes. Wasnt nothin to worry bout, really, cause our cover hadnt been blown yet. They didnt know our little trick and didnt have evidence the first. That's how come Baxter shoulda just been cool and sit pat till he got cleared. Now he got them people on his ass for real, done ruined the business and messed up a good thing we been workin hard to build. Me, I'm clean. I lay back and carry on business as usual, as polite as I can be to the Mexican agents, cooperative to the bone, telling em Baxter's a good man and surely there's been some mistake, señor. They audit our books and investigate our operation and everything's lovely, just lovely. I take care of everything just like I always knew I could—that's why I wanna start my own business—and slip a few hundred pesos to the right people here and there and *mierda!* pretty soon the heat's off. I make sure the pigs know I'm plannin a little trip north to see my father in Chicago. Get in my car, cross at San Ysidro where they do just what I expected em to do—hold me up for two whole days while they go over my machine with a fine-tooth comb and every detectional device known to man and dont come up with nothin, not even a grain of grass in my pockets. They apologize and put my car back together and I'm back on the road, take Sixty-Six all the way, make Chicago where I spend a wonderful week with my old man, takin him out and watchin 'Wide World of Sports' on television and shit . . . Climb back in the short, leisurely motor on up to New York, pay my respects to the genteel diamond trade—which, I must say, looks after its own—*swoop!* I'm home free. I got enough bread together now to really start messin up in style!"

"Are you going back to Mexico?"

"Eventually but I'd like to do a little travelin first—go around and visit my kids."

"Youre talking about taking a round-the-world tour," she laughed, surprised that she hadnt found his little picaresque account offensive. What was happening to her? Only weeks ago, she wouldve thrown him out of her house if she'd known he'd been involved with anything like this. The young purse-snatcher raced across her mind and she winced. Last week she'd taken off an entire afternoon from school to testify with Connie at a highly formalized Juvenile Authority hearing.

"Why didnt you call me like you said you would?" she asked.

"I didnt wanna make any calls to the States except on official business. I figured they might be tappin my phone and I didnt want you to get involved."

"But you couldve written. Hey, I didnt know you could write Spanish that well. That was a sweet card. I keep it in a drawer next to my bed."

"Did the check come in handy?"

"It saved my life, thanks. I'm still gonna pay you back all that money, honest. Youve been so good to me. I dont know what I wouldve done in Mexico if we hadnt run into each other."

"I like you very much," he said. "In fact . . . So you liked my little note, hunh? Took me almost a whole day to get that thing to read right. I was tryin my best to impress you. You shoulda seen me sittin up there in my little hotel room in Belize with my dictionary and grammar book sweatin it out. Even had a friend—well, the chick that worked the registration cage checked it over for mistakes before I mailed it. She told me it'd do, heh heh. Listen, are things all right with your old man still? I was thinkin about him while I was in Chicago."

"I'm flying back to see him again this summer when school's out if I can get on this charter flight I'm on the standby list for. I'm gonna try and get him to move out here."

"Good luck. I'm tryna get my old man and my stepmother to move outta that cold-hearted Chicago but they say everybody they know is there. I guess they just cant see the shit as clear as we can. You couldnt pay me to stay round them cities back there. That's the Old Country far as I'm concerned. Listen . . . Arent you gettin hungry?"

"Very."

"Wanna go for a ride in the Bentley?"

"You just had to be a nigger and buy the first fancy car you saw, didnt you?"

"Wrong. How many times I gotta tell you I only just *look* like a fool? Belongs to a frienda mine in San Francisco. He picked me up at the airport and lettin me drive it around for a coupla days while he's outta town. My little German doodad played out on me after that long haul. I sold it in Brooklyn."

"Did you see your daughter?"

"Anita? Yes, and I wanna go back and see her again, maybe take her to London with me for a visit. I was wonderin if you might like to go along too. I mean, me and her go on over and I send for you after we get settled."

"But Ive got a job, Watusi, and a whole new life right here."

"Think about it, but *please* cant we get somethin to eat?"

"Let's drive over and get some groceries and I'll fix us a meal right here."

"Are you up to it?"

"I'd love to but I'll warn you, I dont eat meat anymore."

He put on his coat, fixed his tie and said, "Baby, I can afford to be as cosmopolitan as the next dude now. You fix what you like and I'll try it."

After dinner and more champagne, she felt herself growing hazy and silly. She still felt so at ease around him that it pained her to remember his three ex-wives spread around the world with his children.

He took off his shoes, and unbuttoned his shirt to stretch out on the sofa with a yawn. "I never thought anybody could make eggplant and okra taste that good. You sure got to me, Angelina. My grandmama use to say, 'You can always get to a Negro through his stomach.' You wont mind if I spend the night here, will you?"

"I think so. By the way, okra was brought over from Africa."

"You got an old man now?" he sat up and asked, running his hand over his hair. "It never occurred to me—"

She picked up his clothing and handed it to him on her way to the closet in the bedroom.

"What's this supposed to mean?"

She shouldve felt awful but she didnt. She stood willing to pay whatever price this decision would eventually cost her. All that money he'd laid on her and all those pretty packages stacked in the corner, begging to be opened. Life was too long and all too short and everything happened at the wrong time.

They drove to a motel. Watusi bought even more champagne. The more she drank, the soberer she became until she found herself naked next to him in the dark, watching early morning movies on color TV.

They talked some more. He made some allusion to getting

277

married and settling down for good but was careful not to put it to her directly.

He was gentler than Curtis. She could make love with him for a hundred years and still feel refreshed—his touch was that tender, it couldnt be true love, according to the Riddler in her dream—but this one crazy night would have to do. Possibilities were beginning to trouble her again. Choices, decisions! That was all her life had been.

Her heart was pounding.

"Do you love me," he asked, "just a little teeny bit?"

She was on top of things now, fingers digging into his biceps and shoulders while she concentrated on stifling or at least softening a low, long moan.

Hours later, or so it seemed, she collapsed on top of him and lay there listening to the beat of both their hearts, tick-tick-tocking at different speeds.

"You never answered me," he breathed.

"Yes, I love you . . . I suppose."

He turned carefully onto his side, pulled the covers up over them and held her in his arms. "That's a funny answer. Either you do or you dont. I need to know. I made a special trip all the way out here to San Francisco to find out."

She waited for her secret heart to tell her what to say.

"That's the way I used to think," she said finally, "either you do or you dont. But it isnt always that easy. Most of the time it's someplace in between. It's taken me all my life to learn that. You can love somebody and not love em. You can hate somebody and not hate em. I love you . . . but . . . I mean, you have to understand how I mean that."

Watusi laughed.

"What's so funny?"

He laughed and coughed, climbed out of bed, clicked on the lamp and broke out another bottle of Mumm's.

"That's pretty hip," he said, taking a big swallow right from the magnum. "That is pretty hip. You talk about all *your* life. Well, all *my* life I been feelin that way about women and kids and a whole lotta other things—and you know what?"

She reached for the bottle. He held it for her while she took her own swig.

"I never had the nerve to say it to nobody, Angie. You the first woman I ever met to say anything like that and if we coulda met up twenty years ago, when I was lookin for somebody that think the way you do, we coulda made such beautiful company . . . Mmmmm," he half-whispered, good naturedly, kissing her all over, "I love you, I love you, I love you."

"Then you do understand?"

"It's comin in loud and clear and it was worth every mile I spent gettin here to find out."

She flopped her head down against the pillow and thought for a long time, then she began to cry in silence.

He stroked her hair, lifted her head and saw the tears. "I aint said nothin to make you feel bad, did I?"

She shook her head no and felt herself smiling.

"Youre a funny woman, Angie. That's how come I like you. Look like everytime we get together and get down to business you end up cryin and carryin on."

"I just feel relieved," she whimpered. "You havent hurt me at all. I really dont think I can be hurt anymore unless I do it to myself."

"I just hope Anita and Giselle turn out to be as understanding as you," he said. "Theyre already as hip and just about as beautiful."

"You never ease up on that jive, do you?" she said, feeling around the bottom of the covers for her pants. "I'm not hip and I know it and I never intend to try to be again. I just wanna be me."

"You already that, Angelina, you already that—whoever that is?"

"I'm finding out fast."

"When you get it all together and you catch yourself gettin lonesome some cold, windy night, just holler and I'll jump—across the ocean if I have to. That's a standin deal."

"How's it feel to be rich?"

He draped her sweatercoat over her shoulders and said, "I never said I was rich but I think I can fake bein peaceful for a stretch."

"Do you really think so?"

He really thought so. He drove her to the Copper Penny where she actually drank two cups of coffee and said good-bye in front of her house with a daughterly embrace.

"I'll pay you back everything I owe you," she said. "I keep my promises."

"I'm takin you at your word but, remember, it's some things you cant never pay back. That goes for me too. I'll send you my address and let's hope it aint the joint."

She stood and waved the Bentley off, watched it purr off down the block—with her precious Mexico memories locked inside—to the end of the street where it turned a smooth corner.

She pictured how it would approach the Bay Bridge, the changes that its driver would go through as he stopped at the toll gate, crossed into San Francisco, turned the car back over to his friend, grabbed a nap, went on to the airport and flew quietly back into another life that couldve been different, that they couldve shared or got trapped in together. Would time ever catch up with him? Would it ever catch up with her?

The night air was chilly but not too cold for her to go for a head-clearing walk and let time continue to do what time does as it burns itself up with each moment.

Soon it would be time to either get up and get dressed and go to meditation, or lie in bed and feel guilty about skipping.

This was order enough for her for now.

There was tomorrow's drive down to Big Sur with Curtis.

There would always be papers to correct.

© Carolyn Clebsch

Al Young was born in Mississippi, grew up in the South and in Detroit, and was educated at the University of Michigan and the University of California, Berkeley. In addition to his novels and poetry, he has written screenplays and several volumes of musical memoirs. With Ishmael Reed he co-founded and edited *The Yardbird Reader*, and, most recently, is the editor of the anthology *African American Literature*. He has taught literature and writing at the University of California, Santa Cruz and at Stanford University, where he once held a Wallace Stegner Fellowship. Also a Fulbright and a Guggenheim Fellow, he has won the Joseph Henry Jackson Prize as well as National Arts Council prizes. He lives in Palo Alto.

CALIFORNIA FICTION

California Fiction titles are selected for their literary merit and for their illumination of California history and culture.

Disobedience by Michael Drinkard	0-520-20683-5
Fat City by Leonard Gardner	0-520-20657-6
Continental Drift by James D. Houston	0-520-20713-0
Golden Days by Carolyn See	0-520-20673-8
Who Is Angelina? by Al Young	0-520-20712-2

Forthcoming titles:

The Ford by Mary Austin
Thieves' Market by A. I. Bezzerides
Skin Deep by Guy Garcia
In the Heart of the Valley of Love by Cynthia Kadohata
Oil! by Upton Sinclair